DEC 2 0

W9-BCG-139

A QUESTION OF TIME

THE SNAKE EATER CHRONICLES 1

JAMES STEJSKAL

CASEMATE
Philadelphia & Oxford

Published in the United States of America and Great Britain in 2020 by
CASEMATE PUBLISHERS
1950 Lawrence Road, Havertown, PA 19083, USA
and
The Old Music Hall, 106–108 Cowley Road, Oxford OX4 1JE, UK

Copyright 2020 © James Stejskal

Hardcover Edition: ISBN 978-1-61200-903-2
Digital Edition: ISBN 978-1-61200-916-2

A CIP record for this book is available from the British Library

All rights reserved. No part of this book may be reproduced or transmitted in any form
or by any means, electronic or mechanical including photocopying, recording or by any
information storage and retrieval system, without permission from the publisher in writing.

Printed and bound in the United States of America by Sheridan

Typeset by Versatile PreMedia Services (P) Ltd

For a complete list of Casemate titles, please contact:

CASEMATE PUBLISHERS (US)
Telephone (610) 853-9131
Fax (610) 853-9146
Email: casemate@casematepublishers.com
www.casematepublishers.com

CASEMATE PUBLISHERS (UK)
Telephone (01865) 241249
Email: casemate-uk@casematepublishers.co.uk
www.casematepublishers.co.uk

Note:
This is a book of fiction. Mentions of historical events, real persons or places are used
fictitiously. All other names, places, and events are entirely imaginary.

The story recounted is not true, no matter how similar it may be to real events. To
the *Federales* who peruse these pages, please bear in mind that the incidents, events, and
vague recollections recounted herein are imaginary and thus do not merit an indictment
in any form or fashion.

Any of my friends and comrades who think they are represented in this story are
sadly mistaken. In any event, the real story is far too bizarre to be told.

"What's a snake-eater, Daddy?"
"It's a funny name they call us, Precious."
"Why?"
"Because we kill snakes and eat them."
"Really?"
"Yes, but only the bad ones."

—overheard at Fort Bragg Child Day Care

OCCUPIED BERLIN

180 kilometers behind the Iron Curtain
inside Communist East Germany

Berlin 1979

From 1945 until 1990, Berlin was the focal point of a Cold War that was anything but. It is only in retrospect that those of us who served can realize how very close to the precipice we actually came.

It all began after World War II when the conquerors of Nazi Germany split the country into two zones they called the West and the East. The western zone became the Federal Republic of Germany, protected by the armies of the United States, the United Kingdom, and France. The eastern zone became the communist German Democratic Republic, the GDR, under the control of Mother Russia, aka the Union of Soviet Socialist Republics (USSR). Nearly one million soldiers of the Group of Soviet Forces Germany were stationed in the GDR.

The conquerors themselves then became enemies. Tensions rose between the Allies and the USSR and its satellites. It was a time when a "lost" reconnaissance pilot or the delivery of missiles to a Third World country could nearly launch thermo-nuclear war.

Those tensions were often at their highest in Berlin, the former capital of Germany. Lying deep inside East Germany behind the border Winston Churchill named the "Iron Curtain," Berlin was occupied as well—by Soviets in the eastern half and American, British, and French troops in the western. By 1963, the city of Berlin was divided by over 100 kilometers of concrete wall with watch towers and searchlights, guarded by thousands of East German soldiers with Kalashnikovs.

Two competing theories of world domination met there. It was the front line of an existential struggle between communism and capitalism; a hot spot left over from a war that never ended, a tinderbox that might start a new conflict or be consumed by it.

In 1979, there was an uneasy acceptance of the status quo, but behind the scenes a chess game was being played by two rival nations—a game that could end with the deadliest of consequences.

If you have to earn a living... and the price they make you pay is loyalty, be a double agent—and never let either of the two sides know your real name.

—Graham Greene

1

The building loomed in the night, a monotonous gray structure like every other building in East Berlin. It stood out only by virtue of being older and more derelict than the others. Situated in the northern part of the Pankow district on the edge of the city, the apartment block lay in an area that had escaped most of the bombing and ground combat thirty-some years before. While newer Soviet-inspired structures towered over the center of the city, the buildings in the rest of the East had barely been updated or repaired since the war.

Inside, three athletic young men in black leather jackets, their faces strained in concentration, crept up the stairwell wearing their quietest rubber-soled shoes, trying hard to avoid the squeaking floorboards that squeaked anyway. Small dim lights barely illuminated the dingy vertical tunnel with its walls that had not been painted since anyone could remember. Each of the men had an ugly little pistol, a Russian Makarov, out and aimed generally upwards. Every door they passed led to an apartment that was home to a socialist worker's family. Every door was identical; only the numbers changed.

Reaching the bottom of the stairs leading to the next level, the first man raised his hand and the column stopped. He grasped the rail around the stairwell; it creaked and wobbled, rotted from age and neglect. Releasing his handhold, he involuntarily edged away from the shaft and closer to the wall.

A fourth man came forward. Bruno Großmann was older than his team of shooters, a prosperous-looking man, portly in a long wool overcoat, who up to that moment had been shadowing the three men with guns at a distance.

He looked up and whispered, "505, on the next floor."

The column continued up the stairs even more slowly than before. Reaching the door marked 505, they came to a halt and positioned themselves on either side of its frame. Großmann came forward once again and inspected the entryway. He pondered announcing that the police had arrived but then decided that quicker action was needed. He stepped back and motioned for the third man to come forward with the sledgehammer he was holding in his free hand. Holstering his pistol, Number Three took the heavy tool in both hands as his partners moved back slightly, ready to pounce forward once the door was open. Number Three looked at the boss and waited.

Großmann nodded to the man in a silent command.

Number Three swung the sledge as hard as he could; too hard in fact. It struck the door jamb and bounced off at an angle, sending splinters of wood flying through the air but with no visible effect on opening the portal.

"Damn it! Again!" All pretense of stealth had vanished.

The sledge struck home on the second try. The handle imploded as the door flew open. Number Three dropped the tool and pulled out his pistol as Number One scrambled past him into the front room.

"*Staatssicherheit, keine Bewegung!*" State Security, don't move!

Number One couldn't see a thing. He had no flashlight and it was pitch black in the apartment. He was followed by his comrades, one of whom hit the light switch just in time to see a half-naked man standing in the corner, leveling a pistol at them.

All three Makarov pistols fired simultaneously. The man, perforated cleanly by a hail of bullets, slumped against the wall and slid to the floor, painting a shiny dark-red trail on the faded wallpaper. Großmann came in at last and walked over to the body. He leaned down and picked up a piece of blackened wood carved to look vaguely like a weapon.

"Crap," he said in a barely audible voice. Then he commanded, "Search this place. Tear it apart. You're looking for papers, film, cameras, anything. And don't forget to check the food!"

Großmann turned and walked into the hallway. A second team of men were coming up the stairs. One was carrying a litter for the body. Großmann didn't normally come out on missions like this one, but its sensitivity and implications were such that he had decided he couldn't afford to entrust it to any other officer in his section. He pulled out a cigarette, lit it, and stood peering down the stairwell contemplating the situation. Holding his cigarette in between his forefinger and thumb, one of Großmann's many affectations, he looked like a Prussian army officer.

He started to walk down the stairs. On the next landing a door opened a crack and a resident dared to peer out at the disturbance. Großmann glared back at the eyes staring out at him and the door quickly shut. He had already arranged for a team to warn each inhabitant and tell them to keep their mouths closed about the incident or go to jail. No one would talk, of that he was sure.

A cold fury welled up inside Großmann. His quarry had escaped him. He surmised the suspect was clever and doubted that he had left any evidence. The noise coming from the apartment was that of a frustrated search that would yield nothing, otherwise he would have heard a pause and then a victorious cry signaling that something, some clue had been found. The dead man was an employee of the *S-Bahn*, the cross-city railway. It was only thanks to a KGB tip that Großmann also knew he was the communications link—the cut-out—between an agent handler in the West and a more important spy in the East.

3

Großmann was troubled by the man. Most of all, why was he ready to die? He must have been totally committed to his cause. Based on the information he had, Großmann was convinced the man was guilty but tonight he had managed to elude East German justice for eternity. In any event, his choice was not stupid: death was far easier than the pain he would have experienced at Bautzen. Most traitors never returned from that deservedly notorious *Stasi* prison. His death made Großmann's job more difficult, but not impossible. It was personal now: he was getting closer to the traitor and would bring him down once and for all.

I will find you. It's only a matter of time.

2

Master Sergeant Kimball "Kim" Becker concentrated on the night scene in front of him. This part of the French Sector of Berlin was quiet. That was not unusual. On the other side of the 12-foot high wall, the East German Border Command of the National People's Army—the NVA— had made it a showcase of impenetrability: high walls, bright sodium-vapor lights, three rows of barbed-wire fences, dog runs, towers every 150 meters, and signs which threatened death to those who tried to enter. Ironically, because the East Germans thought the area secure, it wasn't, especially for those wishing to break into the country rather than escape from it. The sections of the Wall that were heavily defended and had the deepest security on the surface were in fact the easiest to cross through because no one thought anyone would be crazy enough to actually try. Surprisingly, if one searched long enough, there were always weak points. The areas that appeared to have limited security were more dangerous as one could not always ascertain where the actual security belt was.

Becker could see the so-called "death strip" directly to his front, a 15-meter-wide, well-groomed sand trap without the golfers. Then came a paved road and three barbed-wire fences. Contrary to popular belief, the East Germans didn't employ anti-personnel mines around Berlin; they only used those on the frontier with the Federal

Republic of Germany. Here they just used assault rifles to kill their prey—their fellow citizens of the German Democratic Republic.

Behind Becker was a dark glade of pine trees, a strip of quiet isolation that separated the barrier from the busy, capitalist city of Berlin (West). Few Berliners came here. It was a forbidden area and not many wanted to be reminded that they were living in a bubble surrounded by a communist horde. The East German side was quiet as well. Beyond the Wall and a line of trees, it was a rural area, pastureland with a few homes and small military outposts.

Why on Earth would anyone want to sneak into East Germany? Why indeed?

Becker and the four men with him on the West Berlin side of the Wall knew the answer, but presently they were occupied with observing the frontier. They had been here many times before, collecting data, watching the guard procedures, learning everything possible in preparation for this mission. Alone or in pairs, they had walked sections of the border at all hours of the day and night, avoiding being seen by the NVA guards on the other side and eluding the West Berlin Police who tried to keep inquisitive children, troublemaking teenagers, and smugglers away from the Wall.

Becker and his team didn't need permission to be in the area, but they didn't want to advertise their presence either. The name of the game was to get ready for a possible war with the Soviet Union and their plans were of concern only to themselves. In this case, even the US Commander of Berlin was unaware of what was about to happen. Beyond Becker's immediate commander, only the commanders of Special Operations Task Force Europe, US European Command, and the Chief of Berlin Base, the head "spook" in town, knew what was going on.

Becker knew—from his training and from thirteen years of military experience, two of them in Berlin—that every security force had a schedule. No matter how professional and well trained, after months and years on the job certain things became routine and comfortable. The East Germans had been at this for over fifteen years and had developed more than their share of routines. Only the upper echelons of the Border Guard Command were professional soldiers, but they had grown into the patterns of an ultimate security state ruled by schedules, orders, and regulations. The guards who patrolled or manned the towers were conscripts who had no idea of the bigger picture. As well as surveilling the common folk, they watched each other to make sure no one tried to escape. If someone successfully made it across the frontier, the guards were punished. But, every once in a while, they stopped or shot some disgruntled person who decided they'd had enough of life in the socialist Workers' and Peasants' Paradise and tried to make it across the barrier into the West. Those that did stop an escape got a medal. Most escapes, whether successful or not, occurred on the inner-city border between East and West Berlin, not the outer border between East Germany and West Berlin. That part of the Wall was harder to get close to and most of those attempts failed.

This section had tall concrete observation towers and occasionally dogs. But Becker knew the towers were not always manned and tonight the one directly in front of him looked empty. It was also in a depression that obscured its base from the view of the neighboring towers on its flanks. All they had to worry about were the periodic mobile patrols and the trucks carrying relief guards that passed by on the perimeter road like clockwork.

Becker watched the tower intently to confirm it was empty. There was no movement inside, no signs of occupation. Through the glare of the lights, bats swooped down to devour the insects that had made the mistake of being attracted to light. It was very still.

"Truck coming from the south," Fred Lindt, on the right flank, whispered. Becker had also posted two-man observer teams at other sections of the Wall about 2 kilometers away to the north and south of his position and they were feeding Fred information by encrypted VHF radio.

He peered through binoculars and then lowered them as the headlights came into view on the East German access road. The team watched it approach and pass by without stopping before it disappeared around a bend in the road.

"Right on time. We've got fifteen minutes, let's go," Becker said, as he checked his watch.

At the same time, 10 kilometers to the northeast, another small two-man cell of Becker's team were at work next to the Wall. They began pummeling the East German guard dogs with smooth round stones fired from high-powered wrist-rocket slingshots. The shepherds began to bark loudly in their pen. Several more stones sailed into their enclosure to keep them agitated. The noise brought the guards to the windows. Their next move would be a telephone call to the operations center, serving to focus the security force's attention on that section of the frontier. The guards had to climb down from their tower and patrol their section on foot to see what had aroused the dogs' attention. The Americans and their slingshots on the other side of the wall had long since disappeared.

Back at Becker's position, a steel door in the Wall opened quietly onto the death strip and he led two men across the sand into East Germany. Dressed in dirty NVA camouflage uniforms, with small backpacks and carrying a couple of long, rake-like tools, they were hard to spot as they trotted across the gray sand in the semi-darkness. The door was one of many installed by the *Stasi*—the East German security service—to facilitate their own clandestine trips into West Berlin. It was a curious thing. The existence of the doors was known to both sides but for some reason the East Germans didn't expect they would be used to enter their territory.

No one in their right mind wants to break into East Germany.

The doors were fitted with high-security locks, but these were an easily surmountable obstacle for Becker's team. As to his sanity, Becker simply shrugged that assessment off.

Being crazy doesn't make you stupid.

They reached the tower and Stefan Mann went straight to an electrical connection box at its base. While Becker and Logan Finch crouched at the base of the tower and watched the road for any surprises, Mann worked the lock. Once he popped the door open, he pulled a small device from his bag and placed it against the back wall of the box behind the wire bundles. The device contained an induction loop that collected all East German communications made over the telephone cables. Once that was installed, he attached its wires to the power, grounded another, and ensured the transmission antenna was clear but well hidden. Finished, he closed the door and relocked it. That was the signal for the next phase to begin.

Finch had already manipulated the tower door lock and now he pulled the creaking door open. He sprinted up the stairwell while Mann took his place on overwatch.

In the guardroom, Finch took a quick look around to see if there was anything worth grabbing, but saw only a telephone on top of a cheap wooden table, two stools, and an empty cupboard. He located the telephone box and quickly removed the cover with his screwdriver. There was no power to connect to, so he inserted a battery-powered transmitter and the induction device and concealed them as best he could before closing the box. It would last for a couple of months on low power, so it was better than nothing. He stood up and checked the roads. Still all quiet. He had one thing left to do. He reached into his pocket and dropped a small packet on the table before running down the stairs to ground level.

"Good to go?" Becker said.

"Yeah. We're in, but only on battery."

"Close enough for government work. Let's go."

Ten minutes had passed. The team worked its way back across the sand. Walking backwards, they scoured the ground with two soft, rake-like brushes to remove their tracks. Becker led the way, carefully lifting his heels as he moved to avoid tripping. His gaze swung rhythmically from the team to the flanks where the road disappeared over a hill or around a bend. His suppressed MPiKMS assault rifle, the NVA version of the AK-47, was at the ready. It was another of the tools the unit had secretly acquired for just such a purpose, along with their clothing and equipment. Even if they missed a mark in the sand, the prints of their East German army boots would confuse trackers.

Through the partially open door, Fred Lindt watched the team as they carefully picked their way back to the Wall. He pushed it all the way open and the three scrambled back into West Berlin. A quick touch-up of the sand and all was more or less as pristine as the Border Guard groundskeeping tractor had left it the day before. Fred relocked the door and then he and his partner, Nick Kaiser, unloaded and disassembled the suppressed M70 .300 Winchester Magnum rifles which had been protecting the team… just in case. The uniforms were quickly removed and switched for more appropriate city garb, the clothing stuffed into a soft briefcase, the sort used by most manual laborers to carry their lunch and beer to work each day.

"How'd it go?" Fred asked.

"Perfect. Everything in and locked back up tight." Becker cut the conversation short. "Okay, let's get out of here. Meet back at the team house at zero nine."

The team dispersed in bomb-burst fashion, quickly moving away from the Wall in different directions: the two long-gunners to a van, two others walking back to catch a late-night bus back to their car, parked far away.

Becker waited and watched to ensure their work had gone unnoticed and that his men got away cleanly. As he looked back from a rise in the ground, Becker saw the greenish flare of headlights through the tree-line that preceded the scheduled security patrol. He crouched low and watched the truck pass by without slowing down.

So far, so good.

He turned and disappeared quietly through the forest towards the city.

3

Maximilian Fischer glanced out the kitchen window of his apartment as he poured his morning coffee. He was a distinguished-looking man, even in his bathrobe. Tall and fit with mostly black hair that made him look younger than his fifty-odd years, he stood near the counter that ran along the wall, looking out on the street below.

At first, what he saw didn't register, but then slowly he realized something was amiss. It was a frigid morning in East Berlin and in the street below exhaust smoke was curling up from the rear of a parked car. The car's motor was idling. No one wasted precious fuel letting their car idle.

Unless they were with the Firm.

He spooned some sugar and added cream to his cup as he stood at the counter contemplating the car. The windows were fogged up. The person or persons inside must have been sitting there a long time, breathing very heavily, or maybe just talking a lot. He decided it was the latter and that the people inside were part of a static surveillance team. Whether there were other teams in the neighborhood, he had no idea. His first task would be to determine if they were indeed watching him.

Fischer didn't stare too long. He backed away from the window and considered the possibilities. He knew, from his job in the *Stasi's*

Main Reconnaissance Directorate, that no other security service employees lived nearby. As it was, he should have been living in Wandlitz with all the other Party *Bonzen*. But no, he said, it was unnecessary, he was single and it was more convenient for him to live close to the Firm's headquarters.

While this was true, living in the city had certain other advantages for Fischer. For one thing, it made it easier to carry out his other job—spying against the regime he appeared to work for so faithfully and diligently—without being detected. It was a regime he had grown to hate.

He carried on as usual. He remembered all the tips he gave his own agents back when he routinely worked the streets. "If you detect surveillance, act normal, carry on as if everything is fine. Don't panic or you will just confirm that you're guilty," he told them.

So he took his time. He finished his coffee, dressed and collected his thoughts before descending the stairs of his row house to the entrance and walking out to the street to meet his car. The cold air stung his nostrils and he blew a cloud of mist every time he exhaled. The weather would have been exhilarating if not for the brown lignite coal smoke that assailed his senses. The driver was punctual as ever. Max stuffed his lanky frame into the black Tatra 603, wrapping his long, black wool coat around him as he settled in. Then it was off to the headquarters. He didn't risk looking behind him or asking the driver if they were being followed, but he got his answer when the driver started to check the rearview mirror repeatedly, not part of his normal habit. It was not a long drive to the *Zentrale*, as everyone called the headquarters, but it was long enough to establish they were being followed. The car turned into Frankfurter Allee then onto Ruschestraße before entering the compound. The barriers were already open as they approached. With the guards' salute, they breezed through and came to a stop at the entrance.

"I'll call for you when I need you," he said as he unfolded himself out of the car in front of the glass entryway.

Fischer swept through the open doors, into the building and up to the top floor of *Haus 15*. Greeting his secretary, he entered his office, the inner sanctum where he had always felt secure. As he stood before his desk, he again examined the possibilities and questioned that premise of inviolability now. The protection of rank, power, and privilege had its limits even in the all-powerful State Security Ministry. It could be that he was just placed under routine watch, but he doubted that. Senior-level officers were rarely subjected to checks unless there was strong suspicion of something being very wrong.

Sitting at his desk, he shuffled through the in-box, looking for papers with an urgent or priority ribbon, but found none. It could be that he was being slowly strangled of information by a usurper to his position or it could be that Department S, the internal security section, had cut him off. It could also indicate nothing more than a slow day, unless one was paranoid.

But he was.

After all, just because you're paranoid, doesn't mean they're *not* after you.

He knew that truth too well. He had worked foreign intelligence operations long enough to know you could never become complacent. He also knew that once an agent had been compromised, it was probably too late to escape. His agents had been extraordinarily lucky; none had ever been exposed. His long experience within the system revealed to him why the American- and British-recruited agents were easily found and disposed of. It was quite simple: almost all of them were dangles—provocations set by Markus Wolf with the intention of fooling the enemy and luring him into a trap. That was also why Fischer had survived so long: he had seen things from both sides of the fence and knew when to take a risk and when not. He had taken risks all his life.

Max Fischer had started out running errands for his father long before the war. He grew up in a tenement building, one of a hundred such places deep in the Wedding district of Berlin. His father worked at the Siemens plant and his mother did a little of everything around the neighborhood but mostly cooked, kept the apartment clean, and the clothing mended.

He remembered the fights at home, which were mostly about money. There was never enough of that and he and his younger brother always seemed to be hungry. He went to school most of the time, but occasionally, he and his friends skipped. No one seemed to care because the schools were overcrowded anyway. They often played army in the streets but before long they realized how they could use their teamwork to supplement their meagre diet.

They called their game *Blitzangriff*—lightning strike. A swarm of kids would converge on the stalls at the market and a fight would begin, food would be thrown, the kids would be chased by the stall owners and policemen alike, and then another team would move in to fill their book bags with everything they could steal. Max led many of the raids until he was fingered by one of the workers who remembered him from a previous incident and corralled by the police. His mother was appalled and his father worked his belt on Max's backside that night. He went back to school but had a hard time sitting for quite a while.

He heard his father talking at one of the many meetings in their cramped apartment. They were talking about *Kollektivs*. Max decided that what he and his friends had created was a *Kollektiv* that benefitted their society.

Father said, "Nice try."

But the more his father talked with the other men, the more Max understood. Lying on his small bed in the dark corner of the kitchen, he listened to them and their talk of unions and oppression. Talk of Brown Shirts beating up Jews and throwing communists into jail. His mother said he shouldn't be allowed to listen. His father said it would be part of his life soon enough.

The errands his father gave him were never quite what they seemed, nor were they innocent. It started with dropping packages off at other apartments or, sometimes, offices. Sometimes, he had to find things hidden in a park and bring them home.

Then one night, his father came home breathless. He threw a cloth-wrapped bundle on the table and told Max's mother to pack. Curious as ever, Max unwrapped the bundle. Inside was a revolver. Father had shot a policeman. The family left that night, traveling east, never looking back.

Max Fischer lived the next several years in the Soviet Union, first in Moscow until the German Army got close, then further east in a small village near the Ural Mountains. He attended a special school for Germans, which was simply called the Lenin School. He kept his mother tongue, but learned Russian and English as well. He learned other subjects taught by interesting old men and women who knew his home as well as he, but who never answered personal questions. And then, as a young man, he was sent back to Berlin as part of a small cadre of communists. They were the vanguard of what would become the leadership of a new East Germany.

It was 1946 and by that time the eastern part of Greater Berlin was occupied by the Russians. They called it Berlin—Capital of the German Democratic Republic. The western half of Berlin was occupied by the Americans, Brits, and French. The East Germans said the Allied presence was only a minor inconvenience; they would soon be forced out. In reality, Allied-occupied West Berlin was, and would remain, a thorn in the side of the Communist Party.

When Max returned to Berlin, he settled in the Friedrichshain district and began his work with the Russians at their state security service headquarters in nearby Karlshorst along with other Germans who had returned from sanctuary across the Oder. They built a new security service from the ground up and called it the "Firm." Granted, it was modeled after the Russian *Cheka*, but it was German through and through.

Max was an intelligence officer, a case officer, the man who persuaded people to spy on their own country. It was the second oldest profession, and in some ways was not unlike the oldest—prostitution. It also required human contact, not so much physical as psychological. And the psychological effects could be severe. The act of recruiting a human being to do something that is against their laws and sense of decency can make the job unbearable for some. At the very least, it places a great strain on one's conscience. For agents who can detach themselves from the emotion, espionage becomes a necessary fact for national survival. But the lies, the falseness of befriending someone just to ask them to risk their life, to betray their country: that slowly chews away at the soul. Max had spent many days and even more long nights searching for secrets that hid in the shadows.

He had seen the work as part of his patriotic duty and his life in Berlin was good at first. The Nazis were gone and he felt he was serving a cause much bigger than himself, but slowly he began to see the differences between the East and the West. It wasn't so much the material inequalities that disturbed him, it was the moral. He finally admitted to himself that he had made a mistake when the "Anti-Fascist Protection Barrier"—more popularly known as the Wall—went up. He knew that it hadn't been built to keep fascists out: it was meant to imprison his fellow East Germans in their own country. The country was bleeding out its population through West Berlin. Everyone who wanted self-determination in their life and, yes, freedom, was escaping across the ill-defended border between the two Berlins. Had the Wall not been built, the GDR would have withered on the vine. Only when the flow of émigrés had been staunched could the economy even begin to move forward, but it would never thrive. He saw that and realized nothing can thrive under a totalitarian regime. He'd been living a lie and since then he had been working to make amends.

He became a spy. He was not recruited or enticed: he volunteered. Deliberately and with no reason other than a desire to set things right. He didn't need the money the Americans deposited into a special Swiss bank account for him, although he calculated it held just over 2.5 million US dollars. He needed only the gratification of knowing his information helped weaken the men who had deceived him in his youth. His reason to spy on his own country was what any case officer would tell you was the strongest motivation—ideology.

The moment came along easily enough. Fischer had several opportunities to volunteer during his overseas tours but it wasn't until he was posted to the African island country of Zanzibar as part of a diplomatic delegation that he took action. Ostensibly he was Chief of the Solidarity Committee which coordinated aid for the non-aligned states in Africa. In reality, he was advising ZISS, the Zanzibar Intelligence and Security Service, on how best to ensure their hold on power.

It was a heady time, 1966, two years after a small group of African revolutionaries overthrew the Omani Arab leadership that had long dominated the archipelago. Shortly after the 1964 coup, their new leader, Abeid Karume, had brokered a deal with neighboring mainland Tanganyika to unite and form the larger nation of Tanzania. But while the United States and Britain vied for influence, Karume was drawn to the Soviet Union, China, and East Germany, as was his mainland African nationalist partner, Julius Kambarage Nyerere. Karume was also upset that the US and UK took too long to recognize his new regime. The East Germans would provide the "technical" expertise on how to run an efficient security service.

ZISS was an aggressive and often ruthless service. Its officers were not long separated from a cruel colonial history that had been dominated first by Portuguese, then Arab overlords. Although Zanzibar had become a protectorate of the United Kingdom in 1890, an Omani sultanate continued to rule the islands until its protectorate status was terminated in 1963. By that time, the locals had had enough of their masters and when the revolution started, many

Arabs did not escape the archipelago alive. That harsh tradition of dealing with political enemies continued and was even encouraged by many of the *Stasi* advisors who imparted their methods and skills to their new African comrades. Fischer was not one of those who condoned violence and torture. Far from it—rather he was disgusted by his *Kampfgenossen* who thought brutality useful for the interrogation of enemies of the people.

Because of his rank Fischer had more latitude than the officers under his supervision. He could move on his own and he remained watchful. In general, the Zanzibaris had little problem identifying most of the British and American intelligence officers on the island. In their zealousness, they also mistakenly identified some authentic diplomats as spies and threw them out of the country. There were, however, a few real intelligence officers they missed and Fischer, ever wary, looked for one that his "friends" hadn't pegged. That would be his opening.

Zanzibar's main island of Unguja was not a big place and every outsider was closely watched by the locals whether they worked for ZISS, picked pockets, or were just curious. That made clandestine operations difficult for most Westerners who stuck out wherever they appeared.

Fischer was patient. Before long, he decided one American appeared to be of interest. He lived in a beach house not far from where the US consulate was located and spent most of his days in the office, one of the four or five employees who remained. On occasion he would leave his office and travel out to the former site of NASA's Project Mercury tracking station. The location was about 10 kilometers outside town on the southern edge of the island. Surrounded by palm, cinnamon, mango trees and brush inhabited by chattering and exceedingly curious Red Colobus monkeys, it was a quiet, isolated spot.

The new government had demanded the American station's removal shortly after taking power and the site had been dismantled. Only two empty Quonset hut buildings and the generators remained, and it was this man who seemed to maintain them. His name, Fischer learned from a local, was "Mister Frank." Several months later, Mister Frank presented the generators to the government as a gift, but even after their removal from the compound he would visit the local villages nearby and gift the elders bags of rice and, on holidays, with a goat. He would sit with the elders and talk about their problems late into the evening until only one man remained. That elder was also a member of the island's governing council.

Invariably, Mister Frank would go down to the port the day after his meeting. Fischer often followed him discreetly and watched his activities. Frank never seemed to be concerned with watching his back. That told Fischer he was either not an intelligence officer or he wasn't doing anything operational. One time, however, Frank was walking the narrow paths between the carts and trucks in the crowded port area when two young toughs accosted him. They were both shirtless and barefoot, their skin a deep black, which Fischer took to mean they were mainlanders and not of Omani descent. They probably worked the dhows as stevedores and thought Mister Frank to be vulnerable. Whoever they were, the two confronted Mister Frank in a particularly congested area, one in front and one to his rear. Frank acted unconcerned despite the heavy metal bar brandished by the front man. Fischer saw the flash of a blade in the hand of the man to the rear. There was an exchange of words and Frank reached for his pocket as if to get his money. As he did, he stepped to the side, pulled a spring cosh from under his loose linen coat, and swung it at the man behind him. It connected with the young man's forearm. There was a resounding snap and the knife flew into the air as its owner went to his knees in pain. Frank turned and smiled at the first man who decided he had business elsewhere. So did Frank, who kept walking down to the ferry dock and departed for Dar es Salaam.

Fischer decided Mister Frank could handle himself and must be a bit more than a conventional diplomat. And if he traveled to Dar after his meetings then it followed that he must not trust the communications system at the consulate. Fischer did his sums and surmised Frank was a case officer who was handling the old Zanzibari as an access agent.

The visits to the station site and the elder's village never seemed regular, but over the course of several months, Fischer determined that one particular day of the week, Saturday, seemed to be Mister Frank's preferred choice of day to drive out of town. And it was early on a Saturday morning that Fischer parked his old Riley sedan on the road to the tracking station and threw open the hood, feigning engine trouble. He stood near the car, imagining he could smell the cloves from the nearby plantations.

As Fischer had hoped, sometime later Mister Frank's big Ford sedan appeared. He slowed to a stop.

"Do you have a problem?" Frank asked.

Fischer had removed his sweat-stained linen coat and rolled up his sleeves. Despite parking in the shade of several palm trees, he felt the blazing heat and humidity even this early in the morning.

"It seems to be overheating. Do you by any chance have water?"

"As a matter of fact I do." Frank said. He climbed out of the car and pulled out a small jerry can out of the trunk.

"Are you German?"

"You have a good ear," Fischer said. He was even more convinced he had chosen the right man. "You're from the American consulate, is that not true?"

"Yes, I am." It was an easy guess as Frank's car had *Corps Diplomatique* number plates with a "116" prefix for the United States.

"I am with the Solidarity Committee from East Germany," he said. If Mister Frank was an intelligence officer he would immediately recognize the connotations.

"I didn't think you were permitted to talk with us." Frank's alert mechanism was pegged at the warning level.

"We're not. But I'm in charge, so I make the rules and I can talk. I need your assistance and, in return, I think can help you."

Fischer pulled a small brass presentation coin from his pocket.

"Please take a look at this. It shows who I work for."

Mister Frank read off the inscription on the coin, "*Tschekist sein kann nur ein Mensch mit kühlem kopf, heissem herzen, und sauberen händen. Feliks Dzierzynski.*"

"Do you understand German?"

"I do. It says, 'A person can only be a *Chekist* with a cool head, a passionate heart, and clean hands.' That would seem to mean that you're with the *Ministerium für Staatssicherheit.*"

It was a statement not a question. It validated Fischer's supposition and told Frank he was dealing with someone special.

"It does. My name is Maximilian Fischer. I would like to volunteer my services to the United States of America. If you are interested, I will be here at the same time next week."

Frank looked around out of habit, assuming there would be someone in the bushes. There wasn't. It was quiet and they were alone.

Without giving Fischer a direct answer the American said, "My name is Frank. I should probably go now. I assume your car is fine then?"

Frank tried to return the coin but Fischer pushed his hand back.

"Keep it. I have more. Please think about my offer. I will keep the water can for appearances' sake. Go now."

Mister Frank climbed back into his car and drove on.

Fischer watched him drive away and then puttered around with his car for a bit. He poured a little water into his radiator and then glanced around. As he expected, he saw no one. This section of the road was always deserted.

The next week, Mister Frank did come back. And, after talking more, Frank became Mister Frank Miller. Their conversation continued and a contract of sorts was orally agreed upon before Fischer gave him a packet. Not sensational intelligence, but more than Miller was expecting—papers that included a list of all the *Stasi* officers on Zanzibar, Fischer's instructional program, and his student roster. He also included a plan of how they could meet and exchange information.

From the beginning, Fischer's contact plans were geared to his own security. He always insisted on keeping his distance from the handlers and controlling the contact. Over the years, he communicated through carefully chosen intermediaries who often did not know who he was. The Americans knew his identity, but never talked directly with him. They were happy with that because of the quality of his information and the precautions he took. There was always extreme risk involved with running a Soviet Bloc agent, especially one from a security service. Carefully constructed means of indirect communication were devised that permitted instructions and requests to be innocuously passed through newspapers and radio programs. He rarely risked a personal meeting and also chose the means he used to pass documents. It was as safe as a system could be for a spy.

And he thought he had done a pretty good job of helping the Americans over the years. In the beginning there were small coups, like the African air force officer who passed on the complete Soviet strategic plan for Africa. He was a well-placed officer who wouldn't have been noticed by the Agency had Fischer not tipped them off to his monetary woes. Then the Agency asked for Fischer's help to find an advanced artillery piece they heard the Russians had supplied to one of their allies, something the Americans desperately wanted. With the help of one of his assets, he found the item and it disappeared under mysterious circumstances along with the unnamed army officer from a small

East African nation. And, of course, Tel Aviv never did find out where the tip came from—the tip that the Egyptians were about to launch an offensive against them—which justified the Israeli first strike in 1967.

More recently, his intelligence had been reserved for even more rarified, sensitive information: things that came to his suite in Berlin from the meetings of presidents in overseas capitals or the deliberations of the Politburo on foreign affairs.

But his life as an intelligence officer or a spy was rarely that exciting. It was more like a slow game of chess, a game played deliberately with a great deal of calculation and planning beforehand. To rush into a move could be disastrous unless luck intervened or your opponent was stupid. But to rely on luck was unwise because, like nature, she is fickle. And to rely on the opposition's stupidity was a dangerous exercise. He had learned early on in his career to never underestimate the capabilities of his enemies.

Fischer came back to the present and surveyed his realm. Four walls paneled in blond oak, a portrait of Felix Dzerzhinsky, the man who set up the Soviet *Cheka* in 1917, hung on one wall. It was identical to the one that hung in State Security Minister Erich Mielke's office across the courtyard, but Mielke also had a plaster death mask of Lenin on his desk. Not that Fischer was envious; he actually thought it was rather macabre to have those empty, staring eyes peering up from the desk top all the time. Hanging next to Dzerzhinsky's portrait were the official renderings of Honecker and Mielke, both of whom Fischer despised. Both believed their ideology mattered more than the welfare of the people. Both were fanatical communists who thought any deviation from their line of thinking was blasphemy. By their reasoning, most of the population deserved prison time.

On the wall opposite from the portraits was the obligatory Russian KGB–German *Stasi* friendship plaque, and on the third, a map of the two Germanys.

There was only one man in the *Stasi* who Fischer liked, or rather respected. That was his immediate boss, Markus Wolf. There was not a picture of Wolf on the walls of the headquarters or anywhere else for that matter. The same held true for Fischer: the Directorate did not permit photos of its leaders for good reason. The enemy can't track you if they don't know what you look like.

He swiveled his chair around to face the safe built into the fourth wall behind his desk. A tall, wood door panel covered the actual container, a 2-meter-high steel closet with a heavy door, a key lock and a fireproof lining. The safes were all custom-made for the headquarters by the *Stasi*'s own specialists. Unlike the slaves who built the Pharaoh's tombs, however, once the job was done the workers were not killed to keep the secrets. Someone had to maintain and service the things.

Fischer had the only key to his safe on a chain around his neck, and pulling it out he inserted it into the lock. But before he turned the key, he checked the seal on the safe door edge. The previous evening, he had used his issued *Petschaft*, a small metal seal, to make an impression in the soft putty. His seal was unique and if the safe had been opened, the putty would show it. The stamp was in his pocket and never left his possession.

Now Max knew. The putty appeared unmolested, but the safe had been opened by someone else. He always put a trap on the door of the container, a telltale that only he knew—a grain of black sand set in a groove on the dial. It was not there. That meant someone had entered his safe and then closed it with an exact replica of his seal. Only "S," the security directorate, could have a copy of his personal stamp and only the Minister would have signed off on the order. He was in trouble, but he was not about to try and reverse course in the middle of the rapids.

I have embarked on a course from which there is no turning back.

Opening the safe, he quickly scanned its contents. Nothing missing, nothing apparently moved. He never kept anything incriminating anyway, either in the office or at his home.

Something had gone wrong somewhere, somehow. He had to go through the process of tracing back to find where the compromise happened but, at the same time, he couldn't show his hand. Every request he made would be scrutinized in detail. The fact that he had not yet been detained meant they were waiting for some crucial bit of information or for him to confirm their suspicions.

As Fischer sat and reflected, he realized he had come to the end of a phase in his life. He had no real choices and made his decision quickly. He couldn't pass any more information and he was not willing to remain in place and risk arrest. It was time to go. He would get out of the Workers' Paradise. The big question was how. If he was under suspicion he was probably under discreet surveillance, as he had witnessed earlier that morning. If he tried to travel across the inner-city border, he would be stopped before he ever got close to a checkpoint.

He would have to rely on the Americans. It was something he had planned on years before but it required direct contact, an extremely dangerous move and something he had always tried to avoid. He leaned back in the chair and pondered his next move.

First, he would send out a message to warn his handlers. Second, he would determine the cause. Third, he would find a way out. Last, he would survive. But before he cut all his anchors, he would take care of one final thing.

His mood darkened for a moment, then he turned back to the windows. Outside, snow was beginning to fall, brightening the otherwise gray-brown sky. Then he realized it was too early for snow. What he saw was actually chimney ash from the cheap coal the government's power plant burned night and day.

4

Bruno Großmann stood before the Minister of State Security's desk. He was puzzled by its bareness. The desk was huge, bigger than his family dinner table, and there was nothing on it but Lenin's death mask. Like the walls of the office, the desk was made of a light blond wood. At least it wasn't set on a platform to make the minister appear even more god-like, he thought.

Großmann now considered the man sat behind the desk, the dumpy chief himself, Generaloberst Erich Mielke. Mielke was a communist who had risen from the roughest streets of Berlin to the highest levels of the Party. He had been an assassin in the communist self-defense force and had killed two police officers before the war. As Minister, he had built the best internal security apparatus in the world; better than the Soviets and more ruthless than the Chinese. But, and there was always a *but*, he was basically a policeman and didn't know much of anything about intelligence or, more importantly, counterintelligence operations.

That's my area and Mielke knows it, Großmann thought. He was pleased with himself.

Standing to the side of the desk was Markus Wolf, the Director of the HVA, the *Stasi*'s foreign intelligence branch. He was the Grandmaster in the game of spying. Großmann respected

Wolf because of his skill at penetrating and manipulating the *Bundesnachrichtendienst*, the West German intelligence service. He wondered what Wolf thought of Mielke, but it was impossible to tell. Wolf never shared personal opinions and his eyes never betrayed his thoughts.

Großmann was known as "S" because he was the head of *Hauptabteilung II—Spionageabwehr*, the main department responsible for counterespionage. HA II protected the secrets of the GDR's most secret ministry and tracked down traitors to the Party.

He cleared his throat and began his case summary.

"Last night, based on information provided to me by Generaloberst Wolf, my department conducted an operation to capture a spy working for the Americans. A man we believe was linked to a senior level officer in our organization."

"Was? Past tense?" questioned Mielke.

"Unfortunately he was ready for us and resisted our officers. He was shot dead."

"Who warned him? Did you establish who he was working with?"

"Most likely he was awake and heard the team coming, Comrade Minister. As to your second question, we're going through the evidence and are getting close."

"No answers then?"

"Nothing definitive yet, Minister, but based on your earlier instructions, I have begun to monitor several possible suspects. I expect we'll have the answer soon."

"Markus, your opinion?" Mielke turned to his espionage chief.

"To recap what we know: information from a very reliable Russian source at Pullach points to a well-placed traitor within our ranks. The Americans shared a report with the *BND* that contained details of our relations with the Libyans. But they carelessly left in details that described how they had obtained the information. It was enough to reveal the suspect's identity. The man who died was an *S-Bahn* driver with access to West Berlin. But I believe he was just an intermediary, not the spy himself—he would have had no access himself to this kind of material. Whoever the spy is, he most likely uses multiple intermediaries to communicate and has very sophisticated means of protecting himself. Lacking any additional clues, General Großmann's surveillance of the possible suspects within our headquarters, as well as trying to find the spy's contacts on the outside, is our best course of action at the moment."

Mielke turned red and began to splutter.

"I want this spy, this traitor, this—this slime found! I want him arrested before any of this gets out to the Politburo. I will not be embarrassed. Do you understand me, Großmann? When we do find him, and you will, I want him to understand the consequences of betraying his country. Then, we will kill him."

Großmann watched Mielke fume even as he spoke. His words were punctuated with tiny spit droplets that landed all over his desk. He thought Lenin would be appalled to know that the Minister of State Security was defacing his death mask.

Finished with his report, Großmann clicked his heels in the Prussian fashion, although he was not in uniform, and marched himself from the room. For a brief moment he reveled in the thought that it was the GDR, not the soft Federal Republic in the West, that had inherited Germany's true military tradition.

After dismissing his senior security officer, Mielke stared in a seeming trance at the portrait of his hero on the wall. Wolf took the opportunity to leave. He needed no dismissal.

In the corridor, he caught up with Großmann.

"Too bad about last night. I assume you didn't have the chance to take him on the street or at the rail station?"

"He must have known he was in danger. We had to act fast before he ran. When we showed up, my boys saw a pistol in his hand; it turned out to be fake. We found nothing incriminating and I have no leads. I was hoping he would give us something. Whoever trained him did it well. But we'll keep pushing."

Großmann was throwing out excuses and had completely missed the point. Wolf knew he would have had better results had the man been arrested away from his home on unfamiliar ground and off balance. Then they might have had a living suspect to interrogate. Wolf continued, hoping to salvage something from the event.

"Besides the Minister, have you told anyone else in headquarters about the suspect's death?"

"No. I instructed my team not to discuss it and all the neighbors have been warned to keep silent. I don't want to spook our quarry."

"Let's talk, I have an idea," Wolf said.

Großmann suspected Wolf had something interesting in mind. In the convoluted world of espionage, he was the best. They walked down the hall from Mielke's office and stepped into an unoccupied conference room. When Großmann was inside the room, Wolf shut the door and faced the portly security officer.

"Walk me through what you're doing again and who you believe could be our leak."

"I started with the leaked information that our liaison got from the Russians, which was on our relations with the Libyans and assistance to one of their assassination teams. The only departments, other than yours, that deal with anything close are Department X—International Relations, Department XXII—Terrorism, and AGM—the Minister's Working Group. The two offices that concern your directorate are the Overseas Stations and Political Intelligence sections. Since the dead contact was a Berliner, I eliminated any of our officers serving outside the country."

"That's a lot of people, from the generals at the top down to the secretaries."

"I narrowed the list down by looking at who had access to that specific bit of information and after I eliminated you and the Minister, I came up with five names. Niebling, Coburg, Kleine and two from your group: Fischer and Dahle."

29

Großmann had mentioned the subordinates' names to Wolf before the meeting with Mielke but hearing them again did not convince him that either were traitors. Both Fischer and Dahle were long-time trusted employees and had proved themselves patriots to the nation. But he had to admit that Großmann was correct to consider all the possibilities.

"Why did you eliminate me from suspicion?"

"I —" Großmann didn't know how to answer that.

For once, Wolf smiled.

"I'm kidding. What other measures have you taken?"

"The Minister authorized me to put discreet surveillance on each man. I have also checked their offices and safes for evidence but haven't come up with anything."

Wolf thought for a moment.

"If the traitor finds out that his contact is dead, he will either shut down his operation and sit tight hoping not to be found, or he will try to escape. The next days will be critical. So I would like you to consider an idea."

"Yes, General."

Großmann addressed Wolf as 'General' out of respect. Although he was a major general, Wolf still outranked him by two grades and his reputation in the service. He was also very much afraid of Wolf's power.

"I will have a report written that will confirm there is a Libyan plan to assassinate a prominent Western opposition political leader within days. It will be disseminated to the same people as the other report. Then we'll see what happens. I would expect our traitor would be very eager to get that information to his handler, so you must keep close surveillance on all of them," Wolf continued.

"That's an excellent idea, General." Großmann understood that Wolf didn't want him to question the plan; rather he was being instructed on how the problem was to be handled.

"I will ensure my surveillance teams are fully engaged with their respective targets. I will also ensure we have the means in place to instantly alert Border Command if the traitor decides to run for the West."

Sometimes, Großmann longed for the good old days when he could arrest the people he wanted without all this need for proof. Großmann thought back to his days as an interrogator, a member of *Kommissariat 5*, the predecessor to the *Stasi*, where he started out. K5 became the *Stasi* before the June 1953 uprising happened and then everything changed. It was a time that shook the foundations of the government and it was shortly after Stalin died…

I miss the old man.

Early in 1953, Moscow demanded an acceleration towards the full implementation of communism in East Germany. More work and higher production on lower wages and longer hours. The populace began to grumble. The ill-advised policy reforms only convinced people that the government intended to work them hard and wring them out like rags. When the uprising came, the party bosses were caught unawares and on June 16 the country quickly went to hell.

Großmann remembered the workers marching from the factories in the north of town shouting their slogans. Then the office employees poured out of their workplaces and joined them, tentatively at first, then enthusiastically, as they marched on East Berlin's city center.

It was lucky for us that they didn't have a plan beyond marching and protesting.

General Secretary Ulbricht and his ill-informed party hacks had acted like frightened children. They couldn't make a decision and when the rebels began to trash government buildings it looked like the entire country would rise up. In fact, one million people did rise up against the government, but the Western press never got wind of that because the news was suppressed.

Thankfully, the Soviets knew what to do. As soon as High Commissioner Semyonev figured out that his German comrades were out of their depth, he called Moscow for the permission he needed to employ the Soviet Army. He got it and told General Grechko, the Russian military commander, to take care of business.

Working alongside the Russian state security service, the MGB—*Ministerstvo gosudarstvennoy bezopasnosti*—the internal security department of the *Stasi* got the green light to take whatever action was necessary to put things back in the box. The Soviets gave them good cover. Never faint-hearted, they led the T-34s into Berlin and cleaned house. The protesters didn't stand a chance.

At one city square he remembered watching hundreds of protesters milling about as a phalanx of tanks entered into the square from a side street. They were surprised at first but clearly didn't believe there would be violence.

They thought the Russians would never open fire with the Allies so close. So they didn't run. Instead, they began walking towards the tanks. That was the wrong move. When the smoke cleared scores of rebels lay dead or dying on the ground. Then the tanks moved forward, still firing their machine guns and churning through the now-terrified humanity. *Stasi* officers, including Großmann, followed the tanks and arrested the surviving ring leaders, or anyone who looked like one, and disposed of them. They kept at it for weeks after the street demonstrations were crushed. Großmann remembered fondly how people betrayed their neighbors or anyone they didn't like to him and his fellow officers.

Most of the time no evidence or confessions were necessary. If they weren't shot, they went to prison. After it was all done, the Red Cross reported that fifteen or twenty people were killed.

I alone shot almost that many! The total was more like 500, maybe as many as 1,000 dead.

Großmann remembered the empty factory-turned-holding pen where he had conducted interrogations. The Russians brought many of the arrested to him and his comrades. There were so many prisoners that they had to operate like an assembly line: one by one the prisoners were brought in. Then one morning a group of around twenty arrived. They were a motley-looking group of men and women. Scared and dejected mostly, but several looked defiant. He would focus on the strongest first and then the weaker would easily break and confess to whatever he demanded of them.

One of the Russians, an *MGB* officer who spoke German, told Großmann that they were leaders of the rebellion.

"Why do you say that?" he asked.

"They were carrying handbills with anti-government sayings," the Russian said.

"All of them?"

"No, but they were all together. They must all be associates and are therefore guilty."

Guilt by association. Simple enough. He questioned them separately and their stories were all the same. They had been given bundles of handbills by a man on the street and were told to pass them out to everyone they saw or met. No one was guilty of anything more than being caught up in the moment. He didn't believe them. There was one man—an effete-looking man, maybe an academic—wearing wire-rimmed glasses. He looked to be an organizer. Großmann asked him where the handbills came from. Same story.

"A man gave them to us on the street."

"Is he here?"

"No," Wire-rimmed said.

Too quick, Großmann thought, he didn't even glance around.

He marched the man back towards the center of the room.

"This man says he's innocent."

Großmann regarded the prisoners. They were young and old men, young and old women. Most appeared to be laborers, some could have been students, others looked like intelligentsia. He hated the intelligentsia. Wire-rimmed looked like intelligentsia.

"But I know he's lying," he stated, "and until one of you tells me the truth, I will keep you here, maybe forever."

"I am not lying," Wire-rimmed said. He was scared.

"Shut up, traitor. You are a traitor to the Democratic Republic and the Communist Party."

Großmann pulled his Tokarev pistol from his waistband. He always kept it loaded as his Russian instructor taught him. Holding it at his side he pointed at the ground. An audible click resonated through the dead silent room as he flicked the safety to the off position. There were gasps.

"No—" Wire-rimmed started to speak, but before he could continue, Großmann raised the pistol to his head and pulled the trigger. The pistol barked once and Wire-rimmed's head jerked to the side as the small-caliber bullet entered his brain and blew a hole out of his skull. He was dead before the red mist cleared from the air. The body fell heavily to the floor and a pool of blood spread across the concrete.

The other prisoners were transfixed by the sight. A woman turned away and started to sob. Several men just stared at the ground.

Großmann looked at the body and was pleased with his work.

"Who would like to tell me the truth now?"

No one spoke up.

"You," Großmann pointed at a young woman, "come with me."

The woman might have been in her early twenties but it was hard to tell. Her face was grimy and her clothes dirty. He grabbed her arm when she came close and jerked her towards him as he turned. Together they walked out of the holding room and into an adjacent cell.

He tossed the girl across the room. She bounced off the wall and collapsed in a heap. The she looked up at him with red-rimmed eyes and pleaded.

"I am innocent. Why have you brought me to this place? I have done nothing wrong and I have nothing I can tell you."

"You are mistaken, slut. We don't bring people here to profess their innocence. We bring them here to admit their guilt."

Soon, screams permeated the air, assaulting the ears and minds of the prisoners. For fifteen minutes the prisoners stood trying to avoid each other's eyes. The Russian and East German soldiers talked among themselves and laughed. Then came a muffled shot. And quiet. Großmann came into the room, straightening his clothing as he walked.

"Let's try this once more. Who would like to tell me the truth?" he asked.

Some of the arrested informed on their friends and relatives; others, seeing no way out, volunteered to work for the regime. A new order was coming, one built on fear, suspicion, and repression. It was a foundation that would later prove to be built not on stone but on sand. But no one knew that yet and Großmann would never understand that fundamental weakness. Instead, he smiled to himself.

Those were the good old days.

The interrogations he conducted, the confessions—that's what got him to where he was today.

The uprising didn't end well for those that started it, nor for many in the regime. Wilhelm Zaisser, the *Stasi's* chief at the time, was replaced. Ostensibly it was because he missed the signs that the revolt was coming. In reality, he was thrown out because he was too much of a Stalinist and when Stalin died, so did his protection. With Zaisser out of the way, Mielke began his rise to power and in 1957 he would take over as Minister. Things began to change and after the Wall was built, Großmann was told his ways had to change too. East Germany became a kinder, gentler dictatorship. He still missed Stalin, he just learned not to show it.

Now, when the Politburo wants to arrest someone, we need to find evidence. What a bunch of crap!

5

Fischer did not have many interests in East Berlin other than enjoying concerts, eating at one of the few good restaurants in the East, and walking in the parks. He much preferred his small house outside the city. The *Dacha* he called it. It was his forest refuge where he could read, walk, relax, and enjoy the solitude. He did not relish never seeing it again.

Just as had been the case at his overseas posts, many aspects of his daily routine in Berlin were fabricated. He knew he had to have good reasons to move about the city, reasons that would appear normal to anyone who might be interested in keeping watch on his activities. For that, he had developed other interests. Hunting antiques and old books were two of them. Cash-hungry East Berliners always wanted to sell their heritage so they could afford to buy a refrigerator or even a car without saving for years from their meager salaries. Seeking out antiques gave him a reason to walk around the city and loiter in stores or marketplaces for what might seem interminable periods to a surveillance team. Surveillants, unless they were very professional and used to shopping with their wives, usually lasted only a couple of hours before the tedium and repeated appearances revealed their purpose to a situationally aware subject. That was one important thing about a secret life that few understood: it was not as exciting as the movies portrayed it. It was boring as hell and required iron discipline to maintain a cover.

One of his shorter circuits was the walk to the *Konditorei*, a place he visited often. It was not too far from the office but the convoluted route he had chosen made sense because it was the fastest and it offered several natural look-backs that let Fischer unobtrusively see if he was being followed. Not that it mattered; he wasn't doing anything of interest to Department S anyway, at least not anything they could see.

Backerei Lila had been on the Harnackstraße longer than most people could remember. It always had a decent assortment of pastries that made it popular with the locals and the bureaucrats who worked nearby. When he walked into the shop, it was empty save for a retired couple who teetered about arm in arm trying to decide what to buy with their change. Fischer waited patiently until they finished their transaction before he spoke.

"Good morning, Lila! A dozen *Berliners*, please," he said. He would share them with his comrades at work.

Always treat your co-workers well, because you can never tell when a favor might be needed or a secret shared.

Lila was several years younger and a head shorter than Max, and her face held a beauty and glow that contrasted sharply with the monochrome culture that surrounded her. Fischer knew Lila's bakery from its opening and liked her wares, but his real connection was to Lila herself. Their relationship was deeper and longer than anyone knew.

The first time he met her was in 1950. Her father, Heinrich, had run afoul of the communists after the war. He was an outspoken journalist and his socialist views didn't square with the Party's hard line. It was during the so-called intensification of the class struggle that he was arrested, and it was Lila who came and tried to get him out of jail.

Fischer was there to conduct background checks on some names in the police files and just happened to intercept her when she came into the police station. She was beautiful—that was what drew his attention—but he saw she was distressed. When she explained why she was there, he became concerned for her safety.

"You are not safe here, you must leave now," he told her.

He knew the families of "enemies of the state" were usually punished, and ostracized from society. That meant the family couldn't join the Party and without membership, they were not eligible for any benefits and were on the bottom of every waiting list—for housing, buying a car, ration cards, everything. Although he hadn't entirely rebelled against the regime yet, he knew someone in need when he saw them, and he made the impulsive decision to help.

Before Lila left the station that day, Fischer got her name and address. He told her he would be in contact. He thought it was a fortuitous coincidence that he was even there. He had been looking through police files, checking the backgrounds of candidates for Markus Wolf's refugee program. It was a clever plan to recruit loyal men and women to go to the West as "refugees" where they would be sleeper agents. Some would assume completely new identities and seek government jobs. If they were successful they would become agents in place. It was one of the *Stasi*'s best infiltration projects and would later lead to the demise of several prominent West German officials, including Chancellor Willy Brandt.

Later that day, he went to the apartment block in Moabit where Lila lived and coaxed her out to a small *Kneipe* to drink some wine with him. She was nervous in his presence at first, thinking him to be a police officer.

"I am not with the police, but I do work with the government," he said.

He could never bring himself to tell her exactly what he did, but she must have guessed because she stopped asking. But she never pushed him away either.

"I want to help you, but you have to forget your father for now. Otherwise, you and your mother might end up in jail too. I have an idea of how to keep you both safe."

"How will that work?" She was skeptical, having had no education in the finer points of the tradecraft that Fischer knew all too well.

First, he quickly moved Lila and her mother to a safe house. The refugee project paid for incidentals like relocation and he was able to mix the two women in with his classified roster of candidates without anyone being the wiser. The project also provided him the opportunity to get new documentation and set them up with new identities. It wasn't difficult; his work in the security service had its advantages at times.

Next he removed and burned all their paperwork from the Firm's files.

"They didn't work out," was his excuse. Nothing more was asked or said.

Lila's father was sentenced to two years in prison for "anti-government activities" and died there. He didn't die of natural causes though. He was tortured and then murdered "attempting to escape." The only saving grace was that his wife and Lila were never found. The government assumed they had escaped to the West. Fischer couldn't bring himself to send them to the West though. He was selfish and wanted to keep Lila close by because of his growing affection for her.

He kept her company when he could and saved his salary to help them out. With his help, she was eventually able to afford the bakery. Fischer came to their apartment often and they would listen to classical music and talk. Her mother would go to her bedroom early when he came over, thinking he was a suitable and honorable man for her daughter.

That left him with a quandary. He thought he loved Lila. She was the first woman that he truly wanted to spend his life with, but he loved his job too, or thought he did.

As one of the select few Germans at the Lenin School, he had advantages over most of the other officers in the Firm, which translated into valuable experience outside the country. His successes working with friendly foreign intelligence services gave him exposure to the highest levels of the business, both overseas and back home in Berlin. It was the kind of exposure that led to promotions.

Fischer was good at persuading people to spy on their own country. He was equally good at finding spies who had been recruited by the enemy. He remembered one case vividly. His African liaison contact told him they suspected one of their own officers of providing information to a hostile power, but they didn't know which. Fischer worked with that service's counterintelligence section for six months on the case. Then, he stumbled onto a coincidence, a correlation actually. The officer often went to a local fish market, not randomly, but on specific days. He bought a fish and then gave the seller an envelope to pay for it. Fischer thought that odd. Why not just hand him the cash? The answer came later that day when a foreigner came and also bought a fish. He too paid the fishmonger with money in an envelope. After the next time the officer came and went, the security service waited for the foreigner. When he bought a fish, they pounced and searched the foreigner. Inside his fish was a plastic-wrapped envelope filled with tiny pieces of paper with encrypted text written on them. The foreigner was quickly expelled. Fischer was sure the African officer did not get off so easily and he didn't like that consequence of his success. The saving grace of the affair, for him, was that the foreigner was a Russian. It was his first strike against the system which had raised him and then alienated him.

Trips like that helped his profile and his career, but seven months was a long time away, and the absences took a toll on his relationship with Lila. His frequent absences led to arguments and a cooling of his feeling towards her. He felt she had no right to dictate what he did. He didn't realize that she wanted him fully in her life as a partner, not as a part-time lover.

Fischer was too busy to understand and too involved with his projects to look deeper into their problems. Then came the break that changed everything. In 1957, he disappeared from her life for eight months when he went off to Egypt without a word. He saw working with a partner service overseas as a chance for promotion. She saw it as his way to escape from her.

When he came back, she wouldn't see him. He took the easy way out and stopped trying.

When he finally visited Lila's bakery again after the Wall went up, he found that she was still single. They became friends again but, despite his feelings for her, he no longer dreamed of being with her. He knew his job would always be a problem. Instead, like a typical intelligence officer, he decided she might be useful to his work and kept her close. He recruited her to his cause after his tour in Zanzibar. Because of her father, she agreed to help him. She hated the regime even more than he did, but they did not speak of those things often. He wasn't even sure if she felt anything for him other than a bit of gratitude. Nevertheless, she was still pleasant with him.

"How are you, *Herr* Fischer? It's been too long!" She smiled genuinely at him as she packaged up the pastries. She always greeted him so, even if it had been just days since his last visit. She also addressed him formally both out of respect for his position and because of the old ladies of the neighborhood watch who made it their life's work to interfere and start rumors.

"My work is hectic as usual, but it looks like you're doing well," he commented as he regarded the display cases that were more or less filled to capacity, a rarity in the Eastern sector.

"Yes, business is good. I am selling everything we bake."

"I see you have *Bienenstich* today."

The extremely rich pastry sat in the corner display case oozing with a luscious custard filling that tempted even the most restrained.

Lila paused as she wrapped Fischer's packet of *Berliners*. Several heartbeats passed before she could respond to the pre-arranged phrase.

"Yes, would you like to try a piece?"

"No, thank you. My doctor would kill me. Besides I have other vices to contend with."

She passed the package to Fischer and he handed her several bills and a handful of coins, "That should take care of it, I think."

Lila sorted the coins and dropped all of them, save one, into the till. The last one, a five-Mark piece, went quickly and unobtrusively into her pocket. She again smiled up at Fischer and gave him a cheery send-off, "Yes, that's fine. Until next time, *Herr* Fischer."

Fischer was already out the door and marching back down the streets towards his office with the package, his overcoat swirling out behind him. Lila was safe and his escape plan initiated. His next task would be to find out who had been compromised. As he strode along through the chilled air, Fischer's mind was already busy plotting the next steps along his ever more perilous secret path.

6

Embassy Third Secretary Consular Assistant Matthew Brimley pushed his way through the crowd outside the Centrum department store complex. The Christmas holidays loomed; it seemed like every inhabitant of East Berlin was trying to get their shopping done early. Or perhaps they were just window shopping, because this was the most expensive store in the East.

The previous day, Brimley had driven his usual route to work from the apartment complex that housed most of the American Embassy personnel. He followed the route meticulously each and every morning and evening, deviating only when he needed to go to a shop. Even then, he returned to the route and finished it as normal.

The idea was that anyone who was watching him would be bored to death. His post at the embassy was just as boring to the watchers, if there were any. He sat behind a plate-glass window with a hole for talking and a slot for the paperwork the East Germans pushed through it. He reviewed the papers for correctness, made copies, and told the person who brought them to come back in a week or never to come back again. It was usually the former, because anyone who appeared at his window had already run the gauntlet of East German security outside the consulate. His job, as consular officer, was to validate the visas of persons who wished to visit the United States. In East Germany, like the rest of the Soviet Bloc, that meant the only people who made it to his window were those who had been approved by the regime. They were either government officials like diplomats, or engineers directed by the security service to steal American technology while pretending to attend a seminar in New York or Los Angeles. No regular East German citizens came seeking a tourist or student visa—they could visit Crimea or Yugoslavia if they needed a vacation and they could go to school in the Soviet Union. At least that's what the government thought. Try changing your government's opinion and you might end up in prison. That made Brimley's job pretty routine.

But he did have a sideline. He was trained to observe details and ask questions that others might overlook. He would pass those details on to other people in the embassy and they would follow them up. That would usually take the form of a casual meeting with the visitor at the United Nations or a conference in Albuquerque to gauge their receptiveness to further meetings. Brimley was a spotter, a talent scout looking for potential recruits who might be interested in betraying their country. He was also an intelligence analyst who read the East German newspapers and journals brought to the embassy and pulled out interesting details for his reports from documents that otherwise might not make it out of the country—what in the business was called "open source" intelligence. He never left the embassy building other than to go home or shop. His routine was boring and he was boring. That was his job, to be boring.

That was why the East Germans did not suspect him of being an intelligence officer. That was why he drove the same route every day. He was boring but he was searching for something, a signal. Every day, twice a day, back and forth, except on Sundays. He knew that he had to follow the route and he knew which window to look at every time he passed by.

Communication was always about others and, in this case, it was a closed loop between two people. Matthew Brimley knew he was waiting for a signal. On the other side, an agent knew someone like Brimley would check a certain window twice a day. When the agent needed to pass a message, they would set the signal as instructed. Then the two would meet the next day at a set time, if only for a moment, in what was called a brush pass.

Brimley didn't know who this agent was. Even the Chief of Station didn't know. All he knew was that when the signal was posted, Brimley had to conduct the brush-pass, a brief contact with an unknown agent. Brimley exercised the routine several times a year—he'd been in East Berlin for eighteen months—but yesterday the signal had been right there in the window and now he had to do the routine for real. He didn't think he would be nervous; he knew the routine backwards and forwards. But now that he was in the store, Brimley admitted to himself that he was indeed feeling anxious.

He headed for the toy section on the third floor. It was a place he actually enjoyed because he had a hobby—model trains. He loved N-scale trains and knew that the only people who built better model trains than the East Germans were the West Germans, specifically a company called Märklin. But you couldn't buy a West German train for the price you paid for a nearly identical East German version at the Centrum. The exchange rate was what made all the difference.

He was looking at all the different model trains and admiring their details as he waited for the appropriate time. He picked up a locomotive on display; a big Prussian P-10 steam engine known as a Mikado. It was beautifully executed, he thought. Suddenly he noticed a young boy gazing at the toy with envious eyes, his mother staring at him disapprovingly. He put the piece back on the shelf, picked up a smaller PIKO coal locomotive and turned away before the boy made him feel uncomfortable again.

He paid for the train at the register and moved off, pausing here and there to appreciate the other trains and toys before he made his way to the escalator and started down, the shopping bag in his left hand, an umbrella in his right. If anything or anyone appeared to make him uncomfortable, he would switch the umbrella to his left hand to indicate danger.

On the second floor, he wound around in a semi-circle to the next set of down escalators to the first floor and descended again. On the first floor, he stepped off to the side of the store and went down a short hallway to the men's room. The hallway was crowded with people which forced him to slow down. As he did so, he felt a slight tug on his coat pocket. Not looking down, he kept moving into the washroom. He did his business and came back out, wiping his hands on the one cheap paper towel available to him. Unlike West Germany, there were no small dishes on a stool, left out by the janitorial staff for obligatory tips. There was an old cleaning woman sitting in a chair by the door, asleep. She was probably there to keep tabs on everyone coming and going but was failing in her patriotic duty.

Returning to the main part of the store, Brimley headed down the escalator to the ground floor, wound his way through the displays and the shoppers, and headed outside to his parking place. He walked slowly and deliberately with his shopping bag, happily smiling at the people he passed, while inwardly his stomach tied in a knot. He got to the car, unlocked the door and slid into the driver's seat. Only when he pulled out of the parking place did he relax. No one had confronted him.

When he got to the safety of the embassy compound, he reached into his pocket and pulled out the object the unknown agent had left him. It was a five-Mark coin.

7

The next day, some 18 kilometers to the west, in the American Sector of West Berlin, Thomas Murphy sat at his desk reading from a pile of printed files and glancing at the screen of his secure electronic record-keeping system. Murphy was Chief of Berlin Operational Base, referred to by everyone in the Central Intelligence Agency as the BOB. Located inside Clay Compound, the US headquarters in West Berlin, it was one of the Agency's most important posts worldwide and a gateway into East Germany. The smaller station in East Berlin was more constrained in its collection and recruitment activities because of the harsh security environment. East Berlin station officers were constantly under surveillance, which made their job as difficult as working in Moscow. Not that operating out of West Berlin was easy.

Berlin was a plum job; to be on the cutting edge of the intelligence profession was both rewarding and a harbinger of better things to come—as long as you didn't screw it up.

Murphy's road to this position had been an unusual one. He was a former Marine infantry officer and a good operator, but he came from outside the usual line of progression that led to Russia House. The fact that he possessed a persistent eidetic memory, the infinite capacity to absorb information and vividly recall it at a later date, was one factor in his success. People he worked with called it spooky when he mentioned a project or an agent and cited the exact cable number of an old message that covered the subject. It was one of many talents that served him well in his chosen vocation and hastened his upward mobility. It also knocked down barriers that stopped other officers from reaching this position. More than that, he was a good street operator and had recruited a significant number of productive agents.

But the fact that he was here was even more remarkable when one considered that he did not come from the Eastern European side of the Agency. Murphy was an Africa hand and the European branch regarded officers who served in Third World countries skeptically. They felt the work in Europe was more challenging, both technically and operationally.

"Africa is full of spies just waiting for a recruiter," they would joke.

What they meant was that every almost African politician, military officer, and government employee wanted Uncle Sam to pay their way to the high life. Murphy brought the detractors to heel with the facts.

"We have had more high-value recruitments in Africa than anywhere else. And by that, I mean Russians."

His own tally of recruitments attested to that. It made him one of the best. He knew the main enemy—the Soviets— better than most and that was why he landed in this office just off the Clayallee in the quiet Berlin district of Dahlem. If he had spoken Russian rather than flawless German, he probably would have ended up in Moscow.

He had done his share of clandestine ops on the street and in the hotels and bars of the world. A recruitment in Pretoria might be handled with meetings in Nairobi, Paris, or Doha. A lower-level asset might be handled in his home country, but always carefully. Those meetings often were dangerous, especially in hostile countries where an asset faced certain death if discovered and the handler might fall victim to an "accident."

Now he was essentially a dispatcher. He ran his operations mostly from the office, managing the younger case officers, communicating with headquarters, and meeting the chiefs of the British and French services along with West Berlin's internal security service, the *Verfassungschutz*, to share whatever intelligence was deemed shareable. It was a twenty-four-hour-a-day job and his mid-section had grown commensurate with his responsibilities.

No exercise and too much good food.

He once again vowed to follow his long-ignored resolutions. Then a knock on his always open office door brought him back to the present.

"Boss, can we talk?"

Murphy looked up to see his deputy motioning towards the back of the office space. Jamie Wheeler stood in the door taking up most of the available space. He was ex-Army Special Forces and notable because of his size. His name belied his Polynesian DNA; he was over six feet tall and weighed in at around 245 pounds. He was not a guy to take lightly in a bar fight or the jungle. He was no lightweight as an intelligence officer either.

Wheeler's gestures told Murphy whatever he wanted to talk about was serious. Without a word, Murphy got up and followed him to a secure door. The BOB had three levels of security. The first was the main office block, a secure facility in and of itself requiring entry through a sally port, an outer door that had to be closed before the inner door could open. At the rear of the main office was the second level, the communications room that could receive or send the highest classifications of information. Every message generated by the BOB went out as at least "Secret," which included everything from routine supply requests to agent communications. Agent communications, especially those from assets who were considered to be at high risk, were sent out in tightly restricted traffic via special channels at levels above "Top Secret."

The third and last level of security in the office was the "bubble," a sound-proof isolation chamber that prevented any conversation held inside from being overheard. Murphy and Wheeler were headed that way.

The communications staff went about their business as Murphy and Wheeler walked past and through another door. Inside the room behind the door was a standalone enclosure that looked like a meat locker on stilts with its own ventilation system and another keypad lock. Punching the combination, Wheeler flipped the door lever, not unlike that of a railway boxcar, and pulled the heavy door open. At the flick of a switch the lights came on and the loud hum of the ventilation system filled the space. Once inside, the door was shut and the two men were locked away, isolated from the outside world.

"What's up?" Murphy said.

"OZ has been compromised."

"How?" Murphy was alarmed.

He was alarmed for OZ but even more for the Agency. GBOZ, as he was known in the restricted files, was a senior *Stasi* officer and only a few Agency officers knew where he worked, let alone his true name. Neither fact was ever mentioned in message traffic. Murphy knew. OZ was the most important asset he had in East Germany: Brigadier General Maximilian Fischer in the *Stasi's* foreign intelligence directorate, the *HVA*. He was one of the Agency's only high-level penetrations of the Warsaw Pact and his knowledge of the *Stasi's* overseas networks was a goldmine that the Agency couldn't lose. Furthermore, Murphy could immediately think of five major playback operations that could be compromised if OZ were arrested and broke under interrogation.

"We don't know yet. He sent an emergency message. A hollow coin with a message inside was passed to an officer in East Berlin. Station opened the coin and sent the unencrypted text to Russia House. I just received his decrypted message from them through special channels. He hasn't been arrested, but he's under surveillance and wants out. Another complication is that he has closed down his communications network, says it's too dangerous to send out any more messages. So, right now all we have is one-way commo."

Murphy knew the case well. He and Wheeler were the only two BOB officers on the highly restricted BIGOT access list for GBOZ traffic—the 'GB' showed it was an East Bloc case. East Berlin Station didn't hold any information on him because of the danger of compromise; they only knew the coin was from a special asset. Even that was dangerous and OZ's passing it meant he had abandoned his usual communications methods.

"Okay, first, we need to tell him we received his message. He will be listening to RIAS. So, tell him to sit tight and wait for a message at specific times. Figure out a workable schedule. Have Marco fit it in with their regular traffic but don't tell him anything else!"

Marco was the co-opted American manager of Radio in the American Sector, the broadcasting station that was as popular in East Berlin as in the West. In between the music and news, coded signals were routinely sent over the airwaves. Some were just gibberish meant to keep up the impression of heavy traffic, but some were messages intended for specific agents. One might tell an agent that his message had been received or give him instructions. It was the fastest way to get a message directly to an agent. The only drawbacks were that there was no way to quickly confirm the agent had received a message, and he couldn't be overheard listening to the station. Murphy was sure OZ would be careful. He had years of experience at evading scrutiny, but something had gone very wrong. Murphy was sure that whatever had happened took place on the Western side of the Wall. It meant a mistake had been made or a traitor talked.

"I'll pull out his extraction plan and review it. The only problem is that it's old and hasn't been updated as far as I know, and his position makes it difficult to get close. Getting him over the border will be even harder. In the meantime, we must walk back the dog.

Tell Russia House we will do a scrub of all his sub-agents to see who might have gone bad. Any of our traffic mentioning him or his intelligence needs to be reviewed for errors. They need to do the same. Most importantly, if they haven't started, headquarters needs to look at everyone on the distribution list. That last one's an exclusive for the Director only."

"Got it. I will put together the messages and shoot them to you for release. All in the restricted channel."

"Good, and tell everyone in the office that we will be working hard on a sensitive issue and that they should go about their work as normally as possible. We may have to pull a couple of people in and read them on to help, but not yet."

"Anything else?"

"Not right now. I need to think on this. Let's go over a checklist in two hours. In the meantime, get cracking."

"Roger, Boss," Wheeler was up and shutting down the equipment as Murphy left the bubble.

As he walked back to his office, Murphy felt the hairs stand up on the back of his neck. There were only a few things that got him excited or made him anxious. One was meeting an agent in a dark alley; finding that one of his agents was in danger was another. He'd seen plenty the Agency's top-tier agents rolled up by the opposition over the years. Most of them ended up with a bullet in the back of their head in Bautzen or Lubyanka.

OZ would not suffer that fate, he vowed. *I will make sure of that.*

8

Several days after the wiretap mission on the Border Guard tower, Kim Becker strode from his team room and down the stone stairs of Building 817 in the direction of the unit sergeant major's office.

The unit was housed in a building on the Andrews Barracks compound with a sign outside that said it was the home of the Support Detachment Berlin or SDB. With that name and their tasking statement—We support the mission of the Berlin Brigade—people's eyes glazed over with boredom, which was exactly the reaction desired.

The unit's classified designation was Special Forces Berlin and had just ninety men in all. That wasn't many in the grand scheme of things as there were nearly a million Warsaw Pact troops surrounding the city. But they were, nevertheless, dangerous men. They were the foxes in the chicken coop that was Berlin.

Their presence in the city was a secret that few were aware of outside the US Commander of Berlin and his immediate staff, the Chief of Base, and the Military Intelligence Detachment Commander. Counterintelligence reporting showed that the Russians and East Germans may have suspected that Special Forces men were stationed in Berlin and for that reason it was best to be cautious. You never know what you don't know.

It was the only unit of its kind in the American arsenal, essentially an updated Office of Strategic Services that conducted its unconventional operations under the noses of the Soviets. Each man was a specialist, an expert in at least two fields: weapons, demolitions, medical, communications, or operations and intelligence. Those were all fields that OSS operatives would have recognized, but more recently counterterrorism had been added to the mission set.

Once assigned to the unit the men had to master other esoteric skills as well: urban warfare, intelligence tradecraft like surveillance and non-technical communications methods, and surreptitious entry techniques, not to mention language skills. Being able to speak German, act like a German, essentially *be* German, was part of the job description. Some guys were more appropriately Polish, or Czech, or Turkish—anything but American, British, or French. And they had the documents to prove it. Although the men operated as a team, they had to be adept working on their own. Clandestine behavior required discipline and the mental and physical stamina to work as a singleton under stressful conditions.

They were waiting for war, waiting to take on a mission that no one in their right mind would volunteer for—far behind the lines with all the odds against them. But these men thought nothing of it. Or maybe they did, but they didn't seem to care because they believed they had a good chance of success. The unit had been preparing for the balloon to go up since the mid-1950s, and daily life was a cyclical regimen of planning, training, reconnaissance of targets, more training, and more planning. It was routine preparation for a mission that might never happen but it was anything but a routine mission. It was not wartime, not yet. They were waiting for the Cold War to go hot.

In the meantime, there were always other interesting projects.

With his recent promotion to master sergeant, Becker had been given the leadership of one of six Special Forces Operational Detachments or "A" Teams in Berlin. It was the team sergeant who put all the trades together to make a cohesive eleven-man team ready for any mission—he was the detail man, the planner, and the enforcer. Then there was the commander, but Team 5 didn't have a commander at the moment—Vietnam and the army's reduction in force had seen to that. Unfortunately, army captains were either needed to fight the current war or, if there wasn't one, they were tossed out of the service. It was a vagary of military thinking since captains, unlike lieutenants, were not easy to come by when you needed them. Berlin's "A" Teams didn't have a lieutenant; that meant Becker was in charge, which didn't affect operations much as the officers usually deferred to the senior non-coms anyway.

Everything the men of SDB did was clandestine, unseen by enemy or friend alike, except perhaps when two or three men would go out on the town. They tended to avoid the usual American military hangouts because, invariably, some GI would call them out for no good reason, which generally ended badly for the other guy. When it did go badly for someone in the unit, the solution was a quick reassignment out of the city, but that didn't happen often.

Becker stopped at the open door and looked into the office. His immediate boss was sitting at his desk poring over several documents. A Montecristo cigar sat in an ashtray, its smoke curling up into the air. Sergeant Major Jeff Bergmann was a big man, above average height, just under six feet, but stocky. He had been a wrestler in his scrappy youth. He was serious but contemptuous of convention, a trait that served him well in Special Forces. He was willing to forgive infractions, but only if the culprit came clean. He was not a man to cross.

Becker knocked on the office door frame. Bergmann looked up. "Kim! Come in."

Bergmann didn't stand on formality. Becker walked in and stood at ease in front of the desk. "You wanted to see me, Sergeant Major?"

Drawing on his cigar, Bergmann relished the flavor and then watched as his one long, slow exhale of smoke flattened out into a mushroom cloud formation above him.

"Sit."

Becker sat. Bergmann stood up and shut the door before he returned to his desk and sat on its edge.

"I reviewed your initial note on the mission. Between your equipment and the material that Teufelsberg is getting off their wireless intercepts, the spooks are happy—the communications spectrum seems to be pretty well covered. I'd like you to put together a more detailed report for the commander to use when he briefs the SOTFE Commander next week. Just a description with no names. Coordinates go into a separate annex. It will go straight into the compartmented files when the colonel is finished."

"The note didn't cover the technical details, you'll need to describe them in the report. You may have to brief the colonel before he goes to Stuttgart. Do you have an elevator pitch for what you did?"

"Sure. We installed two induction loop antennas and transmitters inside a junction box and on the landline inside the tower. The intel shop says the devices are sucking up all of the Border Guard's landline conversations for that sector. Besides hiding them well, the short-range transmitters should keep the signals from coming up on anyone's scope. And we had no run-ins of any kind on either side of the Wall. Just for fun, Finch left a pack of Russian Laika cigarettes in the tower. That should confuse the guards when they show up."

"You should probably leave that last bit out of the official report. One last thing, your men who worked on this with you, tell me again who they were…"

"Fred Lindt, Stefan Mann, Logan Finch, Paul Stavros were with me and they all did well. The rest of the team provided cover and some distraction for the guards in another sector."

"We need to remember then for future fitness reports and promotions."

"Definitely, Sergeant Major. They did great."

"Now, we have a different issue. Take a look at this," the sergeant major said as he pulled a folder off his desktop and handed it across to Becker.

The folder had a diagonal red stripe across its cover and was bound so its type-written pages could not be removed. There was no indication of where it had come from; it was completely unmarked with the exception of a red TOP SECRET stamp at the header and footer of each page. That meant only one thing: OGA—Other Government Agency—a euphemism for *the* Agency.

Becker skimmed the file quickly and then re-read the pages closely. The information inside surprised him. He closed the folder with the knowledge that the previous evening's mission might have been their last easy operation. He looked up and waited.

Bergmann continued, "We don't have all the details, but the chief of base asked me if we could help. The colonel is okay with us taking on the mission. What do you think?"

"I was afraid you'd ask me that. I think we might pull it off if we get all the support we'll need."

"We'll get it, no problem."

"Is it as important as this file indicates?" Becker didn't want to take on any high-risk, no-gain operations.

"It is of national importance. I know what you're concerned about, but the priority is super high, as is the risk. I want you to think through some possible options and let me know by day's end. And this is code word stuff, it has an even more restricted classification than last night, so don't share the info with anyone," and he extended his hand to get the file back.

"I didn't know the classifications went much higher." Becker stood and relinquished the folder. "I'll get back to you ASAP, Sergeant Major."

Bergmann was already back in his chair reading as Becker left the office.

9

A prisoner snatch inside East Berlin? That's either crazy, stupid, or both.

Becker remembered the last snatch he'd done. It had been a couple of years before in a land far, far away. He had been the One-Zero, the leader of a Studies and Observations Group Spike reconnaissance team called "Cobra," a small team of men in very hostile territory on the Ho Chi Minh trail. It was one of the last SOG missions carried out by Americans in Laos before cross-border operations were forbidden. Becker doubted the tactics he used there were applicable to East Berlin but this new mission brought back the bad memories.

His team had set up a demolition ambush along the trail and waited for three days before they could spring the trap on a small North Vietnamese Army patrol. The intel had given them a forty-eight-hour window to try and grab a prisoner—any longer than forty-eight hours on the ground would inevitably lead to their discovery—but they had hung on and waited. They had studied the aerials and had located the perfect terrain, close to a major artery of the trail with high-speed trails intersecting or paralleling it. They had to avoid the larger North Vietnamese Army—NVA—contingents that trooped by along the main artery in a near-constant stream.

Even a section of Soviet T-54 tanks rumbled through while the team's three Americans and three Chinese Nung mercenaries dug deeper into the moist, decaying detritus that covered the jungle's floor, hiding themselves from discovery. They had noticed that the high-speed trail to the north was regularly traveled by smaller groups who were either couriers or others that stayed away from the larger concentrations on the road. They set up on a bend in the high-speed trail where low-lying hills separated it from the main road. It also offered a fast escape from the ambush area toward terrain that they could hold until the choppers arrived to pull them out.

Finally, just after dawn of the third day, there was a lull in the traffic on the main road. One of the flankers signaled the approach of a good target on the high-speed trail. It was made up of eight porters pushing bicycles loaded high with supplies and led by several NVA soldiers. In the center were more soldiers. The configuration of the group was perfect for their set-up. Claymores, attached by detonation cord to a dual-primed explosive ring main that would set them off on command, were positioned along both sides of the trail bend with a gap in the middle. The back-blast from the claymores near the center would stun but hopefully not kill one or two of the enemy in the middle.

The word was passed by string-pull signals and the team waited for the patrol to walk into the kill zone. To say tensions were high was an understatement. Each man had his own way of dealing with the anxiety, but the moment before an ambush is initiated deep inside enemy territory is exhilarating and terrifying at the same time. Becker tried to push those thoughts aside and focused on the task ahead. The flankers watched for more troops to approach, the rear guard watched everyone's backsides to make sure the team itself wasn't ambushed, while the assault element focused on their individual targets as the enemy came into view.

Becker, as the One-Zero, got the honor of kicking things off and, with a quick squeeze of the clacker, fired the six claymore mines simultaneously. Each claymore's explosive charge fired around 700 small steel balls in a sixty-degree arc. A total of 4,200 balls flew out at 1,200 meters per second in a pattern that covered the trail to around 2 metres high. The blast and the hail of superheated metal vaporized almost everything along the trail. Most of the enemy were dead, two were badly wounded, and only one soldier in the group survived unscathed, but he was in no shape to fight.

As soon as the blast wave had passed, the team raised their heads and two men ran forward with their specially issued, suppressed High Standard HDMS pistols at the ready. Granted, suppressed weapons were superfluous after the explosion of the claymores, but it was standard procedure and why make more noise? A couple of rounds finished off those who might present a threat, while the best candidate for extraction—actually the lone survivor—was subdued. Handcuffed and blindfolded, he was rushed off the trail while the assault team set up a hasty ambush, this one unmanned with only booby-traps to slow down the reaction force that would surely be heading towards their position.

Davis, the team's radio operator, called for extraction as the team ran up the ridge line that paralleled the trail towards their designated landing zone. The LZ was an old bomb scar less than two clicks away and with any luck they would not find a blocking force between them and helos. Base responded that the standby birds were en route. Base was always more responsive when a prisoner was mentioned.

The team and its precious cargo moved quickly away from the ambush site. After a sprint up the incline, Becker counted his men as they moved up and over the ridge. They were seven now with the prisoner and moving fast, but tactically. In the middle of the small column, two Nungs were guiding, or rather carrying, the NVA prisoner. When they got over the ridge, the team stopped for a moment to get resettled but more importantly to listen. They could hear faint shouting from the direction they came, but no explosions.

That meant their direction of movement was not evident yet as the enemy hadn't reached the ambush site. Every moment counted at this point.

Becker gave the hand signal to move out. Although SOG teams, small as they were, carried more ordnance than an infantry company, they were never out of danger, being outnumbered and deep in enemy territory. The point man, armed with an XM177E2 assault rifle, took off. SOG's beloved XM177, commonly known as the CAR-15, was a good rifle. Smaller and lighter than the M-16 and with few of its problems, it was a bit harder to control in full auto because of its shorter barrel and its higher cyclic rate. But most engagements with the enemy were at less than ten paces, so it really didn't matter.

Becker also carried the CAR-15. Before he joined RT Cobra, he had opted to carry a suppressed Swedish "K" submachine gun on his first SOG missions. He was enamored of the weapon, which was a good design, but really he was thinking, *it's cool.*

His first contact quickly disabused him of that notion. He realized that a quiet weapon firing 9mm Parabellum pistol ammunition was no match for a loud assault rifle firing rifle ammunition in a firefight. He was firing as fast as he could but he couldn't get any respect firing a weapon nobody could hear. He quickly switched to a weapon with more firepower and that made more noise.

The point man followed an azimuth that would take them on a tangent to the pick-up point. Not wanting to aim directly towards their goal, they would change course directly for the LZ when they were within around 500 meters. The point was flanked slightly to his rear by a Nung with an ugly, cut-down Soviet RPD. The nasty, belt-fed machine gun could do a lot to dissuade anyone who made the mistake of getting in front of its barrel. The rest of the team followed in dispersed order with Jonas, the team's One-One, armed with a sawed-off M-79 grenade launcher and a CAR-15, taking up the tail-gunner position.

As they neared the LZ, the buzz of an OV-10 Bronco filled the air. The OV-10 was their close-air support spotter aircraft and would stay above them until extraction.

Covey is up, Becker thought. But for once, the sound did not make him feel comfortable. He would be happier when he could hear the steady *whop whop* of the helos coming to pick them up. The team was moving quickly but carefully, each man's senses on full alert, watching for movement or a change in pattern or color to the jungle all around them.

Becker would remember the next moments for the rest of his life.

Like a sudden hailstorm bursting from a clear sky, the firefight erupted at full force. Not with a single burst or a rising tide of rifle fire; it slammed full on into the team like a herd of crazed, wild boar. He saw a line of bright orange muzzle flashes ahead and heard the whining and thrashing of bullets that shredded the brush all around him. Following the team's standard operating procedure, the point element returned fire on full-auto and each man peeled back from the front in turn as their ammunition ran out. Becker saw Tau, one of the lead Nungs, turn and fall face first into the dirt as a burst of rounds hit him in the back. His partner fired the last of his belt before he too turned and peeled back. He knelt and checked Tau briefly, then grabbed his harness and dragged him back to the rear.

Becker directed the team to a small rise in the ground where he thought they could defend themselves. All the while, Davis was yelling into his handset.

"This is a *fucking* Prairie Fire Emergency!"

It was not the best commo procedure but Davis wasn't concerned with word choice at the moment.

Calling a Prairie Fire Emergency told the world a SOG team was in the deepest of shit and needed help immediately if not sooner. Becker switched on an URC-10 survival and emergency transmitter that would vector aircraft onto their position, stuffed it into his cargo pocket and continued firing his weapon from the hip. He emptied his one 30-round magazine, pulled a 20-round mag from the canteen cover serving as an ammo pouch on his left side and slammed it into the rifle. He had thirty-three magazines to go. He hadn't started throwing grenades yet, but soon would.

One of the Nungs rose up and fired his M-79 at a NVA soldier who was trying to storm their position on the hillock. The spinning 40-mm grenade probably armed itself just before it hit the running man in the chest. It exploded leaving nothing but two legs and a donut hole of black smoke where the soldier had been. There was a pause in the firing and then the cacophony quickly resumed as resolute and scared warriors exchanged Chicom- and American-made bullets in both directions. Branches and leaves tumbled down to the ground as they were cut off the trees by the fusillade of copper projectiles.

The key was to gain fire superiority in the opening moments of the contact. Initially, the NVA had it, but the team's immediate response and faster reloading tipped the scales in their favor—at least temporarily. On top of their small green bastion the team was able to blunt the enemy's main advance with grenades and a hail of full-auto fire. Becker knew they only had a few moments to overcome the odds and told Davis to get Covey to send some ordnance down on their position.

Covey requested smoke. A purple grenade was tossed. Covey said he could see two colors. The NVA had anticipated the wrong color, but it showed they were listening. Davis changed frequencies and told Covey the correct color. Covey responded with a brace of 2.75-inch rockets and the advice that he had arranged for some fast-movers to visit them.

Soon enough, a pair of Spads were on station and even more hell broke loose. Armed with a position and an azimuth, the A1-D Skyraiders went to work. First, with 20-mm cannon fire and then a couple of 500-pounders, they sought to dislodge the

NVA or at least discourage them from pressing their attack home. It didn't work.

When the NVA heard the Spads approach they would assault, trying to get as close as possible to the American position in order to avoid the ordnance. It was a death-dance. They'd charge and Becker's team would blow them back. Over and over again. Dead NVA started to pile up in stacks in front of their position and actually provided the team some cover.

A third, then a fourth run was called for.

Covey warned Davis, "Keep your damn heads down. There's gonna be a BBQ."

Through the thick canopy, Becker watched as two metal MK47 canisters with pointed ends dropped from the Spad. As they began to tumble through the air he stuffed his head deep into the dirt. The blast wave pummeled their bodies and he felt a ferocious whoosh as the air was sucked into the inferno by the burning napalm. He also heard one short, cut-off scream of some poor wretch caught in the maelstrom. If you were hit with napalm, you either died quickly or wished you had. The thick, flaming jelly could not be put out unless completely suffocated in mud.

The NVA's rate of fire dropped off completely and Becker sensed it was time to go. He had spotted a suitable alternate LZ on the map about 100 meters to the southeast and rallied the team to push through the jungle.

Davis reported their new destination to Covey and then yelled to Becker and the rest of the team, "Kingbees inbound. About five minutes out."

It's now or never.

"Let's go! Move it, before Charlie gets his shit together."

They ran. And they ran. Carrying Tau and dragging the prisoner along, the Nungs were at the front of the small column. Davis followed up with Becker just behind. Jonas paused to set out a pair of claymores and pulled the fuses. Timed for thirty seconds and one minute, the mines would greet Charlie and make him stop and debate the wisdom of continuing the chase.

Breaking through the last bit of brush with their bodies, the team crashed into the small clearing just as the H-34 Sikorskys came into view, their big Wright Cyclone engines roaring like banshees. A couple of pen flares vectored the birds over their LZ. Becker respected the hell out of the "Kingbee" crews. Entirely Vietnamese, they flew into hell-holes as calmly as if it was their daily commute to work. Becker did a quick head count to confirm no one would get left behind. Now they just had to get out.

The LZ was too small for the birds to set down, so the crew of the first tossed out the 120-foot ropes to pull the team out. The prisoner, Davis and two Nungs went first. They rigged the sedated and heavily restrained prisoner into a STABO harness and clipped him into a line before hooking themselves up. With a line run through each man's rig, they would fly together rather than flail about separately.

Becker had heard the claymores detonate and was wondering when Charlie would appear when they announced themselves. A group had closed in on the LZ and chose the vulnerable moment of the helicopter's hover to open fire. He could hear the rattle of the AKs and the slap of the rounds on metal over the roar of the engines and only hoped their aim was bad. He gave the thumbs up when the team was ready and the Vietnamese pilot pulled pitch to get out of the area quickly. He watched the four disappear over the trees and away towards safety.

Becker and Jonas opened up in the general direction of the enemy as the second bird flew over the LZ. After clipping the wounded Tau into the harness, the men hooked up and fired one of their remaining magazines on full auto into the forest. Then they were jerked up into the sky, crashing through the tree canopy as the pilot sought to get away as fast as possible. Checking each man and himself for injuries, Becker found that, with the exception of

Tau, they had gotten away cleanly. There were a couple of small wounds that would need tending. Tau was still alive, his bleeding staunched by the combat dressings his comrades quickly applied, but he needed medical aid fast. The 80-knot wind at altitude was cold and the harness uncomfortable. They flew through the cool air towards their base camp as the sun started to set and the eastern sky darkened. Through his watering eyes, he could just see the other Sikorsky ahead with the rest of his team dangling below its belly.

Relatively speaking, it's good to be alive.

After a long thirty minutes, he could make out the outlines of their camp and saw the first bird settle in to land. Soon enough it was their turn. The helicopter came to a hover and gently let its cargo touch down and unhook from the ropes. Then the ropes were dropped before the big bird flew off to its nesting place for the night.

After handing Tau off to the medics, Becker thought about how many cases of beer he owed the crews. Then he saw Frank Greener, the SOG sergeant major, walking towards him, distress evident on his face.

Becker met him and asked, "What's happened?"

"Davis got hit bad on the exfil out."

"How is he?" Becker knew Davis from his earlier tour with 5th Group, but this was only Davis' second mission with SOG.

Greener shook his head, looking at the ground.

Becker knew what that meant. Davis was gone. Davis was a professional and well liked even after only a short time on the team. Beyond that, Becker was tired of losing men. SOG had the highest casualty rate in all of Vietnam.

Becker screamed and slammed his rucksack into the dirt.

Everyone around the pad stopped and watched silently.

After a few seconds of wrestling with a loss he couldn't let go of, he tucked it away into a closet deep inside his soul and said to Greener, "The only consolation is that we got a prisoner."

Greener looked at Becker. "Saigon wanted a courier or an officer, but the one you grabbed was a warrant accompanying the battalion commander, who was evidently killed in the blast. The documents you grabbed with the prisoner confirm he was the mess officer for one of the camps on the main trail."

"We lost a good man for a mess officer? What a fucking waste Sergeant Major! What a cluster fuck! They're closing the project when we are needed most and we bleed out trying to fulfill missions that have no end!"

Greener let him vent then reached out and touched his arm.

"Fate has a strange way of settling the score if it's any help. He had a rations roster along with what they will wring him out during interrogation. It lists the number of rations and what unit they were allocated to for the last six months. We will have an entire order of battle of the units operating and transiting this area along with their true numbers of personnel. It's a treasure trove of intelligence that probably will save more casualties if we have to put more teams in the area. Doesn't make up for Davis, but it is what it is. You guys will probably get an award for it in the end and Saigon will pat themselves on the back and bask in their success," Greener said.

Becker struggled to hold his anger and anguish in check, "We don't do this for medals, Goddamn it! My job is to keep my men alive, to bring them all home."

The sergeant major replied softly, "Write up Davis for a Silver Star, I'll make sure that he gets it. At least his family will have that."

Becker nodded and picked up his rucksack, letting his anguish and grief sweep over him as he walked wearily towards his hootch.

10

Becker made his way back to Bergmann's office at the end of the day. In between writing his after-action report and planning the next week's training, he had been thinking about the mission. Smuggling people out of East Berlin had been done before. Tunnels had been dug, walls climbed, and canals swum, but the quickest and easiest method was by vehicle. A few had made it, but most civilians who attempted it had been caught; the East German guards were methodical in their searches. Although it was once a good option, crashing through the vehicle barriers was now out of the question because they had been improved and hardened over the years. That left Allied diplomatic or military vehicles, which could not be searched. In the old days, some of the guys from the unit brought relatives, friends, and acquaintances out in the trunk of their car. That got harder when the Berlin Commander cracked down on the practice and the MPs started to search all returning cars.

But if sanctioned by headquarters, it could still be done. That was the plan he offered Bergmann.

"First, we need more background. Who is the target, where is he, what kind of security is involved?"

"We'll get that once we take on the mission. Only then will we be read in on the specifics."

"Everything is dependent on the intel, but basically it comes down to whether the snatch site is complex or simple. If we're talking a prison or something, the manpower requirements go up exponentially, as does the risk. If it's a snatch off the street, it's easier. We could put several small teams into the target area. One in civvies to do the snatch, a watch team, a transport team to get the prisoner to another location for a vehicle swap, and a team who would carry him into the West hidden in an official vehicle. Timing will be tricky. If the East Germans are alerted, they could close down all the checkpoints and that could lead to problems. We could take him to the American Embassy, but the logistics of keeping and then exfiltrating him from the compound get really complicated quickly. That's not to mention the chances of compromise shoot up the more people get involved."

Bergmann was leaning back in his chair taking in what Becker was suggesting. "I had similar thoughts, so we're on the same track. But we need more target info, like who exactly are we dealing with." He paused for a moment and continued, "We have a rendezvous this evening, so grab your coat and meet me downstairs."

Outside the back door, Bergmann said, "We're going to meet the Chief of Base downtown."

They hopped into Bergmann's BMW 2002tii. With a twist of the key, the turbocharged motor sparked into life with a low growl. The car's power was evident as Bergmann steered out of the compound and sped down the cobblestones for the Steglitz district. After fifteen minutes of demonstrating the handling of the little Bimmer, he parked it on a residential side street. They continued on foot to the Rathaus Steglitz *U-Bahn* station.

The underground stations were probably the only places in West Berlin that were dirty all the time. The few beggars in Germany seemed to hang around them and the odor of whatever they left behind, either trash or human excrement, hung in the air as Bergmann and Becker descended underground. Becker noted how his boss slipped through the crowds in the station as naturally as a local. But then, he was a native German and spoke the language without any indication that he had spent the better part of his life in America.

The *U-Bahn* trains were a complete contrast to the stations: their crews kept them spotless and Becker especially enjoyed observing his fellow passengers interact. Germans, especially Berliners, could either be very polite or extremely rude. The determining factor seemed to lie in their assessment of whom they were dealing with. If you appeared to be beneath their station, a *Gastarbeiter*—a foreign worker—for example, rude was the order of the day. If you looked like an upstanding citizen, the opposite was true. But the subway was a great equalizer although few well-to-do Berliners used it; they preferred their Mercedes to get around.

After eight stops, Becker and Bergmann left the train and climbed out of the Kurfürstendamm station into the cold night air and headed west towards Uhlandstraße. Bergmann led the way while Becker was content to observe, always watching for the pickpockets that infested the crowded sidewalks.

Bergmann stopped under a dimly lit canopied doorway and turned to Becker. "We're here." Becker read the shield on the door which said simply *Der Bojar.*

"Russian or Bulgarian?" Becker said, shifting into German.

"White Russian to be exact, but they don't discriminate over political views. The owner is a friend of the Chief and keeps watch on the folks from the diplomatic community who come here. Russians mostly, the *Ossis* don't seem to like the decor."

Becker saw what he meant when they entered. It was like stepping back into another epoch, a throw-back to a time of despots and serfs. This would have been where the privileged gathered, and he could understand why it might hold less appeal for East Germans. Garishly ostentatious, gold and black brocade wallpaper and portraits of aristocrats and warriors decorated the walls. Heavy wooden stools and tables packed the room. Four men, who Becker judged to be from the Balkans, glanced at them and returned to their cigarettes, coffee, and small talk. Smoke hung in a blue-gray cloud that descended almost to the level of Becker's head. He was grateful for the high ceilings.

Bergmann walked past the tables and through a small archway into a smaller area that was lined on both sides with private cubicles. He held the curtain of one aside for Becker and then slipped in behind him. The base chief, a middle-aged man in a rumpled suit, was waiting for them. He looked unremarkable and could easily be confused for any mid-level businessman on the street, which was how he preferred to be remembered or, more precisely, forgotten.

"Welcome to my *Stammtisch*."

"Been waiting long?" Bergmann said.

"No, I slipped in the back just before you arrived."

"Thomas, this is Kim, one of my most experienced men. Kim, this is Thomas."

"Tom," he said, "my friends call me Tom."

A handshake settled the formalities and everyone sat down. A bottle of Talisker was produced and very healthy drams were poured in equal measure into three Baccarat crystal tumblers.

Murphy filled them in on details as he passed the glasses to his guests. "We can be comfortable here. It's a safe space but we'll talk in generalities nevertheless. So, what did you think of my request?"

Bergmann began, "We discussed it and agreed that we can probably help. We'll need more specific information to plan, the whole who, where, and when thing. What restrictions do we have?"

"First, no restrictions. You plan, I support. You are seconded to us for this operation; the army has no input. Headquarters has given me authority to run this project without the participation of our office across the way," he said pointing his thumb to the East, meaning the East Berlin station would not be involved.

Kim asked, "Can you better define the package?"

71

"Not yet, except it is in the open."

"That is a relief. We won't have to bust any doors down." Becker paused and then added: "On the way in, at least."

"But… I should mention, he says he can't send out messages anymore. It's too dangerous. That means you'll need to make a visit to coordinate the plan beforehand."

"Over there?" Becker said. "That will require some careful thought. We don't want to tip our hand."

"I know, but it might be necessary. And if it does need to be done, you'll only have one shot at seeing him, no fall-backs, no alternates. I will send the full planning packet over to you tomorrow. It's better you don't come to our place because the bad guys monitor how late our lights stay on and when we order pizza."

Bergmann added, "Once we have our general plan and requirements, we'll brief it to you. I expect we will need your assistance on some items like papers."

"Help is always available to those in need. We have the resources." Murphy smiled, knowing he had the whole of the Agency behind him on this project. Then he stood up. "As always, it is a pleasure to see you Jeff, and to meet you Kim. See you soon."

Then he was gone. Bergmann and Becker waited a few moments before departing.

"If he's the big guy, doesn't he worry about this place being watched?" Becker asked.

They stood up and Bergmann swept the curtain open. In front of them in the opposite cubicle was a man packing up a valise with various bits of counter-surveillance jamming gear. Two of the men from the front room flanked him. They looked at Bergmann and Becker briefly and went back to doing what they did well, which was to keep the area secure.

"That would explain it," said Becker.

As they walked out the front, the front room was empty except for a single man at the front door who shooed them out into the brisk fall evening and locked the door. It was dark—night came early at this time of year, and they were nearly alone. Only a few people were on the street walking home late.

With the warmth of the sun gone, waiters chained up the chairs and tables outside the street-side restaurants for the night. If one wanted to eat, it would have to be inside. A few desperate hookers looking for well-heeled businessmen trolled the streets looking for that last chance before it was time to withdraw into their barren apartments. The Ku'damm was tame compared to where Becker was headed.

Becker and Bergmann shook hands. "I've got to check up on my men," Becker said.

"Right, Kim. We'll see you in the morning if you make it back from Potsdamer Platz."

That section of Berlin was the city's most notorious red-light district and the clientele matched the territory.

"Give me a break, we hang out in much better places than that."

Bergmann turned and headed for the *U-Bahn* station. Becker watched him go before he headed off in the opposite direction. He checked his watch—which was the obligatory Special Forces soldiers' accoutrement, a Rolex—and knew exactly where to rendezvous with his teammates. He walked east, passed close to the Zoo Bahnhof and decided it was too early to drink, so he took a break at a sidewalk *Imbiss* he knew and ordered a *Döner Kebab,* one of his favorite meals. He watched the proprietor shave thin strips off a pile of lamb and veal slices cooking on a vertical rotisserie and pile it up inside a flatbread. Stuffing the sandwich with red onions, lettuce, and tomatoes, the man asked if garlic sauce was required.

"*Sehr viel,* Kadir," A lot, Becker affirmed. The sight of the yoghurt garlic sauce dripping onto the meat was enough to initiate spontaneous salivation. He felt like Pavlov's dogs without the bells.

He had learned Kadir's name after he realized he would be coming back here repeatedly and decided as long as he wasn't married and liked to drink on the Ku'damm, he should find someone who could keep him fed. Kadir was one of several surrogates who kept him healthy.

The *Kebab* was a welcome supplement to the Talisker before what he assumed might be a couple of hours of carousing the evening away. He figured he deserved some relaxation after the last mission and before the impending task. As he walked in the door of the Blue Note bar, his teammates may have thought they were being raided—it was that rare to see Becker out and about with his team. He found four of them stuffed into a corner table listening to the music and watching the women. Fred Lindt and Paul Stavros were sitting with Hans Landau and Jan Pavlovich, both members of Team 2.

"Are you guys doing cross-cultural night? Why are you hanging around with these yahoos?" Becker said. It wasn't clear if he was talking to his teammates or the Team 2 guys. He was always prepared to act as the peacemaker; they could figure it out in due course. Then he noticed a fifth man walking towards the table, a man he hadn't seen in a very long time.

"*Hallo*, Detlef!"

"*Hallo*, Kim! You've graced us with your presence?" Detlef said it more as a question than a statement.

"I can slum with the best of them."

"And this is your kind of hole in the wall, Boss," Stavros said.

Detlef Beier was a true Berliner who shared more than alcohol with his American friends. An officer in the West Berlin Police's *Sondereinsatzkommando,* the *SEK,* he was a team leader of the only German special mission unit in Berlin. Because the occupation treaty forbade the stationing of West or East German military personnel inside the city, the police took on the roles of cops and armed forces. The paths of the *SEK* and SDB had first crossed several years before, and they had never diverged. Beier was an outsider to the unit only because of his nationality. He and his team had run ops with SDB inside the city on a number of occasions. The latest had been a mission to crush a Russian smuggling ring. The biggest problem with the relationship was the Germans kept trying to recruit the Americans away from the unit to stay in Berlin and work with them permanently. Luckily, the German police paid their people even more poorly than the American army.

"I have something new for you to try, Kim," Detlef said. "Have you ever heard of a Depth Charge?"

He was holding a shot glass filled with something evil-looking menacingly over a mug of *Kindl* beer. He dropped it into the beer and handed it to Becker.

"Hau weg die Scheiße!"

Kim had seen it all before and knew he was present at the scene of a crime about to happen. The drink Detlef offered was just the beginning of a long, hard night.

11

It had been several days since Fischer first picked up the surveillance. It didn't require him to make any changes as he had always practiced his daily routine as if he were suspect. In some ways, confirmation was liberating; in another it was menacing. He felt like he was waiting for the firing squad he knew he would face if he didn't escape.

But he also knew that Großmann needed to have some kind of evidence before he could do anything. Großmann could pull him in for interrogation only with Mielke's and, more importantly, Wolf's permission and that would require evidence, which Fischer was certain didn't exist.

Unless...

Besides Lila, he had not contacted any of his sub-agents since the unwelcome discovery. He knew that his people had all been well trained because he had done it himself. Like Lila, each was selected and recruited only after he had explored their motivations and decided they were beyond just money or revenge. Those two incentives were easily subverted, as was blackmail. His people were committed to a democratic Germany for themselves and their families.

Once he had considered the possibilities and risks of contacting his network, he decided he needed to do some deeper investigation.

It's time to find out who may have been caught.

Long ago Fischer had set up a proof-of-life system. If one of his people didn't answer then they were likely under duress or had been arrested. He had also planned for the eventuality that they were under hostile control. Under normal circumstances, his agents would use the regular signal system. If they were under control and forced to put out a signal, a subtle change to the signal site would indicate "duress" and warn him. He had activated the system with a set of signals, each unique to a specific agent, and waited. After forty-eight hours, he would check each of the answering signal sites. He only had three sites to check, as he could discount Lila. She was alive and well.

On this fine, sunny, but cool Sunday, Fischer left his home on one of his long constitutional walks. It was a circuit that took him west to Alexanderplatz with its modern Potemkin village-like stores that held things that few could buy unless they were foreign diplomats. The center of the transport hub that consisted of bus, *S-Bahn* train, and *U-Bahn* underground stations was normally a maelstrom of activity on a weekday. Today, it was quiet. Families and young couples strolled through the open spaces gazing in the store windows and dreaming of whatever it was young people dreamed of.

He walked past a small pastry shop that abutted an alleyway and saw what he needed to see. From 50 meters away the signal was visible. He kept moving. He had selected the signal sites based on his agents' lifestyles and located them in easily accessible areas used by hundreds of people daily. It would be extremely difficult to correlate his movements with those of his assets.

In what would look like a lopsided triangle when plotted on a map, he walked north. The residential streets and gardens brought Fischer back to his childhood in Wedding when the parks had been his escape from the monotonous life of the workers' apartment blocks. The lowest strata of Berlin workers—tradesmen, laborers, and petty vendors—lived in buildings that resembled nothing more than concrete beehives. Everyone was too overworked, too stressed, and too poor to have anything other than a colorless life. The open greens were the safe area he could escape to when he didn't have chores, schoolwork, or wasn't needed for his father's errands. Pushing away the memories, he saw the second signal he was looking for and knew three of his agents were still operational.

Fischer wandered seemingly aimlessly, remembering his pre-war days, until he reached another milepost of his life. When the Prater *Biergarten* came into view, he thought of his return to Berlin in 1946. The Prater had escaped the war more or less untouched and, before long, it was again the cultural hub of what would become East Berlin.

The government used the Prater to promote communism and German–Soviet friendship. Fischer found himself coming for the obligatory festivals and staying for the more interesting stage performances. The Prater was a cultural icon that subtly encouraged an alternative lifestyle inside a communist state. As a young man, he was fascinated by Maxim Gorki's plays that depicted Soviet life at the most basic level. He began to realize that Gorki's work, and that of others like him, were the threads that would slowly unravel the socialist dream.

He walked down Kastanienallee and entered the beer garden through its marqueed entrance, not bothering to look at the posted menu on the wall as he knew it by heart. He came often when he wanted to sit and relax in the big open space that was always packed in summer with hundreds of people who also wanted to enjoy a quiet Sunday afternoon.

Most of all, he liked the Prater's food. Almost all of the restaurants in the East were controlled by the *Handelsorganisation* the state trade organization that ensured both mediocre food and service and showcased communism at its unfortunate best. The Prater was independent of the *HO*, and its proprietors and workers actually cared about customers and the service it provided.

The open-air garden was sheltered by huge, old chestnut trees that had also survived the war. Max's footsteps clicked across the stone walkways as he walked through the now-empty space. The garden was closed in the fall and winter but he knew the indoor restaurant was open. It was one of the few places where he felt relaxed, as did the other patrons around him. It was a step back in time compared to the rest of East Berlin and reminded him of a more carefree time long before the Nazis came to power.

Fischer sat down at a small table and allowed himself the pleasure of a large Pils. When the waitress returned with his drink he ordered one of the Prater's famous *Wiener Schnitzel* and sat back to enjoy the scenery. The waitress was talkative and friendly, obviously having no idea she was talking with a senior *Stasi* officer. Of course, Fischer made no mention of it; he didn't allow his position to intrude into his personal life.

Drinking his beer and waiting for the food, Fischer reflected on what he knew so far. Three of his support agents were operational. He had one final site to check but even so, he would be no closer to solving the mystery if one of them was under hostile control and didn't remember or couldn't use his duress signal. At least he would know who still had the freedom to move and he could test them further. His veal finally came and he tucked into it, enjoying the food as only someone who knew it might be his last good meal could.

Fischer scanned the crowd as he had been doing all day. There hadn't been any repeat faces, but he knew that many static surveillants and unofficial employees of the service were available to report on his activities. He expected that a copy of his bar bill would be included in the daily surveillance report. He had to give credit to Mielke; if you wanted to have a perfect police state, you couldn't do much better than this. Mielke didn't understand the subtleties of intelligence collection but he did understand internal security and suppression.

Fischer paid his bill, leaving some small change for the waitress. She would remember him for that if nothing else because no one tipped in East Berlin. He was certain that his shadows would interview her after he departed, as they would anyone who came close to him during the day. The surveillance teams were never very low key. If he went to the bathroom, they would search it to determine if he had left a signal or a message behind—he could count on their suspicions to keep them occupied. But he would only leave them with doubt.

He continued his circuit. The final leg would take him to the Prenzlauer Berg park where he could walk a number of paths to see if he had any close surveillance. He knew they would follow him if they thought he might make a message drop or have a brief agent meeting. If they chose not to stay with him, when he left the park the team would pick him up once again.

One way or the other, it doesn't matter. I assume they are there. There is nothing suspicious I am doing they can observe.

He was in passive mode, looking for something the surveillance team would never see. Out of the park, he walked south and back towards his home. There was a bridge that crossed over the train tracks where he would find his last signal.

Below the bridge lay the Leninallee *S-Bahn* station. Metal staircases on both sides of the street descended to the station platform where commuters met the trains that plied their routes with an exactitude that Mussolini would have appreciated. The trains were one of the few precisely running features of life in the communist East and they maintained their efficiency on both sides of the Wall.

Fischer walked across on the south side of the bridge, his pace unchanged, his demeanor unremarkable. What he felt inside was different. This was a moment he had never before experienced, the feeling that the very delicate house of cards he had built was about to crash down on his head. There had been times when he felt fear or uncertainty, but those were short-lived and easily overcome by his training and experience.

This time, the feeling was magnified for those very same reasons. Despite the message to "sit tight, we're coming" from the Americans, he had no easy escape and no immediate back-up. What he always called "my interesting life" was filled with unsavory characters, small dangers, hidden traps, and moral ambiguities. Those were to be expected, but there had been nothing to match his current situation. It compounded the anxiousness he felt and he had to put that anxiety into a box deep within himself, a box that he rarely opened. Now more than ever, he had to maintain control.

He looked again. No signal—neither primary nor duress—was to be seen. He knew the man he codenamed "Gypsy," the train driver, was out of the game.

It's a question of time.

12

Wheeler rang the doorbell of Building 817 and stood back. It wasn't long before the door swung open. Becker held it open as Wheeler stepped inside. Off to the side, another man stood watching. He was in civilian clothing but had a Walther P5 pistol in his hip holster.

"Jamie, welcome to our lair, we've been expecting you." Becker knew who he was dealing with already, having a photo of Wheeler in hand that had been secure faxed to the unit moments before.

"Thanks, it looks like you guys are ready for unwelcome guests as well."

"We always keep a few guys on standby. You can never tell, we're too close to the border here."

"I wish we did. We rely on the feared German Labor Service guards to protect us."

"Feared?"

"Most of them are draft evaders from West Germany. The only danger they pose is if they pull their pistols out of the holster. They'll probably shoot themselves or some innocent being by mistake."

That brought a laugh to his hosts.

"Let's go up to our briefing room. We can talk there."

Becker led the way up a wide set of well-worn granite steps to the first floor and then down the hall to a metal door. He opened the door and gestured for Wheeler to enter.

There were already several men waiting at a table. Wheeler took a seat and opened his briefcase on the table.

"Tell the sergeant major that we're all here," Becker said to the escort and shut the door.

"We're all cleared to talk anything up to Top Secret. The room is secure but not for any special access material."

"I'll keep my discussion general then."

The door opened again and Sergeant Major Bergmann walked in along with another man. Bergmann shook Wheeler's hand.

"Hi Jamie, I haven't seen you since Ban Me Thuot!"

Bergmann introduced the man who stood behind him.

"Colonel, this is Jamie Wheeler, Deputy Base Chief. He was in Command and Control South with me around 1970, if I remember correctly. Jamie, this is our commander, Colonel Jelinek."

Jelinek, a man almost as big as Wheeler, stepped around Bergmann to grasp Wheeler's hand. He squeezed it hard as he pumped it vigorously in a test of strength. Wheeler was apparently up to the task as the colonel dropped his hand with a broad grin.

"Welcome, Wheeler. I just stepped in to tell you that these are some of my best men and they will do what you need done."

Jelinek spoke with a heavy accent, attributable to his birth in Czechoslovakia. He always called his men by their last names with one exception: the sergeant major. Despite Bergmann's service with the German Army during World War II, Jelinek respected him greatly. Bergmann served with the Werewolves, the last-ditch resistance at the end of the war, but he had seen the writing on the wall and quickly surrendered to the advancing Americans. His experience with the GIs who captured him persuaded him to emigrate to the States in 1946.

Jelinek continued with the smile of an executioner, "And if you guys screw it up, I will arrange a vacation to the *gulags* and replace you with another team from upstairs!"

It was as close to a pep talk as Jelinek would ever give.

"Becker, I want a full mission briefback before this goes ahead," Jelinek added.

With that, the colonel was gone.

"I don't know him. What's his background?" Wheeler wondered aloud.

Bergmann explained: "The colonel escaped the Nazis when they occupied Czechoslovakia and fought with the French Resistance through the war. He came to America about the same time as I did. Enlisted in the army, became an officer and he's been involved in a lot of special projects since then. Helluva soldier, but no one knows him very well. Perfect for this place as he has lived unconventional and clandestine warfare most of his life."

"But we should get down to business. Would you brief us in on the details, Jamie?" the sergeant major said as he took a seat.

Wheeler took a folder out of his briefcase and laid some notes and a photograph on the table.

"This is the man we need to extract. All the details are written down so I won't talk about them here. You must adopt the same procedure—names, places, addresses, phone numbers should never be discussed openly. This mission is that sensitive. Understood?"

After looking at each man around the table and receiving their acknowledgement, Wheeler continued.

"He is under surveillance, but has not been arrested. That may mean he is only suspected or maybe he is one of a number of suspects. Maybe they want him to panic and expose his contacts. He is very experienced, however, and is lying low. So we have to get to him first."

"How soon?" the sergeant major interrupted.

"As soon as possible, hopefully within seven days at the most."

There was a wave of disbelieving comments.

"Seven days? We'll have to cobble this together from A to Z—we have nothing in place for this kind of contingency. "

"I know. Not much time at all. But there is another wrinkle. As Tom mentioned before, we need to meet him beforehand to coordinate the plan. We have only one opportunity to meet him and one of you will have to go in to do that."

"One of your guys can't do it?" Logan Finch chimed in.

"No. First, he hasn't been met face-to-face by one of our people in a long time, so it doesn't matter who meets him. Second, we can't risk sending any of our officers in to see him because they may be known to the East Germans. Last, we need someone who knows the city inside and out. That leaves you gentlemen."

"That means we need a clandestine contact plan now and an extraction plan ASAP."

"Exactly."

Becker leaned back in his chair and looked at the sergeant major who was reading Wheeler's papers intently.

"I'll go," Becker spoke emphatically.

Bergmann studied Becker for a moment.

"Your mission, your team, Kim. Give me a plan and you'll brief it back to the colonel."

"I have an idea. I'll discuss it with my men and be ready to brief you in a couple of hours. We'll need some help from you, Jamie."

"Whatever you need, we'll do our best."

"Okay, first thing: a set of diplomatic identity cards in pseudonym for a man and a woman, two tickets to the theater and reservations at the Palast Hotel."

"I'll get on it. I'll need biographic details for the documents."

"One set will be for me, I'll have the names and other details in a while. I'll explain later."

"I heard you were a fast operator."

"Who told you that?" Becker was puzzled.

"Sergeant Major Greener, a few years back."

The name brought back a flood of memories from Vietnam. The dark expression on Becker's face told Wheeler he had brought up a bad subject and he quickly changed the conversation.

"Sergeant Major, might I have access to your secure telephone? I need to make some preliminary arrangements."

Bergmann got out of his chair and motioned for Wheeler to follow. After they had left, Becker stood up and pulled the documents in front of him so he could better read them. After a minute, he shoved the file over to Finch.

"I want to do this one, Boss," Stefan Mann said. "My German is perfect and why should you have all the fun?"

Becker stared at the members of his team. He could see the eagerness in each face and knew that every one of them wanted to take on the mission. Fred Lindt and Mann spoke excellent German, but they were also relatively junior. Nick Kaiser also spoke the language and had combat experience, but not much time on the streets yet. The others could pass as Europeans, like Stavros with his Greek heritage, but that wasn't what was needed for this task. He thought back to the promise he had made to himself several years ago and looked Mann in the eye. His headache, a result of the previous evening's festivities, made him sound a bit more serious than usual, but he explained his rationale calmly and authoritatively.

"Why? First, German isn't the language of choice for this one. Whoever goes needs to pass themselves off as part of the occupation force, but not American or British. That leaves French. Second, it's my responsibility to make sure each of you comes home from a mission alive. I would take any of you if more than one of us was needed. But only one man will go over to make contact and I won't risk anyone without going first."

Becker rarely gave speeches and somehow his team knew better than to argue.

"Everyone read the file and when you're all finished we'll game this out. In the meantime, I need a woman," he said.

"Don't we all, Boss," said Fred Lindt, always the first with a quip, "but what for?"

"To go with me."

"That's one hell of a first date—" Lindt again. "Why not one of us?"

"Because you'd look like a gay couple," Mann said. If he couldn't go, no one else on the team would either.

"I have a suggestion," Stavros spoke up.

"Let's hear it."

"My girlfriend, Sarah. She's an Army Security Agency intercept operator. She speaks four or five languages well and has a TS clearance."

"I've met her. She's sharp; doesn't ask questions or talk shop," Finch said. He gave his endorsement based on what he knew of the women in the Field Station. They were mostly too book-smart to operate on the streets or they talked too much despite their clearances. Becker paid this scant attention; Finch was from eastern Kentucky and his taste in women was suspect.

"Would she be able to handle the mission?" Kim had to be sure he had the right person for the task.

"I should think so," Stavros said, "she escaped from Czechoslovakia with her family in 1968 when she was about ten years old. She doesn't talk about it much, but I don't think it was an easy trip."

"I like your thinking, Paul. Okay, you guys crash on the exfil planning. Come up with options and all the data and logistics we need. You already know the terrain and the enemy, so that part is easy. In the meantime, I need to convince the old man and sergeant major to break a girl loose from her daily routine."

13

Specialist 5th Class Sarah Rohan climbed off the shuttle bus that brought her to the enlisted living quarters from the ASA listening station perched atop Berlin's Teufelsberg—the so-called Devil's Mountain that had been built from the rubble of a destroyed city after World War II. She was looking forward to some down time after twelve hours of duty, most of which was sitting at a console listening to Soviet and East German radio communications. The rest was spent summarizing conversations into intel notes. Much of her day was boring as hell, which was probably ninety-eight percent of the time. It was critical work, but she felt her language skills were being misused. Many of her colleagues were trained to soley get the gist of the Russian radio traffic and couldn't speak the language well, if at all.

She, on the other hand, was essentially a near-native speaker. Her Russian came right behind her mother-tongue of Czech and the French she spoke at home. There was also the German she had picked up in living in Bohemia and then the English she learned after coming to the States. When she scored high on the army's language aptitude test, she was singled out by a recruiter who lured her into ASA and its Field Station in Berlin with tales of intrigue that mostly proved to be lies. But then there was the big cash bonus for signing up for four years. The question was what she should do when this tour was up: reenlist for another specialty like Intelligence or go back and finish her Master's.

Right now, she was too tired to think about it. Shuffling along with the other unmarried soldiers into the barracks, she thought for the thousandth time that most of them were pretty weird. She never socialized with any of them and they seemed to think she was arrogant. She wasn't; she just didn't like them. A few were really bizarre, like the guy who wallpapered his room with aluminum foil because he thought the Russians were bombarding him with radio waves.

Most of these kids don't belong here...

"Rohan!"

Her reverie broken, she looked up to see her first sergeant standing in the doorway.

"Yes, Top?" She never quite got the rank part of the army, much to many of her seniors' chagrin.

"The commander wants to see you in his office right away."

"Now?"

"Now!"

Sarah climbed the stairs with her senior non-com and turned towards the commander's office. The first sergeant stopped at the door and knocked once.

"Specialist Rohan is here, sir."

"Send her in."

The first sergeant shut the door after her and made his exit back down the hall wondering what all the fuss was about.

She walked up to the commander's desk.

"Specialist Rohan reporting, sir."

Only then did she notice the three men in civvies sitting at the conference table.

Colonel Newhouse stood up. "At ease, Specialist. Come over here and sit down," he said motioning to a side chair. He took a seat at the head of the table.

"These gentlemen want to ask you a couple of questions. But, first, whatever they ask, you are under no obligation to say yes. You can say no and nothing more will be said, understood?"

"Yes, sir."

"Fine." Turning to the others he introduced Colonel Jelinek and Sergeant Major Bergmann. "They're from the unit next door. They are our neighbors, so to speak."

Rohan didn't recognize these two, but she did remember seeing the third, unintroduced man a couple of times and knew he was somehow connected to her boyfriend, Paul.

Jelinek led off. "Specialist Rohan, we have a very important task that is critical to national security. We think you have the qualifications we need. Would you be willing to help us?"

Sarah recognized the name and accent and responded formally in Czech, "Tell me more, sir."

"We can't tell you much here, but it would be a short duration trip, not dangerous, but probably exciting," Jelinek said as he smiled his broadest smile, trying to win her over or at least convince her she wouldn't be sacrificed to the wolves.

"Trip? Where to?"

"To East Berlin. Strictly voluntary of course."

"Colonel Newhouse, I thought it was forbidden for us to travel over there because of our clearances. And especially me, because of my family's background?" Sarah responded, slightly confused by the attention she was getting.

"We will make an exception for you. You'll be in good hands. Isn't that true, Colonel?"

Newhouse was a bit skeptical of the mission, of which he knew only that it meant travel into East Berlin.

"Rohan." Colonel Jelinek paused for effect. "Your family name is French, but you were born in Czechoslovakia."

"Yes, sir."

"They were of Huguenot descent." It was a statement of fact, not a question.

"Yes, sir."

For the benefit of the others, Jelinek explained, "The Huguenots led a rebellion against the French king. When it failed many of them fled into exile. Some came to Berlin and many went to what is now Czechoslovakia."

Testing Sarah he asked, "When was that, Rohan?"

"In the early seventeenth century, sir. They rebelled against Louis XIII."

"Indeed. Courageous people, the Huguenots, especially the Duke."

"If you say so, sir. If I may, you do know your history. Henri, Duc de Rohan is my ancestor."

"It's our common history, Rohan. Now it's time for you to make your own."

Sarah turned red. She paused for a moment of reflection and then gave a definitive answer.

"Okay, I'm in. What's next?"

Bergmann took control of the details. "This is Master Sergeant Becker. He's in charge of the job and will take care of getting you ready. He'll be with you all the way. I suggest you get some rest and then meet your friend Paul on the soccer field at 0800 tomorrow in casual civilian clothing. He'll bring you over to the unit."

Becker stood and leaned over to shake Rohan's hand. "Glad to be working with you, Sarah. I'll see you in the morning. And call me Kim, we're on a first-name basis."

Jelinek spoke one last time as he was about to leave the office, in Czech, "Rohan, don't speak of this to anyone, not the first sergeant or your mother."

Turning to Newhouse he continued in English, "Thank you, Charles. We'll return her to you in good shape, no worries." He smiled, genuinely this time, as he turned and left.

Not that Colonel Newhouse would ever dream of questioning Jelinek or his men; he knew what they could do.

14

Fischer hated being forced to sit idle and do nothing. He had warned the Americans and checked on his agents; there was little else he could do at the moment. Sitting behind his desk thinking about what had transpired, he now understood what had led "S" to suspect him. Gypsy had been compromised. It was doubtful that he had been caught in the act; he knew his job too well. And, because neither his sign of life nor his duress signal had been there, Fischer was certain Gypsy wasn't being run back at him. That meant he had been arrested or killed. If he was arrested, he was being interrogated. Fischer knew the interrogators; their methods were not pretty but they were effective at extracting information.

If Gypsy is dead, then I am safe for now. If alive, he will not be able to resist long. It's only a question of time before they come for me...

Something had given Gypsy away. The Americans might have a traitor in their midst, but he knew his case was handled in the most restricted channels and the likelihood of his name being compromised was very small. Possibly they made a mistake when they passed information to the West Germans and a Russian penetration could have reported something.

The penetrations were dangerous but the Russians' greatest successes were mostly at lower levels, which meant his information was rarely involved. Nevertheless, strict compartmentation between the Russians and his service meant he didn't know who their agents were. More worrisome would be if the Americans had someone in their midst like British MI6 traitor, Kim Philby—then Fischer knew his full identity was in danger.

That the Americans had acknowledged his warning message gave him some comfort. They would know enough to shut down and cease reporting anything that might reveal additional information. Hopefully, they would track back all the previous traffic to find out where things might have gone wrong.

It was their second message that worried him. "Expect a night visitor" was how it broke out.

For the moment, he needed to concentrate on his short game. "S" believed there was a spy but didn't know who it was other than someone at high level. That led to more questions.

What led him to suspect me? Was it the information associated with Gypsy's compromise? Are there others also under suspicion?

Only rarely did Fischer lament the secrecy and loneliness he felt in his chosen profession. Not that of being an intelligence officer for East Germany, but of being a spy for the Americans. Sometimes he wished for someone to talk to about the problems he faced or just to discuss the game and who was winning. He hoped his chosen side was winning but he couldn't see the scoreboard from his office and the recent red card that had taken Gypsy out of play made him feel the game was in jeopardy.

Going back to the question at hand, Fischer could name only a few who had access to the kind of information he sent the Americans. There weren't many. His access was at the very highest level and of that he sent only the choicest bits of intelligence.

He looked in his in-box. As chief of the overseas bureaus, he was responsible for assigning collection requirements, approving operations, and reviewing the intelligence reports produced. He knew the officers in each bureau, what their strong points were, and where the problems lay. In short, he knew what was happening, often before Mielke or Wolf found out. It was an ideal position to keep his friends informed of what East Germany was up to around the world. The only area he didn't have good insight into was West German operations. Wolf controlled those personally and kept close tabs on everything. Diving too deep into that area was dangerous, so he kept his distance despite the continued American pleading for information.

The intelligence reports he received from the bureaus were bundled into area-specific folders after they had been analyzed and assessed for value. Normally, he was more interested in the raw reports which held details of ongoing overseas operations and plans. It was the sort of information that was normally invaluable to the Americans for manipulating those penetrations or discovering sources. It was ironic that one of those reports may have resulted in his own compromise.

The flow of folders seemed to have resumed its normal pace after a couple of days' pause. His senior secretary thought the bureaus had all gone on holiday, but some technician blamed it on a communications problem. Fischer thought otherwise.

The information was, for the most part, routine. Assessments of dictators and their political rivals, notes on the susceptibility of a maritime company owner to bribes (always valuable when arranging covert arms shipments), and which rebel group controlled what section of a country this week. Not exactly what he normally shared with his friends.

A blue striped folder was among the other traffic. Within was an operational cable addressed to Department XXII and copied to several other offices including his. The blue stripe meant it was a very restricted distribution cable. Fischer picked it up and, as he read it, an idea came to him.

15

Rohan met her boyfriend on the soccer field the morning after she accepted Colonel Jelinek's offer. Stavros was working out with some of his teammates when she appeared. They were practicing their soccer, known as football in Europe and most other countries that did not have NFL franchises. The Detachment's soldiers often played with and against local civilian, as well German military and police teams, and it was a good way to meet "interesting" people who might prove useful for any eventuality. They never expected to win against most of the other teams, many of which fielded semi-pro players, but they generally held their own in competitions.

But it required hard work and lots of practice. From the sidelines she could see their labored breathing turn into clouds of vapor in the cold morning air. Stavros broke off to greet her and, to all appearances, it looked to be a normal meeting between a man and woman enamored of each other, which they were. The two went trotting off together towards Stavros' building a kilometer away.

When they reached the back door, Stavros regarded his girlfriend closely and asked, "You're sure?"

"Yes, it gets me away from the Field Station grind and who knows where it might lead?"

Stavros smiled as he punched in the combination on the door lock, "I thought you'd say something like that."

"Not taking me for granted, I hope?"

"Never, I just knew you'd want to do this."

Becker greeted Stavros and Rohan at the top of the steps.

The young, black-haired woman drew some, actually a lot of curiosity from the other men. It was rare to see a woman in the building unless she was a spouse and even then it was unusual. The curious didn't remain long before moving along, however. Becker's dismissive glare urged them to attend to their duties elsewhere.

Just as Stavros exuded a Mediterranean heritage, Rohan didn't look American. She was European: her clothes, her hair, everything about her was different. It was an unconscious habit learned from a mother who never gave up her homeland or languages even as she assimilated a protective layer of an adopted culture. Given a chair and asked to be patient while Becker mapped out some details for their mission, she instead came up with a question out of left field.

"What defines a good leader?" Sarah Rohan asked Becker.

Becker's head was bent over a map while Sarah sat quietly in the small room where Stavros had left her several minutes before. Now he looked up at Rohan and then back down at the map.

"First, either someone is a leader or he's not. There is no such thing as a bad leader. If he is bad, he is not a leader."

"That's it?"

"No, there are many things that make a good leader. Do you want to hear what I believe?"

"Yes, I don't think any of my superiors could do that without reading off a note card."

"First, in my view a leader must know his men, or in this case, women, as well as he knows himself. He must understand their abilities and limitations and be able to communicate with them. Communication is important, not only to instruct and guide, but to listen and perceive. He must train them to be their best and cannot ask anything unreasonable of them. A leader must know what he does is not for his own promotion, but for the people he leads. Success comes not from one person but from the efforts of everyone working together as a team."

"Did they teach you that kind of stuff at the Sergeant Majors Academy?"

"No, I learned from a much wiser man."

"Who?"

"A guy by the name of Musashi, he was a warrior scholar."

"Where did you meet him?"

"In a book he wrote. He is much older than I—about 300 years older."

"Was he a philosopher?"

"He was a Samurai first; it is the highest caste of soldier in medieval Japan. He won over sixty sword duels before becoming a recluse and philosopher."

"He sounds ancient. Are those kinds of ideas still relevant?"

"Good leadership never gets old. The principles of leading haven't changed. Some people just refuse to learn them. And if you don't learn it from your mentors or in books, you have to learn it on the street. That's a pretty unusual thing to ask for a junior soldier to ask. What makes you so interested in leadership? Aren't you concerned with what we're going to be doing?"

"I like to know the thing that drives the people I work with or for. Most of the kids in Field Station are too scared of the first sergeant to ask questions or they blindly obey whatever their section sergeants say. Most of the sergeants seem to have been promoted into a level of mediocrity and couldn't answer that question with anything other than some formulaic B.S. taught at NCO academy. Our sergeants aren't leaders, they're technicians."

Becker reached into his knowledge of military history to answer. "Obedience was important in the days when close-order drill was the mainstay of battlefield tactics. Not obeying an order could lead to confusion in the ranks and panic. That was a crucial thing when you faced a well-disciplined army. These days it's better to train hard together as a team and learn to trust each other. Still, at the end of the day, soldiers still need to follow their leader's orders."

"That's it?"

"Most of it; the only other thing I would add is the leader has to know when to say no."

"Say no to what?"

"You have to say no to missions that are stupid, useless missions that risk your people's lives without any gain. Your soldiers will always be enthusiastic and want to do the impossible. Sometimes you can do the impossible, but there are times you have to ask if it is worth the sacrifice and when it's just a waste."

Becker went silent. There were too many times he hadn't followed that rule. A moment passed before he continued.

"You're a college graduate, right?"

"Yes, are you?" she countered.

"I never had the chance, or better said, I fouled my chances up and ended up enlisting to get out of town. I'm a simple soldier."

"Seems you've done pretty well."

"For the army, maybe, but I'll never have a penthouse on Fifth Avenue."

"That doesn't matter much to me. What matters is a good life well lived."

"Why did you join the army, Sarah?"

"Because America accepted my family and me without question. I've had the opportunity to learn a lot and I felt I could give something of myself to repay the debt. Now, are you going to mentor me for this job? Or must I pick it up by osmosis?"

"I think you might be too smart for the army," Becker said. He shook his head and continued.

"Now, you could just learn by OJT, except on the job training doesn't work well for critical skills like flying airplanes or operating in enemy territory. The failure point generally comes too quick for a healthy recovery. Or we could go over basics and role play some scenarios."

"I like the second option."

"Good, then with your permission, we'll begin," Becker was beginning to fathom that working with Rohan would be a lot different from what he was used to. He continued,

"We will be going to East Berlin together to see a play as husband and wife."

"Is that what all this is about, and have you told Paul where you're taking me?"

Becker smiled, "At least I have your attention. That's our story and you need to learn the details. We'll be carrying identity documents in false names that show us to be French diplomats from West Germany who are visiting the East. We'll be booked at the Palast Hotel—no worries, we're probably not really staying there—and we'll have tickets for the Schiffbauerdamm Theater."

"I love theater, but what are we really doing?"

"We're going to meet an important man at his house, but we can't be seen with him. We'll sneak in and out of the area. If we're stopped, we will say we came to see the show and got lost. That way we have a plausible reason for wandering around."

"Okay, I think I have it now. You need me for cover to be out at night. I did something like this with my parents when we escaped from Czechoslovakia."

"Tell me about it."

"As we were making our way out of the city, my mom made me use a different name with strangers. So I had to learn that I wasn't Sarah from Prague anymore, but Nadia from Pilsen. To this day, I don't like that name. There was a lot of angst associated with the thought of getting it wrong."

"But it got you out."

"Eventually, yes. But one night before we made it over the border, I had to go knock on a door in the middle of nowhere and ask for something. Mom said only that whoever answered would help us. I've forgotten what I had to ask, but I was scared and felt alone in the countryside. It turned out to be an old farmer lady and her husband who hid us for a couple of days until we could make our way across the border."

"Why were you hiding?"

"My dad was a teacher who was wanted by the police for supporting the reform movement."

"That's why your family had to escape?"

"Yes, otherwise he would have been sent to prison."

"So you've had some experience in the kind of things we'll be doing. I think some time spent on the details of our story would be good and then I'll fill you in on how we'll do the mechanics of the job. By the way, I'm glad you got out." He paused before adding, "So is Paul."

For a second time, Sarah blushed.

Changing the subject, she asked, "What's the play?"

"Braun's *Großer Frieden*. We may or may not make it to the play. It depends on how long everything takes with our contact."

"Your friend better be pretty entertaining for me to miss that, whatever the hell it is!"

"He's not a friend, but a man we've been asked to help. I'm told he is a rebel hiding deep inside the system."

"Who is he?"

"You'll find out soon enough, but for now, I think we'll just call him the 'Wizard.'"

Becker thought the questions were finished, but Rohan had other ideas.

"Are you married?" she said.

Oh, Jesus, he thought.

"Where did you learn your interrogation techniques? You ask about one thing and then you switch to another. You keep your subject off balance."

"My mom and dad taught me to question things. I guess that's what got him in trouble but he told me never to stop asking. My mom was like that too. Plus, she was very open and always wanted to know about people's feelings. It may have rubbed off. So answer my question."

"I was never married. My army life has really been too intense for a meaningful relationship. It's a hard life and I've seen too many marriages go bad. Why do you ask?"

"Sorry for asking, I was just wondering. If I stay in this line of work will I have the same future as you? And what does that mean for me and Paul? I have a lot of questions about where I need to go next. I wouldn't ask anyone in my unit because they would probably think the wrong thing. I thought you might have an idea."

"I am probably the wrong guy to ask but I really don't think you need to worry much. Besides now isn't the time to think about anything other than the task ahead. In any event, you'll have opportunity enough to think about it when it's re-enlistment time."

"You're right. I need to concentrate on what's next."

Becker smiled. It was probably the first substantive conversation he'd had with a woman in a long time, if he was honest. He could see why Stavros was drawn to this one, but he'd have to be careful.

She's smart and pretty—a dangerous combination for any guy.

It was probably for the best that he deviated from his true history a bit as he related it to Rohan.

There was this one woman in Monterey... but that was a story better left untold.

16

As defined in the Special Forces Operations manual FM 31-20, the briefback is the final decision brief presented by an "A" Team to its commander. Its preparation involves a systematic process that covers all areas of mission planning: what the team has been tasked to do and how they intend to carry it out, as well as the enemy they will face on the field. This exhaustive methodology had been used since SF was first commanded by Colonel Aaron Bank in 1953, and Becker was well versed in it. He thought of it as a "soup to nuts" approach to a task, throwing in how the team would react to anything and everything that could possibly go wrong. Usually, the process takes a week or more; sometimes, as with this mission, a team only has hours.

Colonel Jelinek sat back in his chair as Becker concluded his briefback. Sergeant Major Bergmann, Jamie Wheeler, and the unit operations officer, Dieter Kelly, were the only non-players in attendance. Most of Team 5 was also there as they had tasks to fulfill on the mission. It was typical for a Special Forces briefing, intensive and thorough. The team's primary and alternate plans were covered, including any emergencies that might come up. A map showed the route each of the different elements would take after they separately crossed Checkpoint Charlie into the East.

Team 5 had received the mission just days before and pulled out all the stops to organize resources. They were going into a denied area and, although Becker was confident, he knew one thing could screw up all the planning: a trap set by the *Stasi*. This was out of his control and he just had to place all his confidence in the two Agency officers, whom he regarded as professionals without any hidden agendas. Besides, Jelinek and Bergmann would not have taken on any B.S. mission, of that he was sure.

"What are your questions, sir?"

Jelinek asked Wheeler if he had any.

"Tell me why you chose to go with French documents. I assume you can pass yourself off as French?"

"Both of us speak French. We will present less of a threat to the East Germans than we would as Americans."

Wheeler dove deeper and directed his next question to Rohan.

"Your French, what you spoke at home in Czechoslovakia, is an older dialect, right?"

"I am equally comfortable in old as well as modern French. I spent a year in Paris studying before I joined the army. I am quite familiar with the requirements of the *Académie Française.*"

Only a language enthusiast would have understood her humor. None were apparently present.

"And you, Kim?"

"My family is from the Alsace. I'm fluent in French and German."

Wheeler explained his concern. "We had to call in some favors from the French station chief to get the docs. He knows we're using them but not when and why. If you're picked up and held, we'll have to rely on them to help us get you back. It wouldn't go over well if you couldn't hold up your story."

"We have our cover down pat, both for who we are and what we're doing over there. Everything we wear or carry is either German or French. We can't risk being tagged as Americans, for our sake as well as the asset's."

"Exactly what counter-surveillance training do you have?"

"Rohan has none, other than what she learned escaping from Czechoslovakia. I have had several courses and, most importantly, your Internal Operations course."

"That course is normally reserved for case officers going to denied areas. How did you get it?"

"It was for a specific mission," Becker said. "If you are read on to 'Cauldron' material, I can discuss it with you separately."

"That is all I need to know," Wheeler said, "Okay, then what kind of surveillance detection route will you run?"

"It'll be around 10 kilometers with the car and then we'll transition to foot. That leg will be around 2 kilometers. We can't do a full denied area route; our cover and the time we have won't support much longer than what we've planned."

"What about surveillance on the house?"

"Apparently there is a car on the street in front most of the night. Sometimes one of the team walks the alley in the back, but infrequently."

Wheeler nodded.

"You have to be very careful then. One more question. Are you going to carry any weapons?"

"No. We can't carry anything. We couldn't shoot our way out of a jam anyway. We'll talk our way out. If we're arrested, we stick with our story until they throw us back. We're protected civilians, they can't hold us for very long according to the Berlin Occupation Treaty."

Wheeler gave way back to the Colonel: "That's it, sir. I'm good." Despite the fact that Wheeler's General Service-15 rank was equivalent to Jelinek's colonelcy, Wheeler knew who was more important.

"Sergeant Major?" Jelinek looked at Bergmann.

"There are a lot of moving parts. You don't think it's too complicated?"

"No, each element has a specific job and there is built-in redundancy if a problem arises."

"Fine, when will you go?"

"Assuming the colonel gives us the go-ahead, we have theater tickets for tomorrow night."

Bergmann turned to the colonel.

"Sir?"

Jelinek stared intensely at Becker for a moment before speaking.

"I am approving this only if you promise to break it off if anything appears to be out of the ordinary. I trust your judgement but I don't want to have to explain anything to the USCOB. He might make sure I don't make general," he said.

Jelinek once said the only way he would see a star on his uniform was if he got a job at a Texaco gas station, Becker remembered.

"Absolutely, sir. That's my rule: everyone comes home."

"Then you are good to go. *Hodně štěstí!*" The colonel stood up.

"Gentlemen, let's go smoke a cigar," he said to Bergmann, Kelly, and Wheeler.

As the room emptied and the rest of the team pulled down the maps and made sure no papers were left behind, Becker looked at Rohan.

"What did he say?"

"Good luck."

"I hope we don't need it."

"You weren't playing down the risk of our getting arrested were you?"

"No, I'm sure we will be fine and we have good back-up. If anything looks wrong, we'll just break off."

Sarah relaxed a bit. "I'm trusting you, you know."

"Don't worry. I don't want anyone pissed off at me, especially you," he said.

"Another thing, what is Cauldron?"

"It was a project I worked on a couple of years ago. Nothing personal but I can't talk about it."

"It's okay, I understand the system."

106

"It wasn't a memorable experience, I'll just say that. Anyway, we should be spending our time getting ready."

"Yes, because now we're off to see the—"

"Don't even say it."

"What? Why can't I say it?"

"You'll figure it out soon enough."

"I think I just did."

"I imagine you did, you're a smart cookie."

"I am indeed. On a lighter note, you know I learned my English from Judy Garland."

17

As Becker walked back to his team room, he mentally traveled back to a small room in one of the Special Warfare Center buildings at Fort Bragg. After his return from Vietnam, he spent a tour with the 10th SF Group before being hauled down to "Fayettenam" to help teach the SF Operations and Intelligence course. His previous attendance at the Agency's operations course had marked him as one of the few SF soldiers who were *fully* trained in intelligence tradecraft. Yes, the O&I course taught it, but it was an abbreviated version suitable for field operations, not stuff required to be a case officer. Someone upstairs figured that Becker could improve the course curriculum without bringing in an intelligence officer who knew a lot about intelligence tradecraft but little about Special Forces operations.

Although very few SF soldiers want to be tied to a classroom, Becker had accepted his fate stoically.

Two years at the most and then I'll go back to an "A" Team.

He was about a year into the assignment and sitting in his office on Smoke Bomb Hill when he got the call to show up at the school's headquarters, the building everyone called the Puzzle Palace. Not without reason, because much of what came out of the big white office block was confusing to anyone who had to implement its directives.

He wondered if he was in for another course change directed by some field-grade officer who decided he knew better than anyone else. Luckily, he was spared that pain. Instead, he was given a more perplexing task.

"Operation *Hamerkop* is the codename for the South African government's nuclear weapons program," announced an unknown man with "Agency" written all over him.

They were sitting in a small room cleared for classified discussion. The Agency liaison officer was present, along with one of school's many lieutenant colonels, Robert Foster, a guy waiting for reassignment back to a Group or to be tossed out of the service in a "RIF," one of the periodic reductions in force. The speaker was a classic Agency type who had come down from Langley to present the briefing to Becker.

"*Hamerkop*?"

"Hammerhead, it's a bird from southern Africa. We received warning from the Soviets, of all people, that the South Africans appear to be constructing a nuclear test facility in the Kalahari Desert. They took pictures of it with one of their satellites, and we confirmed it with a SR-71 'Blackbird' overflight. Information we have from a couple of our assets leads us to believe they may be ready to do a test."

"That's all very interesting," Becker said, "but where do I fit into this?"

"The facility is located at a place called Vastrap, a bombing range north of Upington. It's here on the map," the Agency man said, pointing out the location on a map, "but they have built a shelter over the site and we can't see the construction or anything else going on. To make things more urgent, we think they may have moved a device from their Pelindaba assembly plant to the site. They may be ready to do a test shot. We want to confirm that."

"Why? Why not just wait for the detonation? You'd pick up a seismographic event and have good confirmation," Foster said.

"First, because we plan to confront them beforehand and get them to shelve the project. Second, we think the Israelis are helping them carry out the test. We don't want either of them to advance their capabilities."

"So, I ask once again, how do I fit in to the equation?"

"We want you to go in and retrieve some soil samples and take a look at what is under the shelters."

"In the middle of a South African Air Force facility that is, I imagine, pretty well guarded?"

"We think you have the right qualifications for this mission. You went into areas that were more hostile in Vietnam and Laos. The South Africans don't have that kind of security on their bombing range, only right around the test site."

"You don't have any Para-Military Branch guys who can do it?"

"PM? Ha, most of them are too old, too fat, and too long out of the saddle to take on a job like this one."

"I'm not sure that makes me feel more comfortable. How do I even get in country to get close to the place? I have heard the South Africans have a pretty good intelligence service."

"We will document you as a German businessman. Your cover for being in country could either be a business trip or a vacation, so we'll look at those options. But we also want you to do our surveillance detection course."

"I have done two of those courses, once in O&I and then your tradecraft course."

"We have another surveillance training module called the Internal Operations Course. It's quite a bit more intense—long days and longer nights—and is only for officers going into places like Moscow. You'll need it for the times you're in Jo'burg or Cape Town when you might be watched by the BoSS—the Bureau for State Security."

"Aren't we allied with South Africa?"

"Sort of, but it's just like we're allied with Israel: both countries make our work on their territory difficult. They are a pain in the ass. BoSS is a good service, they know what they're doing and they trust no one, especially Americans. A German has a better shot getting to the target, especially one that seems sympathetic to the Afrikaners."

Becker went to Washington and lived out of a hotel for the course. He met with instructors in various locations and received both group and personalized instruction before he was sent out onto the street. Some of the training was repetitive, like how to load a dead drop or do a brush pass. What made it different was that everything was done under surveillance. The "operational act" had to be accomplished without the surveillants picking it up. He often did six- or seven-hour runs—a couple were even longer, twelve hours—that would culminate in a "clandestine act" on some dark street, a subway, or in a cemetery. It seemed cemeteries in Moscow were well visited by American intelligence officers.

Then came the rousts. He got busted by the FBI on a couple of occasions for no apparent reason other than being on the street. The charge was that he was a drug dealer. He saw quickly that he could never admit to being in Washington to go through secret squirrel training, he had to find a different way to explain himself. Not everyone figured that out and those who did screw up were summarily tossed from the course and sent off to an easier assignment in Asmara or some other god-forsaken place where they didn't have Moscow Rules. In those places, if they caught you they just shot you, no explanation required.

Finally came graduation day.

The infamous chief surveillance instructor, John, a former marine known as "Cowboy" not for his horsemanship, but for his tendency to break rules, shook his hand and said something along the lines of "Go get 'em."

No diploma, no nothing. It was all recorded in his file locked up somewhere in the bowels of Langley.

He met his handling agent again, Gordon Bennett, the man who briefed him, who cared for and fed him, the man who was sending him to Africa. The man Becker called the Zookeeper.

"You're almost ready," Bennett said.

"I am trusting in your good judgement."

"The instructors were happy, so am I."

A week of more briefings followed. Becker learned everything he could about Israeli nuclear weapons and an approximation of what the South African system might look like. Signature pieces of equipment were shown to him in slide-shows and photographic books until he could name them after seeing the briefest exposure of a part or the whole object. Then came the contact plan; who he would meet and how, and what he needed to do in an emergency.

There would be no contact with any of the official-cover officers from the consulate in Cape Town. There would be only one brief encounter, if he made it that far, with a non-official cover officer, a NOC, another illegal. Otherwise, he would rely on a local contact, a Rhodesian expat who lived in South Africa and provided the Agency with logistical support in the continent.

"We are ready to send you in," Bennett said.

Becker flew to Germany and spent several days in Stuttgart before continuing on his way to Cape Town. It was nighttime as the big Boeing descended towards the coastal city. A dimly lit shanty town was just visible below and Table Mountain spread its majesty across the background. Just before the plane touched down, the houses seemed to grow and spread out, the lights became brighter. He knew he was seeing Apartheid for the first time.

Airport formalities were perfunctory. *Herr* Klaus Winter, born in Baden-Baden, a travel specialist, was visiting the country to inspect vacation hotels, bush resorts, and sightseeing possibilities for his company in Germany. The entry stamp came down on his perfectly forged German passport and he entered the country.

A taxi brought Becker to the Cape Heritage, a fine old hotel in the center of town. It was a good start point for the trip. For the first days he wandered the city visiting touristy things and getting oriented. He was surprised by Cape Town; it was unlike any other place in Africa he had visited. Heavily influenced by the Indian and Malay slaves who had been transported there by first the Dutch, then the British, Cape Town had a distinct Asian flavor about it.

It was two days later in Bo-Kaap that he met his contact. Becker walked through the neighborhood, a tightly packed warren of row houses and shops, many painted in pastel colors, and turned into a nondescript, hole-in-the-wall restaurant, not far off the Buitengracht. The only identifying features on the outside were a street number and a sign that announced it to be a *Kombuis*, a kitchen.

It was a small place, clean and tidy, outfitted in what Becker would soon realize was the same cheap furniture used in every local restaurant in the city. What made it special was the cuisine, a fusion of Malay, Eastern, and African dishes called Cape Malay.

Taking in the pungent aromas and looking around the small seating area, he recognized his contact from the photo he had been shown in Washington. It made sense to meet him openly because he too was in the travel industry.

Doctor John Kingsley was a Renaissance man. The travel company he ran was a hobby; his real interests lay in archaeology. Anytime the government or a company decided to build something, it was him they called on to survey the land for any undiscovered history, which gave him good access to people and places. He was also a former soldier and a bush pilot whose combined skills came in handy on the continent.

It was the gray beard that made him stand out.

"John?"

"Klaus, I assume? Please sit with me."

"Thanks for meeting me."

"I understand you want to establish some travel itineraries in the region," Kingsley said, reconfirming the reason for their being together. Kingsley's English accent was proper in a colonial sort of way, toned by his upbringing in Rhodesia. "Where would you like to start? What kind of things do you want to see?"

"I thought the Garden Route would be interesting, maybe around the De Hoop Reserve. And then I think the Orange River and the Kalahari. Do you know the Vastrap?"

Within those areas were objects of interest to the Agency and key to Becker's success.

"Interesting. Let me begin by saying I was asked to help you during one of my trips to Nairobi. I normally don't do this sort of thing close to home. You know the saying about backyards."

"Yes, I understand."

"Good, because what I am about to say may upset you. You are not going anywhere near Vastrap. It's in the Kalahari and 70 clicks from anything. You can't carry enough water to walk it and I assume you don't know what a boomslang looks like, right?"

"Boomslang? No, what is that?"

"Just one of our deadliest snakes. And there are many other things out there that will kill you."

"Can't you get me in closer?"

"I assume the part of Vastrap you want to see is somewhere near the administrative facilities?"

"It's north of the airfield," Becker nodded.

"Yes, that is a restricted area and they patrol it. Not to mention it's used as a bombing range. You would probably either get picked up or blown to pieces in an hour."

"That's the focal point of my survey. I need to get there."

"I know what it is, that's why I agreed to help. Listen, I was military, I served with the Selous Scouts, but I wouldn't go in there."

"Then how do you suggest I get the information?"

"I said you or I couldn't get in there, I didn't say we couldn't get someone else in there."

"Who else?"

"You'll see. We'll start at my camp on the Oranje." He said the river's name as the Dutch did, in three syllables.

They met at the Morningstar Airfield the following morning. Kingsley walked into the administrative building from the airfield side, just as Becker arrived.

"Let me take your bag," Kingsley said as he grabbed it out of Kim's hand. "It's my job," he said before Becker had a chance to resist.

Walking out into the sunlight, Becker enjoyed the comfortable Cape weather. In the late morning, the ocean air was fresh and clean. In the fall temperatures wouldn't get too hot until mid-afternoon.

"Which one is yours?"

"The yellow Pilatus over there."

Staying in role, Becker said, "Great airplane, I have used them a lot for exclusive travelers."

"There are quite a few in Africa. They're a perfect bush plane for hunters as well as NGOs."

Kingsley finished up with the pre-flight checks, while Becker stowed his small bag inside and got comfortable. Kingsley climbed in and went straight into startup. Satisfied with the gauges, he rolled the plane towards the runway. The turboprop at full power buffeted the airplane and it danced a bit on the runway until he released the brakes. Becker watched the scenery race by and felt the tail lift after a few short seconds. Then they were airborne.

"Not the fastest, but we can land just about anywhere."

"Except where I need to go," Becker groused.

"Yes, but we'll get what you need."

The plane turned northeast and soon they were flying over the semi-arid wasteland, the savanna that bordered the southern edge of the Kalahari.

When they landed, it was mid-afternoon. A dark-blue Land Rover Series III awaited them on the strip. A short, slim man with a thin face, brown skin and what to Becker could have been Asian features waited for them by the car. Another taller man who looked like a younger version of Kingsley strode out to greet them.

"Welcome to Vortrekker Camp," the young man said.

Sensing Becker was about to ask a question, Kingsley said, "My son William."

Unlike his father, William had a deeper accent, reminiscent of the Australians Becker worked with in Southeast Asia, but not as strong as that of the Afrikaners who once in a while consented to speak English with outsiders.

They climbed into the car and drove to the nearby camp which was made up of canvas tents on wood pole platforms that circled around a larger main tent. There were camel thorn trees and low brush around the site, but the center was fairly wide open. That was both to make walking easier in the camp, but also to reduce the number of hiding places for snakes and other deadly things. Becker smelled the dry, scented air of the brush and heard the sounds of unfamiliar birds chattering and calling.

"We'll get started right away," Kingsley said. He walked towards the main tent as his son dealt with the baggage. The small, dark man followed them into the tent where another, older, dark man waited at a table. The sitting man's face was creased and lined, wizened with years of exposure to the harsh desert sun. His younger comrade would age into the same face in the years to come.

"This is Sam and this is Henry. They are Khoi, the first people of South Africa," Kingsley said, introducing the elder first, "Their tribal names are difficult for outsiders to pronounce, so they have adopted European names. These are the men who will go for you."

Kingsley introduced Klaus to the two in Afrikaans. They seemed to regard him with curiosity.

Becker greeted them before turning back to his host.

"Have they done this kind of work before? They have your full trust?"

Hearing Becker's words, Henry spoke to Sam in their language.

"Henry speaks English, Klaus," Kingsley said. "They have worked for me for several years. I trust them. They are not fans of the government, nor do they like the ANC," Kingsley said. "Neither the Apartheid government or the leaders of the African National Congress always represent the wishes of the original peoples."

"Sorry, I just needed to be sure," Becker said. He was speaking to all three men now. "They are much like the Montagnards of Vietnam," he added, "caught between two systems."

"I imagine. Let's get down to the task then."

With Becker talking and Kingsley translating, the mission was laid out. Becker asked if they could record the things they saw at the site and was met with doubt. Kingsley noted that they didn't know how to read and write.

"If you see trucks, how would you remember the numbers?"

"We would just remember and tell you how few or many we saw," Henry said.

"And if I need to know the number exactly?"

Becker wanted to ensure accuracy so he pulled out a notebook and drew several images on the side of one page. One was a simple depiction of a pick-up truck, another a car, and another a cargo truck. There were also drawings of a building and a generator. Becker explained the drawings and showed the men how to make a mark next to each item to keep track of the numbers. Four vertical lines with a hatch mark through them made five, he explained.

"That's a good trick," Kingsley said, "where did you come up with that?"

"I stole it from Hemingway's *For Whom the Bell Tolls*."

"The value of literature in action."

After concluding the briefing, they broke for an open-air dinner.

"The bushmen won't join us tonight. Our food is not really to their liking," Kingsley announced as they sat down to eat.

The food was prepared by the camp staff. Besides Kingsley, his son, Becker, and the two Khoi, only four or five locals were present in the camp's background. It made for a quiet meal. The birds were still calling even though it was turning to night. And, for the first time, Becker heard the unmistakable laughing call and answer of two hyena in the distance. He paused and looked in the direction when he heard the cry.

"The hyena usually stay far away from the camp, although they play tricks on us sometimes. They like to steal things so don't forget to secure your tent flaps tonight."

"I'll remember that," Becker said as he sipped the Scotch that Kingsley had brought out to cap off the evening.

"We will launch in the morning to an airstrip northeast of here to look for game. Our tracker friends will go with us and begin their trip from there. The test site is around 30 kilometers east of the field and they should be able to get in and out in three days. We'll meet up with them once they return. In the meantime, we'll make a circuit of several camps so you have something to talk about with your clients."

"The Khoi, they must be a hardy people." Becker said.

"You have no idea. They call us fish-people because we drink so much water in the desert. They can find food and water in anything and don't need a compass to move across the land. Vastrap was once their land but the government appropriated it from them without any compensation. They know it well. They will get you what you need."

Becker took the hissing gas lantern that was offered him and walked to his tent. He sensed the local man, the guard that paralleled him in the darkness, before he saw the silhouette of the rifle he was carrying in the light of the campfire behind him.

For once, I am being protected.

He turned off the lantern and secured the flaps of his tent. Becker decided to listen to the night sounds before calling it quits for the day. He poured himself another dram of Scotch from a bottle in the sideboard and sat in the canvas campaign chair. Before long his eyelids started to droop and he yawned. He gave up and crawled into bed. Lying there as sleep approached, he again heard the plaintive cry of the hyena, sounding like laughter in the darkness.

***

The next morning, William took them to the strip where the plane and the two trackers awaited them. They took off and headed north flying at five thousand feet. Kingsley monitored the radio closely listening for any military traffic while constantly scanning the skies for fast movers.

"The military airfield is east of us now. The air force is generally good about notifying us of exercises but sometimes aircraft appear out of nowhere. There's a lot of activity to the north along the border between South West Africa with Angola and Zambia with the war going on. Some of the SAAF bombers and fighters fly in without notice."

"I guess I should help watch," Becker said, "I'd hate for us to get knocked out of the sky by a jet."

"It would happen so fast that you would not feel a thing."

"That is very comforting. Thank you."

"My pleasure. We're almost there."

Becker could see the faint line of a dirt airstrip up ahead as Kingsley nosed the plane downward in a slow descent. He was still scanning the horizon for fast-moving objects as they lined up with the field. Then the plane was over the threshold and on the ground, rolling down the dirt runway with a cloud of red-brown dust blown up behind them. Kingsley used so little of the strip that he could steer the plane into the small parking stand halfway down the field without having to turn it around.

The doors popped open when the propeller came to a standstill. Kingsley and Becker hopped out. There was no one to greet them. Kingsley motioned for Sam and Henry to climb down the ladders from the aircraft, which was significantly harder for the much shorter men.

"They are ready to go," Kingsley said. "Do you have anything else for them?"

"Just these." Becker pulled two small bottles out of his bag and handed them to Henry. "Fill them with sand from as close to the building as you can get."

Kingsley repeated the instructions to the Khoi in Afrikaans.

Sam said, "Yes, but why?"

"It will tell us what kind of things like chemicals are being used in the building."

Sam and Henry nodded their heads as Kingsley spoke again. Then they picked up their long canvas shoulder bags, bows, and arrows and headed east across the airstrip, each touching the ground lightly with their walking sticks as they moved. Once they disappeared into the bush, Kingsley went to the rear cargo door and pulled two bolt-action hunting rifles out of their cases, handing one to Becker with a box of ammunition.

"We might as well take a short tour of the neighborhood as long as we're here. I assume you've handled one of these before?"

Becker looked the rifle over; it was a Brno ZKK 602. The .375 caliber Holland and Holland was larger than anything he had hunted with before, but he didn't count 40-mm grenade launchers or .50 caliber M2 machine guns as hunting weapons. Those were for killing other things.

"I was brought up with a Springfield 03A3 by my dad. We hunted deer mostly—whitetail and mule—maybe an elk or two, but it was only .30–06 caliber. So this will be interesting."

He took out five rounds and loaded them into the rifle. Then he chambered the sixth and final cartridge by hand, slid the bolt closed before he put the safety on and stuffed the box into the cargo pocket of his field pants.

"We may see kudu or gemsbok, possibly a cat or three. Don't shoot the cats unless you're attacked, I don't have a current license for them."

"I don't want to shoot any lions or leopards. I'm not into trophy animals, only something we can eat."

Kingsley tossed a big green canteen with a long strap to Becker as he shouldered a small backpack. "We won't be out long, but there's water and I have a medical kit in my bag."

They stepped off in the opposite direction the Khoi had traveled and into the bush. Dry grass crunched under their feet. The surrounding terrain was alive with birds and bugs. Becker heard the loud song of the cicada in the distance but they would suddenly quiet as they approached. As did the birds. Their presence seemed to signal danger to the animals as well; there were none to be seen.

Kingsley stopped after about fifteen minutes and raised his hand in a universal signal to halt. Becker waited, looking into the bush ahead, straining to see what Kingsley saw. Then the raised hand motioned Becker forward. Quietly and slowly, Becker moved to Kingsley's side. He pointed through the brush.

"There, about 50 meters straight in front of us."

It was a kudu, one of the largest of the African antelope. A big majestic one, his hide was blue-gray with thin white stripes and his horns turned three spirals above his head. He was totally unconcerned with their presence. He looked like he weighed about 700 pounds.

"He's about eight years old. Magnificent horns. Want to take him?"

Becker located the animal and stared at him over the iron express sights. He knew he could take the bull. It was not a long or difficult shot. There was little brush, just a gap through which he could easily put a bullet into his vitals. He stood steady with his left arm through the sling to stabilize the rifle, a technique he had learned from the instructors at the Army Marksmanship Unit. He breathed in and out slowly before clicking the safety off. He held the sight picture for a moment, then clicked the safety back on. He could have pulled the trigger but he didn't want to.

"No, he's too proud and too pretty and I'm not hungry."

"Fair enough. We would have to carry him back to the airplane anyway and I can do without that. Let's continue. We'll be back in four days and maybe then something else will show up when we have extra hands to carry it."

They trudged back to the strip and the plane and reloaded the gear before climbing in. Kingsley completed his checks, restarted the engine, and taxied to the end of the runway. Hearing nothing on the radio, he rolled the plane forward and took off over the bush to the South.

The next days were filled with stops along the Western Cape and the Garden Route in the extreme south of the country. First, it was the Atlantic coastline, and then the Indian Ocean. The sights along the coast would mostly appeal to tourists who enjoyed scenery, botanical parks, and the ocean. There wasn't much wildlife except in the B&B bars at nighttime. Becker saw everything he needed to begin his ostensible tourist excursions and more, but in the back of his mind, he was with the Khoi trackers in the desert. Four days later they headed north.

No sooner had they landed, than the two Khoi came trotting out of the bush. Becker saw that they looked tired, but Henry had a smile on his face. Kingsley and Becker climbed out of the airplane and met them as they arrived planeside. Sam unshouldered his pouch, pulled out a leaf-wrapped package and handed it to Becker. While Becker unwrapped it, Sam handed another small packet to Kingsley. Once Becker had removed the protective leaves, he held up the two bottles filled with sand.

"Great," he said, "and this came from close to the building?"

Henry nodded in the affirmative. "Very close," he said, "the floor of the shed was too hard."

Kingsley said, "It must have been a concrete slab. Where did you get the papers?"

"From their trash bin next to the building," Sam said.

Kingsley unfolded the papers. Most were nothing special to his eyes but one stood out. It was a delivery invoice with the company imprint written in Afrikaans.

"I see it's from ARMSCOR, the Armaments Corporation of South Africa, but what does it say exactly?" Becker said.

"It's for a shaft cover plate to be delivered to a SAAF test site."

"A shaft cover plate? It says that specifically?"

"Yes, I asked them to retrieve anything they could find from the site to prove that they were there. It says Vastrap test site on it, but I have no idea what the item is. And here's your 'Hemingway' paper."

"Whatever it is will be for the experts to figure out, but I would call that validation."

Becker took the papers. There were only a couple of marks on his pictorial record and one of those was for the building. The invoice was the most important piece because it tied the samples directly to the test site. He would burn everything else and prepare it and the bottles together to be handed over to the Agency.

"There wasn't much going on there?"

"No," said Henry, "very quiet. It was night when we visited. Nobody there."

"I think this was a success. We can get out of here. Sam and Henry deserve a rest."

Minutes later, the airplane lifted off the ground and headed back to the river camp. They spent the rest of the day relaxing. Becker knew he would have no more chances at the site and now had to pass the materials on to an Agency contact. It would be best to do that as soon as possible and get out of the country.

"We'll go back to Cape Town tomorrow and I will not see you again. Have you been taken care of by our office?"

"They'll get a bill. They gave me a pretty good advance, but I didn't factor in all the fuel and taking care of our two friends. Fresh meat and honey can get expensive, especially when you're taking care of an extended family," Kingsley said. His smile came through the beard as an enormous white grin.

"I also wanted to thank you for reminding me of something. Trusting the locals, someone you don't know well, to help you… I'd forgotten what I learned before. 'Better they do it tolerably than you do it perfectly.' They usually know best. And maybe I'll come back for the kudu."

"You have also read T. E. Lawrence then. Good, I think we both learned a bit."

The following day, Becker returned to the Cape Heritage from the airport. He checked into one of the suites and cleaned off the dust and other bits of savannah he had brought back with him. Later that evening, he went downstairs and poked his head out onto the street. The sun was descending as he ambled down Long Street. He went in one bar for a medicinal gin and tonic and then moved on to another. The second was attached to a hotel, which made it convenient to find a telephone. After ordering he walked into the hotel and placed a quick call from the public telephone.

"Hello?"

"Is this Robert Grammercy?" Becker said.

There was a short pause.

"I'm sorry, you must have the wrong number. This is 6811810."

The line went dead, but Becker had the time and date for his contact.

***

The next day Becker was contemplating his English breakfast while admiring the grapevine that was climbing the courtyard wall.

The sign claimed it was brought to the Cape in the eighteenth century. He believed it because the main trunk was as thick as his bicep and its bark rivaled the old Khoi's face with all its creases and cracks. For a moment, he pictured the city as it might have appeared back in 1780, but then quickly came back to reviewing his plan for the day.

No daydreaming.

Becker was living a lie and the hardest part of that kind of life was to make sure that no one saw anything inconsistent with the lie. At every moment, his actions had to make sense to someone watching him. It was a game in which no inconsistencies were permissible. If anyone made a mistake, they risked arrest. Today, he would meet an undercover officer who could be declared *persona non grata* or arrested if caught in the act by BoSS. Becker knew he too would face severe consequences: he would certainly spend time in jail, maybe years. The life of a singleton, a solitary operator, was hard. Family and friends were far away and there was no refuge in an embassy. Even though there were allies out there, he would never meet them and couldn't rely on them for help. He was alone.

Becker planned a long route, one that involved driving, walking, and taxis, and he started out from the hotel in the rental car the concierge arranged for him. He drove west, around Table Mountain to Constantia where he visited a B&B with its old vineyard. He talked to the manager and took brochures and made notes before driving on down a long steep gorge towards Hout Bay. He did more visiting and note-taking as he played the game of being a high-end travel agent. He hadn't picked up any interest in his activities, no cars appeared twice, and no one followed him that he could see.

One road led up a mountainside. It turned into a dirt track and became rougher until he saw a cattle gate. He hopped out of the car and was greeted with a gust of ocean breeze, cooled by the coastal Benguela current. The view out over the ocean was spectacular and he thought he'd come back and really be a tourist when he was done playing spy.

He turned the car around, seemingly lost, but he wasn't. He had plotted the route out meticulously before he even set foot in the country. The only things he couldn't account for were construction and the occasional traffic. He continued around the mountain on the Victoria Road, stopping here and there until he got to Green Point. From there he walked, using all the tricks "Cowboy" had taught him to make sure he was completely free of surveillants until he found a taxi and disappeared into the city following his chosen cover theme of "travel agent."

It was only when the sky began to darken that he made his way back down the hill to the flatlands near the harbor. He passed the Citadel he had visited earlier that day and entered the oldest park in the city, the Company Garden. He was nearly certain that he was not under surveillance, but that didn't mean he was home free. He could have missed someone but he doubted it. That said, there was always the chance encounter—an "aw shit" moment when you realize an undercover policeman just happened to be in the area and saw you make the drop—that could ruin things.

He had to be certain. Becker walked slowly through the park. In addition to the police and BoSS, he now had to concern himself with another danger. The park was not a safe place to be after dark: the slums and shanty towns had encroached on it seriously and many unsavory characters roamed the darkened pathways at night. He wasn't worried about one bad guy, but a gang of them was another story.

There was a wooden information sign ahead. It described the park's origins and how it had served as a garden for the first Dutch ships that came into port to re-victual. It also informed Becker that he could proceed. There was a red tack on the side of the left post. It was clean and bright, consistent with having been placed only moments before.

I am free of surveillance, come to me, it told him.

He walked on through the park until he saw the outlines of the Cecil Rhodes statue ahead. Nearby a man in an overcoat sat on a bench, a newspaper in his hand. Becker could see the man was covertly watching his perimeter. He too was cautious, but Becker still did not want to risk exposure. He backed off to rethink how he would make the approach when he saw a young black kid about twelve years old walk down the path.

"*Jong man*," he said, "do you speak English?"

The youth was startled. Rarely did a white man speak directly to him unless he was yelling something and never at this time of day.

"I do. What do you want?" Suspicion filled his question.

"Want to make some money?" Becker said.

"Maybe."

"I am playing a trick on a friend. See the man sitting by the statue of the white man Rhodes over there? Take this package to him. Carefully, don't let anyone see you. Leave it on the bench next to him and say it's from George. Got that? It's from George."

The kid nodded.

"Here's ten Rand. I'll give you twenty more when you come back. And remember, I can see you."

He grabbed the package and disappeared.

The package was small, about the size of two "D" cell batteries, wrapped in paper. The invoice was inside, wrapped around the bottles, all of which he had wiped clean as best he could. Becker doubted anyone could lift prints off the items if they were intercepted. At least, he hoped that was the case. From his secluded position in the shadows, he could see the youth slip behind the man on the bench and place a package on the wood seat. The man looked up and appeared to say something before he put the packet unobtrusively in his pocket.

Minutes later, the youth came back. He was breathing heavily but smiling.

"That was fun. The man said to tell you 'Robert says thanks.' Can I have my money now?"

Becker gave him a fifty-Rand note and turned to leave.

The slack-jawed boy could only stammer, "*Dank U wel.*"

The night closed in as Becker disappeared from the park.

***

The rapping on the door came early, far too early for housekeeping, he thought. Becker rolled out of bed and put on the hotel's dressing gown to answer the door.

So much for sleeping in.

"Who is it?"

"It's the police, Mister Winter. We need to speak with you."

Becker opened the door to see two rather burly men dressed in civilian clothing. One of them held out his credentials.

"I'm Inspector Coetsee. This is Inspector Reid. May we talk with you?"

"Of course, come in."

Becker went back inside and sat on the unmade bed. Both policemen remained standing. While Coetsee talked, Reid wandered about the room looking at things.

"You were at the Castle Museum yesterday, were you not?"

"Yes, I was there as well as a number of other tourist sites."

"We're investigating a theft that took place about the time you were there. We got your name off the museum entry log. Do you remember seeing anything unusual?"

"Nothing specific. Could you give me any more information?"

"Just this: did you see either of these men while you were there?" Coetsee said.

He held a composite photo sheet in front of Becker's face. He had pulled the page from his notebook and it showed two white men in their thirties. Becker thought one of them might have resembled

"Robert," but he wasn't sure. He stared at both closely, controlling his breathing before he answered.

"No, I don't think I saw either of them."

"That's fine. One more thing, could I see your passport and airline ticket, please?"

"Yes, no problem."

Becker got off the bed and walked over to his shoulder bag and pulled the documents out. He handed them to Coetsee who looked at them closely. He jotted down a few details and closed his notebook with a slap of the leather covers.

"You're leaving this evening, I see."

"Yes, I was planning to. Is there any problem?" Becker wondered if he made a mistake in asking.

"*Nee meneer.*" No sir, Coetsee said, "Just be careful in town today. Watch out for these men and let us know if you see them." He handed Becker a card that showed only his name and a telephone.

No affiliation, Becker thought.

"*Kom, Robert,*" Coetsee said.

Reid was still poking around in the corners—looking. For what, Becker had no clue. After the two departed, he thought about their visit. He had questions: who were they and why were they interested in him? He knew his cover was airtight and the pass to the NOC had gone well. At least he hoped that was the case. If Robert had been picked up, they probably would have arrested him too. How then did they come across him? Becker didn't believe their story but he didn't have much recourse. There was no border to run for and if he did, he would only confirm their suspicions. He had to stay the course and ride it out. He had been in bad situations before, but at least then he could fight his way out. Now he couldn't. He had to pretend all was well while at the same time feeling the bottom of his stomach falling into a dark hole.

It was time to go and he had planned well ahead; his airline ticket was ready. He spent the rest of the day in close proximity to the hotel. He visited a couple of bookstores. He was searching through the stacks of Clarke's Bookshop when he discovered a biography of Frederick Selous, the adventurer, big-game hunter, and soldier. As he leafed through it, he thought of Kingsley. And although it was an expensive first edition, he bought it anyway. If he got out the country, he would have at least one souvenir.

He left the hotel about an hour before the flight and grabbed a taxi to the airport. He walked into the terminal and found his check-in counter. All was going smoothly up to the point when a blue-uniformed customs official came up behind the desk clerk and spoke a few words of Afrikaans in the clerk's ear. She stepped aside and the officer came forward.

"Good evening *meneer*, we're doing spot checks of luggage for prohibited items like animal trophies and such. Do you mind?"

Knowing refusal was not an option, Becker acquiesced to the request. A second man in civilian clothing joined the officer as they lifted his bag onto a table and opened it. Becker could see they were doing a thorough inspection. Then the officer asked for his shoulder bag. Again, it was searched completely. The second officer was finishing up when he reached into a small pouch and brought out a monitor and swept it over both bags. Becker felt his stomach drop out of his backside. He hoped he had cleaned everything sufficiently. It was only when the officer finished and shook his head that Becker relaxed.

"What was that about?"

"Nothing important, *meneer*. Have a nice flight," he said, leaving Becker to close his bags himself.

The ticket clerk came back and finished checking him in, all the while looking at him warily as if he were a criminal.

"There you go, Mister Winter. Have a nice flight," she said without any trace of conviction.

Becker did not know what to expect next but he wasn't prepared for what he did see when he turned to go to his gate. Standing in his way was Inspector Coetsee. He was wearing the ubiquitous emblem of African security officials: sunglasses.

"I just wanted to see you off, Mister Winter, and to wish you a nice trip. Your flight to Atlanta leaves from Gate Ten."

"Atlanta? I'm going home to Frankfurt, why would I want to go to Atlanta?"

"Silly me, I forgot—or maybe I just assumed," Coetsee said. His eyes were obscured behind the dark lenses, but he was smiling malevolently. His expression said: whoever you are, we'll be watching for your return.

Becker said, "I still have your card, I'll look you up next time I'm here."

He hurried down the hall towards his gate.

So much for the kudu.

***

It wasn't like he could afford to go back for the kudu on his own dime anyway. An African hunting trip cost thousands of dollars and he certainly didn't have that kind of spare cash. Whatever drove Coetsee to confront him, he never found out.

Becker flew back to the States and met up with the Zookeeper at j. gilberts, a McLean restaurant favored by Agency types.

"How did we do? What did the samples tell you?"

"I'm not really supposed to tell you but the samples were a wash."

"What does that mean, a wash?"

"We got nothing from the samples."

"Nothing?"

"Nothing."

"What the fuck… That's probably why they didn't pick anything up from my luggage."

"Probably. The information you brought out didn't reveal anything substantive."

"Substantive? What is that?"

"Something, anything revealing. Evidence we could use against the South Africans. We got nothing."

"You have nothing but the Russian satellite images and the 'Blackbird' photos?"

"Yes, but those still prove nothing definitively. Just pictures of holes in the ground."

"Great, so we did this and got nothing?"

"Basically, yes."

"At least you are honest. And Kingsley?"

"Ah, that's the thing…"

"What?"

"Kingsley's Pilatus went down in the Okavango Delta. He and his son were killed. The South Africans say they were shot down by a Cuban MiG that crossed the border out of Angola. The thing is, one of our assets in Angola says the Cuban Air Force didn't fly that day."

"So the South Africans murdered them?" Becker's emotions welled up inside. "Was anyone else with them?"

"No, not that we've heard."

Maybe Henry and Sam were safe. He could only hope. But for what did John and William sacrifice their lives? For a sample of dirt? To confirm an assessment the analysts already knew to be true? Why?

Remembering that episode, Becker was sure the South Africans would not have let him out of the airport if they had discovered anything. He and Rohan had to go over their plan again.

18

"Where is the General?" Fischer asked Wolf's secretary as he walked into the office. He hadn't called because his own office was just a short walk down the hall.

"He's gone to see the Minister in *Haus 1*," she said as she continued to type. "He was called to some meeting."

Fischer thought this presented as good an opportunity as any.

"Thank you," he said and left.

He strode across the open quadrangle from his office in General Wolf's *HVA* building to *Haus 1*, the epicenter of all the Ministry's operations except for its clandestine foreign intelligence. The *Stasi* compound was the biggest open secret in the city and the location was avoided by every East German except the ones who worked there. A certain negative energy exuded from the place that was surpassed perhaps only by the KGB's Lubyanka headquarters in Moscow.

Haus 1 was open to all *Stasi* officers, unlike Wolf's office building, which was accessible only to officers of the Main Reconnaissance Directorate because its operations were conducted in extreme secrecy. Fischer sometimes thought it ironic that he had full access to the entire Ministry compound, but then he felt his work was on a higher ethical level than that of any other department of "the Shield and Sword of the Party."

Climbing up to Mielke's second-floor office, he went over his proposal once more, answering in his mind the objections and counterproposals he expected would meet his own. He walked into Mielke's outer office and past the executive assistant who started to say something and then decided against it when he saw the hard-set determination on Fischer's face.

The door to Mielke's office was partially open and Fischer pushed through and into the inner sanctum. Wolf was sitting in an armchair to the front of the Minister's desk. He recognized the third man as Lieutenant General Hoffmann, the head of *AGM*, the Minister's Working Group.

An appropriate audience.

Mielke stopped mid-sentence, surprised at the intrusion. Wolf as usual showed no emotion, while Hoffmann just stared.

Fischer looked at Mielke and came to the same conclusion he always did.

A fool. A strutting martinet. He's an ape, no, he's a toad in a general's uniform.

"Sorry for the intrusion, Comrade Minister, but I ran across something in today's traffic that I thought deserved your immediate attention."

He pulled the blue striped folder from a portfolio and brandished it like the weapon he knew it was. When he read the message in his office moments before, he realized that his intelligence report on the Libyans must have been the one that had compromised Gypsy. Großmann must be attempting to flush him out, hoping he would give himself away by trying to report this new tidbit of critical information. He intended to turn Großmann's ploy in a different direction.

"I just received a highly classified report that a Libyan hit team is present in Western Europe. They are planning to assassinate an opposition party leader there. I wanted to make sure you were aware of its implications."

Mielke looked questioningly at Hoffmann, who lied.

"We briefed you on this last week, Comrade Minister."

Mielke nodded, unsure if he remembered the briefing or not, "Yes, and what of it?"

"I believe this may be the same team that Department XXII recently hosted at our operational site 'Walli,' is it not?"

Fischer was asking Hoffmann for confirmation.

"I believe it could be, but Colonel Dahle would be able to confirm that."

Dahle's Department XXII was another of the contradictions that underpinned Fischer's dislike of the system. It was ostensibly the Main Department for Counterterrorism, but actually spent most of its efforts supporting terrorist groups like the Red Army Faction and Red Brigade who created chaos in Western Europe. Fischer was also aware that Ilyich Ramírez Sánchez, better known as the Jackal, was at that moment being hosted by Department XXII in a safe house not far away.

"I don't think that will be necessary at this moment, General. My concern is that I don't think we've prepared for the blowback of an assassination."

"What blowback?" Mielke was now interested. He wanted nothing to shake his status with the Politburo.

"I am not sure where or when this operation might take place but, if anyone in the West determines that this team trained in the GDR, we will face consequences at the United Nations, not to mention in the world press."

"What would you suggest?" Markus Wolf spoke for the first time.

Wolf knew Fischer was on Großmann's list of suspects. What Fischer said next might be an indication of where his true allegiances lay.

"General, that is not my area of expertise. Active Measures should be the focal point of any contingency planning, but if the Libyans carry out an act, we should have a story that perhaps suggests they were a rogue element. Or we could blame it on the Bulgarians, they have a history of ties to Middle-Eastern terrorists. That would be a start, anything to distance us from their activities."

Fischer was speaking of the *Stasi's AM* disinformation branch, the section that propagated false stories to discredit nations, organizations, and personalities. Its best operation to date was propagating the lie that the Americans were eavesdropping on their West German allies.

"You're not suggesting we try to stop the Libyans?" Wolf asked.

Now Fischer had to reach into his case officer's bag of untruths.

"No, certainly not. If successful, their action will serve us well to destabilize the targeted government. Also, if we should try to stop them, we might tip our hand that we knew of their activities beforehand. We should just be prepared for any blowback."

"It's a reasonable suggestion," Wolf turned to Mielke. "If you agree, Minister, I will have *AM* look at the issue and prepare some possible scenarios that we could consider."

"Yes, yes, do it," Mielke said. He was not adept at propaganda either, but knew he had to protect himself and the organization he had done so much to build. Most importantly, he didn't want the Politburo meddling in his affairs— he had enemies who would like to strip away his power and destroy him.

"Anything else?" Mielke asked of the troublesome interloper whom he knew by sight but not by name.

"No, Comrade Minister," Fischer turned and retreated from the office as quickly as possible.

Hopefully, a seed of doubt has been planted...

Once Fischer had disappeared, Mielke asked Wolf, "Who was that?"

"Major General Fischer, my head of overseas stations in the Third World. He's been with us since the beginning."

"You damn spies are so secretive, I don't know any of you, other than you!"

"Perhaps it's better that way, Minister."

As for Fischer's motives, Wolf was still unsure.

19

The teams were ready. Becker and Rohan would make contact with the target, the only boots on the ground close to him. The two other cells would be for security and make sure they got in and out without a problem. Everyone was linked with concealed and encrypted Ascom SE-138 VHF radios that would only be used for warning or to signal an emergency. Even if their communications could not be understood by the East Germans, a transmission signal might alert the security forces that an unauthorized radio was operating.

Kim felt that his team was well prepared. Since he took over, he had optimized training for cellular operations rather than working as a full or split "A" Team. Special Forces teams generally operated as one twelve-man or two six-man elements. In Berlin, the teams took it further and broke down into three-man or even two-man cells that were linked loosely by well-practiced clandestine communications systems. It was the only way to survive when operating in a high-threat environment, a system that was derived from Office of Strategic Services operations in World War II and continually improved since.

The first two cells would cross the frontier into East Berlin, initially traveling together ostensibly as a freedom of passage patrol. Both the Soviets and the Western Allies sent patrols into their opposites' occupied zones—the Russians into West Berlin and the French, British, and Americans into the East. The Allied patrol cars could not be stopped or searched and Becker was counting on that to get the first elements into place. The car would drop off two of his team about a kilometer from the target. In civilian clothing, they would provide an outer ring of surveillance near Fischer's home, while the van continued to roam further away.

The staging site was in an abandoned factory complex in the seedy district of Neukölln. Secured from the outside, it looked all but empty to the locals. Only a few vehicles entered and exited every day. It seemed to pass for some type of maintenance facility, which situated the proprietor nicely. The Agency preferred that the locals ignore its facilities. It was a typically drab group of buildings; windows on the street side were broken and boarded over, the concrete had passed through every shade of gray from light to dark and was heading for the black color of an about-to-be-condemned rat-trap.

Inside one of the buildings, Becker watched as his first team left the garage in an olive-green US Army Ford Transit van and turned towards its crossing point and Checkpoint Charlie about 2 kilometers distant. Soon he and Rohan would follow from another start point in a second car, a civilian vehicle with French occupation forces license plates. The East Germans could not stop and search that car either, but there was a slim chance of it being detained. The East Germans had done that before when they suspected a vehicle was being used to smuggle a disenchanted citizen out of their Workers' Paradise. They often blocked Allied civilian cars from moving by trapping them with a *Volkspolizei* cruiser front and rear for hours. The "accidental" discharge of a policeman's pistol into the trunk of a car might end the quest for freedom then and there. But Becker wasn't worried about that today as he and Rohan would not be smuggling anyone out.

Becker left the Neukölln facility to take a ride on the *U-Bahn*. He emerged from subterranean Berlin at a station in the Wedding district. A short walking route followed so he could meet Rohan near a cafe. Satisfied he was not being watched, he approached Rohan who, as usual, looked totally at home in the area. Becker had to admit that she was an attractive woman, but she did not stand out. She seemed to blend into the environment with her rather drab clothing, perfect for a trip into East Berlin where they needed to attract no one's attention.

The one thing he did notice that he hadn't seen before was her eyes, now framed by a pair of dark-blue eyeglasses. If you looked closely you could sense that she was constantly observing her surroundings and evaluating. It was a trait normal for well-attuned soldiers, spies, and criminals, not so much radio-intercept operators.

"Hi, Paul! I'm glad you're on time," Rohan greeted him in French.

"I would never leave my lady waiting."

Becker responded in kind. Their banter was as much a greeting as a warmup for the task at hand. They needed to get into character quickly and stay there until the mission was complete. Kim's decision to use "Paul" as his cover name was as much to remind him of her boyfriend as it was to make it easy for Sarah.

Rohan thrust her arm though Becker's and turned him down the street.

"I parked close by," she said.

She handed Becker the keys as they walked.

"Full tank of petrol, everything seems to function properly. And I have done a radio check. Hopefully, that's the last time I will have to use it tonight."

Becker looked to see if he could spot the radio's clandestine kit earpiece but her hair hid it from view.

"Perfect. Hopefully, this will go smoothly and quickly."

"There it is," she said, "the blue Renault."

"That's one ugly car. At least it will blend in with the *Trabis*," Becker said. He alluded to the ubiquitous and cheap East German car made of fiberboard and plastic.

"It doesn't smoke, though."

Trabants smoked like locomotives with a two-stroke engine that sounded like an angry sewing machine.

"That's a plus, but I hope the owner didn't smoke either. I can't stand French cigarettes."

"It smells like Chanel. Your senses will be safe."

Rohan climbed into the passenger seat as Becker checked the tools and spare tire in the trunk.

Always be prepared. He lived by the Boy Scout motto as much for it being ingrained into his memory as for its applicability in daily tasks, especially ones involving mortality. Satisfied, he hopped into the front seat, familiarized himself with the controls and adjusted everything before he cranked the engine.

"Okay, no shop talk, this is a fun evening," he said.

"Yes, dear," came Sarah's unexpected answer. She had a self-satisfied grin on her face.

Checking the mirrors, Becker launched the Renault away from the curb and south towards Kreuzberg and the Allied crossing point into the East. It was an easy drive, even if the streets were full of evening traffic. He would head east and then south through the Tiergarten district to avoid the heavy congestion in the city center.

Ahead he could see the glistening column that stood in the center of a traffic roundabout; a testament to the Prussian victory over the Danes in 1864. A gilded statue of Victoria glistened at its peak and captured cannons encircling the column reflected the western sun as he approached the circle. He wasn't sightseeing but he appreciated its symbolism: a sight that rankled the East Germans who had to look at it from across the border. If it had been situated further east, the communists would probably have dynamited it after the war, just as they had most symbols of Prussian power.

Onward he drove, through the Tiergarten then south through Nollendorf Platz before he turned east. He stayed away from the Wall as if he didn't want to be exposed to East Berlin before it was absolutely necessary.

Sarah seemed to sense Becker's mood, determined as it was, and didn't speak. Little did she realize that it was his way of bringing focus to the task ahead. But she too was in deep concentration, going over details of her cover life and visualizing the routes and streets they would soon be walking, not to mention the layout of the apartment building belonging to the man she only knew as the Wizard.

Before long, Sarah realized she was reliving an earlier moment of her life, a time when she was a child pretending to be someone she was not. This time she felt at ease, better prepared and, even if nervous, actually looking forward to the task. This was what she had enlisted in the army to do, after all. She glanced at Becker and decided that she could not do much better than having someone like him in charge.

Their car turned onto Kochstraße. An illuminated blue and white *U-Bahn* sign marked the turn into Friedrichstraße and an immediate stop at Checkpoint Charlie. There, in the middle of the street, was a booth marked "US Army Checkpoint" with the flags of the Allies—the United States, United Kingdom, and France—flying outside it. Another big sign proclaimed, "You are leaving the American Sector" in English, French, Russian, and, in very small type, German. Further down the street, Rohan could see the East German Border Guard tower, a tall structure that commanded the street and reminded anyone who saw it of what awaited them on the other side. To the right and left of the street was a sobering sight. The Wall ran out perpendicularly from the roadway topped with several strands of barbed wire. Several more linear obstacles stood behind the first were meant to impede the flight of anyone foolish enough to try escaping at this point. Rohan had seen similar fortifications on the Czech border, not quite as formidable as this, but those had left scars on her soul. That was then, however.

Becker stepped out of the car. Seeing the license plates, a French military policeman approached. He gave a perfunctory greeting and salute before he took the papers Becker offered. He checked the papers with their official stamps and compared them with the identity documents to make sure everything matched and the dates were correct.

"You will be staying the night?"

"That is our plan, yes."

"Everything is in order, sir. Pay attention to the Germans in the booth ahead. They will want to see your identity cards. Give the cards to them but don't engage them with any talk. Do what they ask and move on only when they say to proceed."

The French corporal did not see the guards as East Germans; to him they were all the same—German.

"Understood, thank you."

Becker hopped back in the car, "We're off."

Pulling past the Allied checkpoint, the first stop was just inside East Berlin. Becker could see they were now behind the Wall proper. The communist checkpoint was marked with a sign that proclaimed HALT! To emphasize the sign's instruction, an East German soldier wearing an olive-green uniform marked with the forest-green epaulets of the Border Guards stood waiting for the car. His uniform echoed those of soldiers of the former *Wehrmacht*.

Becker stopped adjacent to the soldier and handed him two identity cards. He took them without a word to the window in a booth. The cards disappeared into the booth where Becker knew another soldier would record the data. After a long—seemingly longer than necessary—wait, the cards came back out the window to the first soldier, who marched stiffly over to the car and shoved the cards into Becker's hand.

"*Fortfahren.*" The soldier gestured with his hand and indicated that Becker could proceed.

Becker rolled slowly out of the checkpoint into the city.

"The hotel isn't far, we'll check in and then do some sightseeing before the performance," Becker said as he pointed their car north towards their goal. He still imagined the French had left a recorder or transmitter somewhere in the car.

It was a short trip to the hotel through the more or less refurbished streets of the communist capital. Unlike the western sector of Berlin, the East did not suffer from an overpopulation of cars and Becker found a parking spot close to the hotel's main entry.

Rohan climbed out of the car and stood looking at the modern Palace of the Republic, the communist parliament building, across the cold, dark waters of the River Spree. Beyond its mirrored, brown glass facade, she could see the tall spire of the *Fernsehturm*—the TV tower—in the distance.

"They say the tower was cursed by the Pope because its windows reflect a cross in the sunlight," Sarah said as she glanced at Becker. Then she added, "This side of the city smells different."

"It's probably the lignite coal smell, it's stronger over here."

"No, it's the river. Its source is near a town called Bautzen on the Czech border. The river carries the stench of that place, I'm sure of it."

"What stench?"

"Fear. Bautzen is a mean place."

Becker glanced around to see if anyone was close. Despite the French, he didn't want their conversation to be overheard.

"No politics, remember?"

She looked at him again and he could sense the intensity of her feelings.

"It's all around us, I can't help it sometimes. On the hill, I listened to people's conversations, the leaders and the officials; they all spoke of that place with something in their voice that told stories, very bad stories. We had a place very much like it in Prague—Pankrác.

We couldn't talk about it either. I hate the people that build those places."

"Try not to think about it, think about the theater, about pleasant things. We'll talk about it later. Please try."

There was a deep hurt in her eyes. Her look was one of intense pain; he could feel it and couldn't look away. Then she shook her head and blinked the pain away. She smiled at him, stoically it seemed.

"I'll try."

Becker grabbed the luggage, two small bags, and walked towards the entrance. Rohan followed, her head turning from side to side to take in the sights as well as to get oriented to the new surroundings.

Becker knew he had to keep Sarah focused. He didn't want her to be overwhelmed by the all-pervasive negative environment that surrounded them. He had seen a similar reaction in a refugee once before in a training program.

He clearly remembered the young man's name: it was Zenebe. He was perhaps twenty-eight years old, an aspiring journalist from Ethiopia. He had escaped the *Derg*, the murderous regime that ousted and murdered Emperor Haile Selassie. The *Derg* were nasty people. They buried Selassie under his toilet.

In the early seventies, Zenebe was arrested and put in prison. He was interrogated and tortured many times before being released, possibly so he would lead the secret police to others they could arrest. Instead, he disappeared and ran for the border, escaping to Kenya where the UNHCR—United Nations High Commissioner for Refugees—arranged for his relocation to the United States. To make his way in his newly adopted homeland, he joined the army and that was where Becker met him.

It was during a SERE course. The acronym stood for "Survival, Evasion, Resistance, and Escape"—instruction on how to avoid getting captured and then what happens and how to live through it when you do. It is one of the worst five days a soldier can experience.

Becker knew: he had done it four times, twice with the army, once with the navy, and once with the air force. It never got any better, but then he was a glutton for punishment, or so his team sergeant told him.

Zenebe was in training to work with Special Forces as an Amharic interpreter and had to successfully pass the arrest and interrogation phase of the training. It was a course that simulated the sights, sounds, smells, and sometimes, the pain of being locked up in a Third World prison.

The students were returning on a bus after several days of field training. There was one instructor and the driver on board with the thirty-five or so passengers. It was dark and the usual chatter had died down. Two hours of driving lulled many to sleep and only half the people on board were awake.

The bus had turned off onto a dirt road and was slowly heading up a long incline. Even if someone was awake they could not see anything beyond the glare of the headlights, when a series of bright flashes and explosions rocked the bus. The driver slammed on the brakes throwing everyone and anything into turmoil. Both he and the instructor went down as if they were dead.

The bus doors burst open and about six men rushed on board with pistols and Kalashnikovs firing into the air. They were firing blanks but no one knew that. Several of the students tried to bolt for the rear escape doors, but no one made it. The invaders were yelling and screaming at everyone.

"Get down! Get down on the floor!"

There were more explosions and firing and yelling. Smoke filled the bus as flashlights searched through the students on the floor of the bus. Then it quieted down.

The invaders became captors and handcuffed everyone with cable-ties. Then they "bagged" all their new prisoners, putting black cloth sacks over their heads. The prisoners were grabbed roughly and dragged off the bus one at a time. To the prisoners, time became an unknown. Was it ten minutes or an hour before they were taken off the bus?

Each would remember the ordeal differently, from their own perspective. As they were wearing hoods, directions became confused. That was the instructors' objective: keep the students confused and disoriented.

Was that a ramp or just a hallway, and what is this space?

"Is there anybody else here?" someone whispered.

"Keep your mouth shut!"

The bus had been "ambushed" in front of a building that couldn't be seen in the dark. Each student, now a prisoner, was taken into the building and down into the basement where individual holding cells awaited them. Then the fun began.

Each prisoner was subjected to a medical screening. Their clothing removed, each was inspected by a female medic if they were a male, a male medic if they were female. All the while they were blindfolded. It was meant to demean and humiliate the prisoner. For many it worked. There is nothing worse for some men than to hear a woman laugh and say, "Look at that tiny thing!"

They were questioned under duress, made to kneel on a steel grate that bit into their knees or forced to sit in front of a roaring hot furnace. Then they were taken to another room and sprayed with ice-cold water, still blindfolded. In between sessions, they sat in their cells wearing nothing but underwear, freezing their butts on the cold concrete, listening to the chaos around them.

Then the process was repeated.

The interrogators' questions and accusations came in rapid fire.

"Who are you?"

"Why are you in my country?"

"You are a spy!"

"I think you are a drug smuggler. You know we shoot drug smugglers in this country."

147

After about ten hours of listening to the ear-splitting white noise and recorded screams being blasted into the halls and cells of the basement confinement facility, Zenebe couldn't handle it. He was reliving a terrible moment from his past. He broke. He cried, he screamed, he rolled on the ground and said he couldn't do it anymore.

The chief instructor came to him. "If you want to quit, all you have to do is say, 'I quit.'"

"I quit," said Zenebe.

He was taken away immediately, given a hot meal and the opportunity to clean up before he was sent back to his home unit. Several others quit that night; quitting was contagious. It wasn't a negative thing and didn't impact their careers. It was stress—kind of like combat fatigue, a thing you have little control over. Zenebe quit the training and returned to his unit where he would serve in jobs with little chance of being captured and interrogated by the enemy's security forces.

Some say that a man who has been tortured can never again be trusted. Becker knew that the more important question was why would anyone want to risk being tortured a second time. What kind of person can overlook the pain they experienced? Would they have that last measure of courage to push through it all? What was their motivation to do so?

Becker knew Sarah had gone through a painful experience—just how painful he didn't know—but he hoped she was stronger than Zenebe.

Why would she want to go through this again? What does she stand to gain? She has to weather this night.

Becker entered the hotel and came back from the dark place he had been for the last few moments. He marveled at the human mind—how it can replay in mere seconds memories that lasted for many hours.

Becker thought that the check-in process at the Palast must be like that of German-occupied Paris during World War II. He knew that the secret police would soon have their photographs and copies of their documents. These would be filed away under categories like "French," and whether or not they were of interest to the *Stasi*, or potentially dangerous to the GDR.

Becker contemplated that reality as he and Rohan registered. The staff was cleanly if somewhat shabbily dressed; the hotel was orderly, but poorly maintained. It seemed that the only things that worked precisely were the cameras at the entry way and in the reception area. Those were the responsibility of hotel security who were essentially sub-contractors of the *Stasi*.

He had reminded Sarah of the possibility that their room would be monitored and they acted accordingly. They were there to drop off their overnight bags and prepare for the evening. It was a short stop and for a moment he wondered if the routine was worth the effort. Most, if not all, theater-goers from the West stayed the night after a performance rather than run the gauntlet of the checkpoint at night. Not many people wanted to put up with the bother of returning. Becker had decided to follow the norm and at least go through the motions of registering and getting a room; what they would actually do later was another question.

When Sarah came out of the bathroom, Becker looked her over closely. He told himself he was assessing her readiness for the evening's mission, but he admitted he was also appreciating her beauty. She wore a pantsuit, walking shoes, no jewelry, and had her hair arranged to keep it out of the way, but he still couldn't see the earpiece. Her non-prescription glasses were the only nod towards fashion, but they served a purpose as well.

"You look very nice," he said. He realized he was smiling. He felt a bit like a teenager saying it, but it was true.

"Thank you. You clean up well, too. I'm ready when you are, dearest."

She threw in the "dearest" as if it was the most natural thing in the world. Becker knew it was for show and the benefit of anyone listening, but for a moment he wished she were sincere.

Then he came to his senses.

"Let's go have a look at the city before the show."

He grabbed her coat, a reversible trench suitable for fall or clandestine operations, and handed it to her after she closed and locked the room door. The coat was tan on one side and dark gray on the other. She put the coat on tan side out.

Rather than risk getting stuck in an unpredictable elevator, they took the stairs down to the lobby. Becker strode across the open expanse to the concierge desk.

In simple German with his French accent, he said, "Where is the Schiffbaum Theater?"

The concierge looked at Becker curiously for a moment. "I think you mean the Schiffbauerdamm Theater, true?" he answered.

Then he showed Becker the route on a map that he refused to part with.

Cheap bastard.

Becker wanted the map. Any map from a denied area was a good map to take home.

Becker already knew the directions anyway. He had no intention of following the concierge's instructions but wanted to make sure the staff thought they knew where they were going. With that established, he took Rohan by the arm and headed out the front door.

The theater was about 3 kilometers away, too far to walk at night. The car was a logical mode of transport to get there. But that wasn't the objective. The car would put them closer to their meeting and give them an excuse for being "off course" if they encountered any police.

Becker opened up the passenger side door of the Renault and let Sarah settle into the car. It gave him an opportunity to do a discreet visual sweep of the people and cars in the vicinity. It wasn't definitive but it would at least give him an idea if a similar car showed up again later. He had to rely on his instincts and hope that, if they decided to follow them, the East Germans would use just a few cars and expose themselves repeatedly and quickly. He knew the police and *Stasi* rarely used Trabants, which didn't have the power to tail another car, so he concentrated on the bigger vehicles. Nothing popped out at him as he slid into the front seat and started the car. It was early evening, which meant that the sky was beginning to darken as night approached from the east.

"Let's take a look at the island," Becker suggested as he drove away from the hotel.

Passing Alexanderplatz, he turned towards Museum Island. It was a logical direction to sightsee or to get to the theater. He slowed the car to a crawl going over the Spree River bridge. He was watching the mirror, but there were no cars behind him. Continuing across the bridge and then south onto the island, he named the old buildings as they came into sight, the Dom Cathedral, Customs House, and Nikolai Church, before they turned again and drove off the island. He sped up before turning one more time over the Spree into the tight streets of the Friedrichshain District.

Finding an open space, he shoehorned the car into the spot. He and Rohan jumped from the car and walked away at a fast clip in the direction they had just come from.

"Are we clean?" Sarah asked. She had reversed her coat from tan to dark gray.

Clever girl.

"I think so. It was a short run but I didn't see a soul."

They kept walking until an alleyway appeared and they ducked in, walking to its end and then onto another residential street.

"Nothing from the others," Sarah said, referring to the other teams that had entered the city before them. One was on the ground walking the inner ring around their objective; the second was cruising the main streets further out, watching for security patrols and monitoring radio communications with a scanner tuned to the known *Volkspolizei* and *Stasi* channels.

Becker led the way, hand in hand with Rohan, stair-stepping several streets and crossing a playground before walking down a pedestrian path between two apartment buildings. They were relatively new, simply constructed and plainly adorned in the communist style, or better said, lack thereof. To their front was a smaller building. It was described as a duplex in their target folder.

From 50 meters out, Becker could see the rear concrete block wall that protected the residence and came to a halt. At this distance he risked doing a blatant visual search to their rear and all the other directions. He saw nothing. It was still quiet.

"Anything?" he asked.

"*Rien.*" Nothing, she answered. The other teams were silent. *Report by exception* was their last order—use your radio only in emergency or when absolutely necessary.

It was quiet. By night, there was an eerie kind of beauty in the neighborhood. The buildings stood as sentinels, a few dimly lit windows illuminating each one. A partial moon blinked at them between gray clouds scudding across the sky and a slight breeze rustled the tree branches overhead. By day it was another story; then the city was a testament to the poor conditions in the country.

Becker saw the building they were seeking and walking carefully forward in the darkness, he felt for and found the unlocked latch. He lifted it and pushed the gate open slowly. He just hoped that the hinges were well oiled and only relaxed when they didn't protest. They moved inside and closed it quietly behind them.

They had but a few moments. A *Stasi* surveillance team was probably on the street in front of the house and it was possible that a foot surveillant might venture behind the building to check on things.

The rear courtyard was split in two parts, separated by a wooden fence. The house had been a single-family dwelling before the war, but was then divided into two three-floor apartments by the regime to provide suitable housing for senior officials. There were two doors that opened onto the courtyard. Becker knew the left-hand door was theirs. He walked towards it and as he did, he felt Rohan grasp his hand. They stood close together in the darkness next to the wall, waiting.

Becker looked at his watch. "Almost time."

At 19.10 Central European Time, the light in the hall came on as did the light over the door. They flashed for a moment and then went out.

"Now."

Becker and Sarah walked to the door which was partially opened and slipped inside.

A tall figure stood in the dimly lit corridor, waiting.

"*Wir sind Ihre neue Nachbarn.*" We're your new neighbors, Rohan said.

If Fischer was taken aback by Sarah, he didn't show it.

"*Willkommen in meinem Schloss.*" Welcome to my castle, he responded.

Fischer motioned for them to follow. He led them up the stairs to a second-floor foyer. Music was playing in one of the adjoining rooms. Not loudly, but enough to provide some cover.

"This area is good to talk. We have little time and much to discuss."

"First, we're French theater-goers, lost in the neighborhood."

"Ha, no one will believe that if they find you here. But it was a good idea to bring her."

"We didn't have many other options for cover. Now, we need to talk about getting you out of here."

"You can't get me out of the East to West Berlin. Surveillance on the border crossings in the city is too tight. We will have to cross the frontier to West Germany. I have a house, my *Dacha*, north of the city. The exact coordinates are inside." Fischer handed Becker a coin. "There are other important notes in there as well, including information for one of my people—'Flower'—but trying

153

to contact me through that asset should only be attempted in extreme emergency. It's in code, your people over there have the key."

Becker knew what the coin was as soon as he felt it in his hand. He pocketed it as Fischer brought out an army map to show him the landscape around the house. After memorizing the map's name and series, Becker asked, "What are these?" and pointed at several lines around the house.

"This is a dirt road from the main route and these are walking trails I use in the forest."

As Becker and Fischer talked about the house and trails, Rohan roamed the hall. She noted the curtains were heavy brocade, pulled closed. The walls were sparsely adorned with old lithographs and historical photos. Not a single photograph of a person. It was all generic; nothing indicated who lived here. She glanced into a room through a partially opened door and saw similar decorations, although many books lined the wall shelving. Older furniture, well cared for but plain. There was a record player atop a table.

Interesting, a "Dual" turntable and speakers, all high-end West German equipment. He likes music and books but otherwise the man who lives here is an enigma.

She turned back to the two men still quietly talking in German.

"*Sept heures et demie.*" Seven-thirty, she reminded Becker.

"You *are* French," Fischer said. He was surprised.

"No, but I speak it well," she said. "We must go soon."

"A couple of details more." Becker needed time.

Fischer described what he thought to be the cause of his compromise and the recent message about the Libyan hit squad that he had been given.

"It's a trap, I know it. But it may be an opportunity as well."

Becker nodded all the while. No notes were taken. Rohan listened closely to the last details.

Coming to an end, Becker summarized, "We have a location and a signal for the date and time. You gave us the information on the leak and the players involved. Anything I missed?"

"No."

"We will set up the means to get you out, just be there."

"Yes. But try to set it for these days," Fischer pointed a span of days on the calendar.

"Got it. We'll be in touch very soon. *Auf wiedersehen.*"

He reached out and shook Fischer's hand. It was a strong grip.

"I hope so, neighbor," and to Sarah, "*Au revoir, madame.*"

"*A bientôt, monsieur.*"

They climbed down the stairs quietly. The door opened and they were gone into the night.

Fischer stood at the top of the stairs hoping they would make it home without a problem, praying that he could finally escape from the intricate web he had wrapped so tightly around himself.

The music played on in the background.

***

Becker peered out onto the pathway behind the house before he dared open the gate fully. He smelled the man before he saw him, a figure walking slowly along the path in the deepest of shadows. A wisp of smoke would rise from his cigarette and get caught in the moonlight. He was one of the surveillance team, of that Becker was sure. The man walked too slowly and paused too often to be anything else, except maybe a husband trying to get away from his wife. But Becker couldn't risk it and watched carefully as the man continued his route. He was going back to the car and probably some lukewarm coffee. When the path was finally clear, they stepped out and walked briskly back the way they came. The car was almost 2 kilometers away but the walk passed without incident.

Becker started the car and they headed back towards the city center and the theater.

They were on Frankfurter Allee and about five minutes into the drive when blue lights flashed in the rearview mirror.

"*Polizei*, damn."

"*Non, 'zut'!*" Sarah corrected.

"Sorry. I know he can't arrest us, but running from the police is never a good idea."

After stopping the car, Becker waited for the *Vopo* to approach.

"*Franzosisch, nicht wahr?*" You are French, correct? "Where are you going so quickly?"

In bad German, Becker tried to explain that they were lost and trying to find the theater.

The *Vopo* glanced at the identity document Becker had given him and sighed.

Touristen, he thought.

Swatting the card back and forth on his fist, the policeman contemplated asking for a gratuity and then decided the people in the car were probably too cheap. They were French, after all. Slipping into his best simple German he pointed ahead and rattled off a series of street names before finishing with, "And then you are there."

He handed the identity cards back, gave a salute, and walked back to his car.

It was Becker's turn to relax.

"He seemed nice," Sarah said facetiously. "Let's get out of here."

Once they arrived near the theater, Becker checked his watch. It was close to 20.30.

"Right on time, let's go see the performance."

"We might as well," Rohan said, and keyed the radio mike three times to signal success before they disappeared into the crowd of theatergoers.

20

The loud hum of the bubble's ventilation system deep inside the BOB made it hard for Wheeler and Murphy to hear each other, let alone think about their damage control plans.

"I sent the summary of Becker's meeting to Russia House and they believe OZ's theory is probably spot on. One of our reports passed to *BND* headquarters at Pullach had too much detail about his contact, enough to figure out who he was. I am told the reports officer and reviewer in Bonn who did the summary will be disciplined. The West Germans will have to deal with an enemy agent in their midst. That is, once we decide to tell them," Murphy said.

"They should all be summarily executed," Wheeler said. Clearly upset, he tended to resort to ballistic solutions when confronted with incompetence or treachery.

"Chief said he would wait until the case is resolved to determine punishment. Execution is out, but they will be dealt with."

"Hopefully. Putting OZ at risk was unconscionable. The report should have been triple checked before it was released."

"Agreed. But at least his info gives us an opportunity to turn the tables a bit. Since we have the best handle on the East German service, Russia House asked for something that could be inserted into another report that would throw suspicion in another direction."

"Nice they want help after the fact." Wheeler did not easily forgive transgressions.

"Sometimes they'll admit weakness. Anyway, everything compromised seems to have dealt with terrorism-related issues; they think nothing from his more substantive political reporting was passed to the West Germans. So, for the report I'm going to describe the *Stasi* operational site 'Walli' with information we already have and loosely describe a Libyan team that was there. OZ confirmed that was where they trained and our information on the location isn't critical, so we can use it for good background. I will also add a very subtle operational note pointing at someone in *Abteilung XXII.*"

"The 'counterterrorism' department that trains terrorists?" Wheeler asked.

"That one indeed. I think something along the lines of 'a usually reliable source who directly observed the activity described' would be good."

"Subtle and direct. We play that back to the Russians and hope they give it to the *Stasi* quickly. If they do, it'll buy us some time. If they already had a suspect in XXII, that will burn him pretty good."

"OZ said the red-herring message included XXII on the distribution line, so it makes sense that they're casting a wide net to catch the leaker. Luckily, OZ has more experience than most anyone in the organization. His lead should confuse the investigation and lets us finish preparations for the extraction. How are our friends doing with their planning?"

"Well, I think. They're doing some out-of-the-box brainstorming and pulling in assets I didn't know existed or at least they didn't when I was a young pup in SF."

"Were you ever a pup? I guess times have changed since both of us were in the service. By the way, I want to sit in on the final briefback, so you're going to sneak me over when it happens."

"That won't be hard. I'll get someone to drive us over in a closed van. The Russians won't see us leave the compound."

21

Out of the frying pan and into the fire.

As he plotted Fischer's coordinates of his country house onto a map, Becker thought about the challenges the mission posed for his team. Going into East Berlin under diplomatic cover was one thing; going into East Germany black, was another.

There were few options. Travel as a Western tourist was a no-go. There was no way to get close to Fischer and no way to get him out. Pretty much the same went for diplomats as they would be followed immediately after crossing the border. Going in black would be the only possibility but he had to come up with a means of transport. Hopping over the border wall would not work. Fischer's place was over 50 kilometers from Berlin and walking there was out of the question.

Then, once you get to his house, how do you get him across the border to the West?

He sat back and scratched his head, as if acknowledging the conundrum to the rest of the team.

"Ideas, gentlemen?"

Team 5 were crouched in a huddle around the East German military map, the same series as the one Fischer had shown him. They were staring hard and looking for answers.

Becker had plotted the coordinates Fischer had given him on a map he got from the Agency. Fischer's country house was located about 12 kilometers northwest of Neuruppin. It was located in an isolated area of farms and stands of forest, one of which enclosed Fischer's property.

"Getting to him is the first problem."

"Cross over and steal a car," offered Finch.

"This isn't Boston. You wouldn't last three hours." Stefan Mann knew the *Vopos'* capabilities.

"Helicopter," Finch tried again.

"Even worse," Mann continued his critique.

"Piggyback with a Mission tour." Nick Kaiser threw in his best idea.

"Hold it there. What's your thought?" Becker said.

"One of us rides in with the Mission and drops off somewhere near his place. Once they meet, they get picked up and brought back to Berlin," Kaiser outlined.

The "Mission" was shorthand for the United States Military Liaison Mission, a kind of legal spying arrangement agreed to between the Allies and the Soviets after World War II that permitted the monitoring of military activities in their occupation zones. Just as the Soviets observed Allied forces in West Germany, the Allies did the same in the East. Looking for new equipment was one task; the other was to serve as an early warning mechanism. The USMLM, like its British and French counterparts, sent clearly marked vehicles into East Germany each with a Foreign Area Officer who spoke Russian and a senior enlisted intelligence analyst who spoke German. These missions provided the Department of Defense with some of the best military intelligence that could be gathered, and gave SDB an opportunity to look at its targets up close by sending men in as part of the Mission tour crew.

"It won't work. They would detain every Mission car once they figure out he's gone. You'd never make it safely back across the bridge into Berlin," Mann again struck at the obvious weak point.

Becker tweaked Kaiser's idea a bit: "True, we wouldn't be able to get him out with a Mission car, but we could get *to* him. Then we need part two."

"Helo pick-up," Finch tried again.

Mann was obviously ready to smack him.

"Give it up with the helos already. The EGs would blow them out of the sky once they deviated from the usual flight path and crossed the border. And they're too slow to outrun a MiG."

"Then how about a Beaver?" Finch was referring to the de Havilland U-6A, an airplane used by the Berlin Air Detachment for its daily Wall Flights.

"Still too slow."

"But not a bad idea. There might be a better aircraft out there." Becker was beginning to frame up some alternatives. "See if you can locate some good LZs within, say, a 10-kilometer radius of the house. I'm going to talk to the S-3 about available assets. Paul, come with me."

"Uh oh, Pauli's in trouble."

"Shut up, Finch," Stavros shot back as he walked out behind Becker.

Becker had stopped in the empty hallway and was waiting for Stavros to catch up.

"I meant to tell you that Rohan did quite well. Once she got over her initial anxiety, she settled in and was more relaxed than I was."

"Actually, I waited for her last night so I could talk to her. She was excited to have done the mission and said you were very professional and taught her some cool stuff."

"She got mad at me when I told her we were going to abandon our luggage. So we went back to the hotel. She likes the bag from the French PX; Louie Button or some silly thing."

"Louis Vuitton. Yeah, she mentioned that. I think she's going to be really bored in her job now," Stavros chuckled.

"I'm going to ask the sergeant major if he has any ideas for her. He's got good connections at the Pentagon."

"Well, don't get her reassigned yet. I'm still working on her."

"I can imagine. Are you making any progress?"

The smile on Paul's face told him everything.

22

Days had passed since he broke into the meeting with Mielke and Max Fischer was planning to tell Wolf of his decision to spend the weekend at his *Dacha*.

It wouldn't be necessary.

Wolf seemed to sense something and Fischer wasn't sure if it was because of Großmann's suspicions or in spite of them. What he did know was that Wolf was a chess player to the 'nth degree. That was why he was in charge of the Main Reconnaissance Directorate. The MRD carried out East Germany's espionage outside the country. MRD officers recruited spies and placed infiltrators in foreign governments—it was the most delicate business an intelligence organization could attempt. Mielke didn't understand its intricate methodologies and the tradecraft required, and neither did Großmann. They were cops and brutally straightforward in how they carried out their business. They were also killers. Wolf was above that and that was why Fischer respected him. He had watched and learned from Wolf from the beginning when he started to work with the service as a young and resolute communist. While his commitment to communism had wavered, Wolf's never did. Because of that, Fischer was wary. Wolf would have no sympathy for a traitor to the cause.

Fischer was in his office reading the latest traffic out of his in-box when a knock came at his door. He always left his door open: he had nothing to hide and was ever approachable, was the image he always tried to portray.

He looked up and was surprised to see Wolf in the doorway.

"Come in, General!" he said as he stood and walked in front of his desk.

"It's Markus, Max. I told you that you can always call me Markus. We've been at this together too long, you and I."

Ever the gentleman and ever the player, Fischer thought.

"Thank you for bringing that issue to the Minister's attention so promptly, Max. My secretary told me that you came looking for me."

"I thought the Libyan issue might pose a problem that needed to be proactively addressed. Department XXII seems to carry on operations without much thought given to the overall strategic effect."

"True. I think General Hoffmann should be able to put something together with *AM* as you suggested. But what I actually wanted to talk with you about wasn't really work related. It's about you."

Fischer was genuinely surprised.

"Me? How so?"

"You seem a bit stressed. Perhaps you should take some time off. Looking over your calendar I saw that you haven't taken any time for yourself in over a year!"

"That's probably right. Things have been busy with all that's going on in Africa and southwest Asia."

"Yes, but that shouldn't keep you from taking care of yourself. As I said, we've been at this for a long time but even I take a vacation now and then. Why don't you take four or five days and go off to the countryside? You have a nice, quiet place to relax at your *Dacha*. Catch up on some good reading, that sort of thing."

"I was actually thinking about doing that. Some time in the country would be nice."

"Agreed and so ordered. Tell your deputy he's in charge and get out of here."

"Yes, General."

Wolf started to say "Markus," but just shook his head and turned and walked away.

Well, it's now or never.

Wolf's visit had been unexpected and Fischer, ever paranoid, wondered about his chief's true motivations.

Does he really think I need a vacation, or is he giving me the rope to hang myself?

He began to close up his office. There was nothing he needed or wanted except for his personal *Petschaft* that he had used for his entire career. He slipped it back into his pocket after he pressed it into the bit of gray clay on his safe. And then he set a telltale as always, just in case.

All secure.

Fischer glanced about his office and felt mostly relief. The time had come and nothing he was looking at was holding him back. Grabbing his coat, he walked out of the office and handed his secretary his out-box with a couple of documents nested in its tray.

"I won't be in tomorrow and should return in less than a week. The general just told me to take a couple of days off. You should also try to get out of the office early. Colonel Geyer will be acting in my place until I return."

The secretary acknowledged Fischer's instructions, happily looking forward to some stress-free days ahead.

Fischer made a stop at Geyer's office, informed him he would be in charge and made sure he had the *Dacha*'s direct phone number before heading down the stairs. He made no effort to look at the headquarters as his car left the compound. He was focusing on the things he needed to do in order to leave his life in Berlin without appearing to be cutting ties permanently.

Fischer dismissed his driver when he reached his apartment. He would drive himself to his country retreat as he usually did.

***

After leaving Fischer, Wolf walked the short way back to his office thinking about what he had done.

Russian liaison had informed him their penetration had provided more information and it looked like the source of the Americans' information was indeed out of Department XXII. Although that was an easy solution, he wasn't sure he was ready to accept it yet. Wolf ran through the permutations of the moves he had just made and where they would lead. He didn't think much of Großmann, but he still wasn't sure about Fischer.

Either he will take this opportunity to run, or he will come back in several days. By then Großmann may have figured out who the traitor is, but probably not. All the officers on his suspect list are smarter than he is and won't make mistakes. Except maybe Dahle, he is about as thick as Großmann.

I may regret this. When Großmann finds out that Fischer left town, there could be hell to pay.

23

Major Steve Bright was a long-standing veteran of military intelligence work. So much so that his career and promotions had stalled after his twelfth year of service. The army placed so much emphasis on the combat arms branches that all the others suffered. Of course, the brass at the Pentagon recognized that intelligence was important to operations, but not so important as to actually promote those who were skilled in it.

In the past several years, many, if not most of his contemporaries had been systematically and unceremoniously cashiered from the army despite their stellar performance and Vietnam experience. Undeterred, Bright soldiered on, secure in the fact that he was still employed.

Still, he felt like he had to keep looking over his soldier for some bean-counter who might pull his name out of a hat. He hoped MI needed at least a few officers with experience and would not replace him with some wet-behind-the-ears captain in an effort to save money and keep more positions in the hard skill jobs—infantry, artillery, and armor. That seemed the rationale behind most of the RIFs, but then he was an optimist. Or maybe he wasn't.

His service in Vietnam was noteworthy, he thought. Almost singlehandedly, he had dismantled a Viet Cong support network in Saigon before the Americans pulled out completely in 1975. After he returned stateside and completed a stint as an infantry brigade intelligence officer, he had received a call from his branch manager in the Pentagon offering him a position in Berlin. That was the encouragement he needed not to look seriously for a job in the civilian sector.

Finally, he would have a chance to use his degree in Russian Studies that had given him fluency in the language as well as a good understanding of Soviet strategy. A tune-up at the Defense Language Institute in Monterey was all he needed before he headed out to his posting at the US Military Liaison Mission in Berlin. That was two years ago.

Sitting outside the USMLM chief's office, he wondered what was up. He was nearing the end of his posting and would be leaving the city for a job with an MI battalion within six months. The commander rarely called on his tour officers individually unless it was to discuss family matters, performance, or assignments. He knew everything was fine at home and he hadn't heard any dissatisfaction with his work, so he hoped his follow-on job had not been cancelled.

Finally, the door to the chief's office opened and the colonel walked out.

"Hi, Steve. Sorry to keep you waiting. Come on in."

Bright followed his boss into the office expectantly. Instead of sitting the colonel remained standing. Bright assumed that meant a short meeting.

"We have a special tour coming up that I would like you to take."

In MLM context, a 'tour' was any planned trip into East Germany to roam the countryside looking for signs of imminent hostilities. It was essentially legal spying, agreed to and tolerated by both sides, but it was not without its dangers.

"Okay, sir," Bright responded with not a small amount of curiosity in his voice, "but why me and why is it special?"

Despite the fact that the MLM offices were swept religiously for bugs, the colonel was careful in his words.

"You are my most experienced tour officer for one," Colonel Stofall began, "and it might be a bit hairy. It will require you get in and out of an area without being spotted."

"Is it a PRA?"

Bright was referring to Permanently Restricted Areas, the zones the Soviets arbitrarily created to keep curious mission teams out. They were usually near training areas and a few important garrisons.

"No, but it might as well be. You will get a specific briefing from OGA this afternoon. You need to be at their office at 1400 hours. After you get the brief, choose the driver you think best suited for this tour; he needs to be rock solid."

"I've never heard of an OGA-directed tour before."

"You're correct. While we take on their requirements all the time, rarely do they directly task us. But only one part of this tour will be theirs, the rest will be normal. Let me know if you need anything else. Questions?"

"I'm sure I will have, but I'll save them for the briefing. Thanks for your confidence, sir!"

"Go then. Let me know how the briefing goes before you head out for Potsdam."

"Roger, sir." Bright saluted and withdrew from the office.

He was intrigued by the prospect of the tasking and wondered what it might entail. Back in his office, he set down to finish up his last report and pondered who might be the best driver to take along with him. Some were excellent linguists and good drivers. Others were excellent drivers and adequate linguists. Although everyone had a professional level of fluency, the officers in Russian, and the enlisted men in German, there were some who were either native speakers or close to that. He scratched that requirement. Speaking perfect German would not be key to avoiding detection; good driving skills would be.

What most people didn't understand unless they were assigned to the Mission or a senior Berlin Brigade staff officer was that, despite the existing Huebner–Malinin Agreement between the Allies and the Soviets, a Mission tour was not like driving on Route 66.

Granted, most of the trips were routine, driving on back country roads, visiting small villages, and the like. Normally, the biggest danger was getting followed by the *Stasi* or the *Volkspolizei*. They were easy enough to lose because the Mission was equipped with Mercedes-Benz sedans and G-Wagons. The East German cars didn't stand a chance and just couldn't keep up.

But where it got interesting and often dangerous was when the teams got close to a Soviet or East German military facility or convoy. Soldiers who were completely unaware of the agreement or took their job too seriously would often take potshots at the teams when they saw them.

In the West, if the Allies caught Soviets in a PRA they would simply detain the car. The Russians and East Germans acted differently. They liked to "clobber" the Allies. Clobber was the accepted word for being run off the road or rammed by a military vehicle. In this case, a Mercedes didn't stand a snowball's chance of coming out on the good end after an encounter with a big Soviet tank or armored personnel carrier. Several men had been badly injured in similar "accidents" as the Soviets always called them. Or they blamed it on the Allies' bad driving.

The Russians also often sent in *Spetsnaz* troops to harass the teams. Woe to the team that got caught with their pants down, literally, while relieving themselves in the woods. Next thing, they were being beat up by a bunch of Soviet commandos as their car was ransacked.

No one had been killed. Yet.

Later that afternoon, Bright drove to the Brigade headquarters compound and parked in the rear of the main building. What had been a Luftwaffe district air headquarters during the war was now headquarters of the United States' military and the diplomatic legation in West Berlin.

Bright walked into the main building and through its long hallways winding his way through the labyrinth until he was at the southeast corner exit. He left the big complex and walked across a smaller parking lot to the back door of a much smaller facility. Designated "Building 66," it was the home to the BOB.

He punched a button outside the door and waited, not bothering to look at the camera perched above him.

"Yes?" came the disembodied voice.

"Steve Bright, I have an appointment."

No answer. The lock buzzed and the door popped open a bit. Bright stepped into the vestibule and waited for the second door. A minute or two passed before the inside door opened.

"Come on in."

The voice was vaguely western sounding but it was attached to a very large and intimidating Hawaiian man. Bright was not small but, comparatively, his host looked to be a lineman for a pro football team.

This guy must be their enforcer.

"Welcome, Steve. I'm Jamie Wheeler. Follow me, please."

At least he's a polite enforcer, Bright thought he as followed Wheeler.

Wheeler led him back to the room which held the bubble and brought him inside. Already present were Murphy, the base chief, Becker and another member of Team 5, Nick Kaiser.

Bright's face broke into a grin when he saw Kaiser.

"Nick! How are you?"

Kaiser needed no introduction as he had spent several months with the Mission as a tour driver, including several trips into the East with Bright.

"I'm doing well, Major. It's been a while!" Kaiser reached over the table and shook Bright's hand.

Once Wheeler completed the introductions, Murphy took over and began the discussion.

"Major Bright... Steve, if I may, as you may have gathered, we need your help with a special project. First, this is all classified at Top Secret SPECAT level. Jamie will have you sign the NDA after this meeting, but from here on in, you must not discuss the specifics of this mission with anyone outside this room."

"Understood."

"Perfect. The basic task is simple; however, its execution may be a bit dicey. What we need is for you to drop off one of our assets at a specific point inside East Germany during what should look like a regular multi-day tour visit. Obviously, the most difficult part will be to get to the drop point and out again without being observed."

"Getting in and out without notice will depend entirely on where the drop-off is. If we're near a PRA or some other key point, it could be difficult. Who is the asset?"

"Me," Becker chimed in, "and the area is pretty isolated. Close to a forest and not near any major training areas. Nick has looked at the topography and has some thoughts, but it will all depend on your input and especially the most up-to-date Order of Battle on the Soviets and the EGs."

Kaiser unrolled a map onto the tabletop. It showed most of northern East Germany from Berlin up to near the Baltic coastline. Then he laid a slightly smaller map next to it. It was a large scale 1:25,000 map that showed the operational area in more detail.

Pointing at the first map, he explained: "This is the general area we're talking about, in the Brandenburg district—" and then to the second map, "inside this triangle formed by Neuruppin, Wittstock, and Rheinsberg."

"Off the bat, I see at least one issue," Bright pointed at one section of the map. "There's a couple of PRAs here near Wittstock. It's the Gadow–Rossow firing range here and there are ammunition bunkers here. That specific area is guarded. There is also an airbase nearby."

"Where?" Becker said. He leaned forward. An airbase close by could complicate things.

"Here, west of Wittstock. It's a Soviet base."

"Our primary objective is here, further south, about twenty clicks from that base," Kaiser noted. "I think any of these routes," a pointer traced several roads into the area, "could be used for entry into the area."

Bright pondered the possible different routes.

"The PRAs are fairly far away so we should be able to get into that area without a problem, hopefully without being seen."

"If we're seen in the general area, it's not that much of a problem. However, we need to get close to the drop-off point and away again without being noticed," Becker clarified. "I was planning on doing a night drop-off. Sometime around 2100 hours so I will have a full night for cross-country movement. The weather should be good and maybe I will the benefit from the moon if it's clear skies."

Murphy, who up to that point had let the army discuss the problem, interjected: "Nighttime? Can you find the drop-off point at night?"

Bright and Kaiser all looked at each other and silently accepted the old Marine might not understand their capabilities. It was Kaiser who answered.

"That's what we do, we navigate cross-country. I can put you anywhere you want to go with a map and compass, day or night, to within 10 meters. We'll also be using NVGs."

"NVGs?" Wheeler was really out of date.

"Night vision goggles. We can walk or drive with them."

"Steve, are you comfortable with taking this on? Do you have any reservations?" Murphy asked.

"I think it's doable. I know and trust Nick's opinion and he's got the time on the ground with the Mission to know what we'll face. But I think Master Sergeant Becker will have quite a time crashing through the countryside."

"The East German forests are easy to navigate. Their *Forstmeister* keep everything quite orderly," Becker said.

"How do we get you out?" Bright asked.

"You don't. After you drop me, you get out of there and do regular MLM business. I'll get out by alternate means."

"Which is?" Bright's interest was piqued.

"I am afraid those details are not your concern, Major," Murphy said. His tone was controlling.

"Sorry, I was curious."

"It's okay, we're trying to keep the different aspects of this compartmented, just in case."

"Like, in case I get rousted by the Russians?"

"Yeah, something like that. This mission is of the highest national importance. We can't chance a compromise. The fewer folks who know all the details the better."

"Do I get an 'L' pill?"

"No, we don't issue those anymore. You'll have to go out in a blaze of glory," Murphy said.

"Unfortunately, we don't carry weapons," Bright replied.

As Bright enlightened Murphy on the fine print of the Huebner–Malinin Agreement and the prohibitions on weapons, Becker thought he should mention something, but then decided against it.

It can wait.

He saw Murphy looking at him and winked.

"Okay, next subject," Murphy took the cue to move on. "Getting into the East."

"How do you propose that we get you there," Bright said, "besides in one of the Mission cars? So, hypothetically, we're at the bridge. Where are you?"

"I'll be in the trunk."

"That'll be comfy. Then what?"

"Nick?" Becker said, sliding the question down the bar to his expert.

"I would suggest you go from Berlin straight to the planned route and skip the Potsdam House. No need to go there. If you cross with two other cars about the same time, the EGs will have a hard time following all of you."

"Agreed. But, we only have seven tour teams to work with at any one time so we'll have to figure that out with scheduling."

"One other point, he won't have a Mission ID." Kaiser was referring to the document required to process the Glienicke Bridge Checkpoint between West Berlin and East Germany or if stopped by the Soviets.

Bright latched on to that. "What happens if you're picked up?"

"I don't intend to get caught."

"That's what you all say. And if you are?"

"In that event, I will claim that I went AWOL. It will buy me a little time and cause an incident, but I probably won't get shot."

"A master sergeant in the United States Army goes AWOL? Bull. Shit."

"My ID card says I'm still a sergeant first class."

"Like that makes a whole lot of difference. Is Colonel Stofall aware of this?" Bright asked.

"Yes, he's not happy but he really doesn't have a say," Murphy said. "The authority for this is echelons above all our heads."

"I wouldn't want to be you if you're caught."

"We don't have a great deal of wiggle room here. We do have a back-up if things go to hell, but I accept that my decision to do this puts me in a lot of danger."

"Yeah, a whole lot of trouble. You better not get caught. It would be bad for us all, not just you."

Bright went back to the main issue. "Then what comes after crossing the bridge?"

"We worked out a couple of possible routes that would take us to an offset well beyond the drop-off point. That way, whichever one we take won't point directly at the location." Becker laid a piece of transparent overlay onto the second map with the routes traced out in color.

Bright looked at the overlay and nodded. "Those are good and we can use others if we need to. I would also assume that you would come out of the trunk before then?" he said.

"On your call. When you think it's safe to do so." said Becker.

"We can keep the rear window screens closed for the trip. That's pretty normal. If we slow down in a village, you can go under a blanket. If we go in with two people, we need to continue being seen as only two in the car."

"Then we fishhook and make the run into the drop-off point. I'll leave you near here," he said pointing at a spot on the map, "and you get out of the area. That's it, sweet and simple."

"We can do that but I'll tell you one thing, I still don't want to be you."

24

The classified conference room was packed. It wasn't that big to begin with, but it was filled with all of Team 5, the base chief and his deputy, the MLM commander, Major Bright and his chosen driver, Sergeant First Class Jason Marazano. On one half of the front wall were the maps that had been used to plan the driving routes. Whatever was on the other half of the wall remained covered with a sliding door.

Jelinek, Bergmann, and Kelly sat in front as the inquisitors waiting for the briefback to get rolling.

"Good morning, Colonel Jelinek, Colonel Stofall, Sergeant Major," Becker began. "First, I am going to begin with a general outline of the mission. After we discuss our infiltration, we'll have to excuse the MLM personnel as the rest of the briefing is compartmented information."

With Marazano showing the route on the map with a pointer, Becker described the plan up to the point where he would be dropped off.

"Any questions on this phase, sir?" Becker said. He directed all his comments to Jelinek as the overall commander. There weren't any.

"Colonel Stofall, thank you for your support to this mission. We wouldn't be able to pull this off without your help," Jelinek said.

It was the indication for the MLM team to exit.

Becker shook hands with Bright as he left.

"See you soon."

Once the MLM crew had departed, he continued.

"After drop-off, I will make my way on foot cross-country to here."

Becker pointed to the newly revealed large-scale map on the wall and the aerial photographs that had been taken by a "Live Oak" surveillance aircraft. OZ's *Dacha* was clearly shown on the images. So clear, you could read the model number of the tractor sitting on the edge of the field.

"OZ and I planned a link-up on a trail in the forest near his home. He will be taking his usual walks each day when he arrives and I will be located off the trail along one of the tracks around here," again pointing.

"Once I arrive, I will watch the house and set up in the forest approximately here," he said tapping the map with a pointer. "In the early morning, I will leave a sign on the trail that we've agreed and when he sees it, he will give me a safe signal to indicate I can approach his house. Once OZ and I make contact, we wait at his home until our pick-up team arrives. That'll be Kaiser and Mann. We will all proceed to the Landing Zone for exfiltration that night."

Colonel Jelinek got up and looked closely at the map.

"What will you be wearing?" he asked.

"An unmarked Czech army parka over civilian field pants and boots. I will wear a uniform shirt with US Army insignia underneath and I'll carry my ID card in my true name."

"What equipment will you carry?"

"A generic European rucksack and sleeping bag, NVGs, Silva compass, binos, the big map, some food, water, and a Walther P38 with suppressor and three magazines of ammunition."

"What's the trail sign?"

"A rock pyramid."

"What if you can't find rocks?"

"Then it'll be three sticks laid out."

Sergeant Major Bergmann said, "What if you're injured and can't make it to the target?"

"I have two RV sites, one close to the infil point and another about mid-way. I'll try to make it there and wait to be picked up."

"When do you abort?"

"Only if we can't find OZ to get him out. I need to go in first to prepare him, but if I'm out of action, Kaiser and Mann will continue the op without me."

"Kaiser and Mann," the colonel said, "what about you, what will you be going in as?"

"We'll be in East German uniform, sir. We'll both be armed with Makarovs and everything needed for the extraction in the trunk."

"What ID are you carrying?"

"We're hanging it all in the wind. We have East German ID but we're not carrying anything US. Our American ID cards won't help us if we get nailed. We'll only get our US uniforms back when we make the final RV, the rendezvous point, after the pick-up."

"You understand the implications and consequences of that?"

"Yes, sir. Major Kelly made us sign a release form."

Colonel Jelinek looked at his S-3 operations officer.

"Regulations, sir," Kelly said.

"Destroy the forms, Kelly. I'll take the heat. We won't abandon anyone if it comes to it."

"Roger, sir."

"Okay, back to you two. How will you know if it's safe to approach the house?"

"We will be looking for a piece of twine tied in a bow at the center of the gate."

"If it's not there?"

"We'll approach the house on foot and do a recce. After one hour, if no one is there, we'll abort. We break off and head for the first RV to find Master Sergeant Becker and if necessary on to the second RV. We can't wait around."

"Becker, where is the LZ?"

Becker took a pointer and tapped a yellow triangle on the map.

"This is the primary," and then tapping a red triangle, "this is the secondary."

"How will the pilot know to go to the secondary?"

"He won't see any lights and we have the beacon with back-up radio comms. We are carrying two PRC-90s."

"One last thing, gentlemen," Jelinek said, "Rules of Engagement. You can only engage the enemy if you are directly threatened, that means they are confronting you. Second, they must have the means to do you harm, that means they have the capability to hurt you whether with a firearm, a club, or a knife-hand strike. Last, you must judge they intend to harm you. Got that?"

"What if they just intend to arrest us?"

"Would that, in your judgement, harm you? Don't answer me now. Contemplate the consequences of your actions or your inactions and do the right thing. Understood?"

Everyone did understand. It was the clearest ROE any of them had ever received but that was typical of the colonel.

Jelinek nodded and turned to Murphy. "Any questions, Mister Murphy?"

"Thanks, Colonel. Master Sergeant Becker, what happens when you depart the house with the asset?"

"We'll make it look like OZ has committed suicide and burn the house so that the evidence will make it extremely difficult to prove otherwise. We have incendiary devices that are very effective."

"What about any dental evidence, like his teeth?"

"OZ assured me that he had long ago removed all his medical records from the system and has been using his own choice of practitioners. They apparently have nothing that can be used for identification."

"He was always meticulous. He's been preparing for this day for a long time."

25

Fischer took the long way out of town. He stopped at one of the better supplied stores to stock up on a few necessities he couldn't get in the village near the *Dacha*. Carrying his groceries he walked back to his car and loaded the bag into the back seat. When he was finished arranging things, he stood up and looked over the roof of his car at the buildings across the street. He suddenly realized what he had done.

Damn. How could I have been so stupid?

Fischer cursed himself. Unthinkingly, he had driven to a place he had been to many times before, a place he knew all too well. But in this moment he had forgotten what else was close by. So close, that for a brief instant, he thought about crossing the street.

No, I can't. Not now.

It was a fleeting moment before he came back to the business at hand. He slammed the door shut a bit too hard and walked around to climb into the car. Starting the engine, he drove off without another look back. He prayed his plan would succeed and no one would suffer because of him.

Watching him from across the street was a woman. She was standing behind the plate glass window of her shop. Lila wondered what Fischer was doing.

Why doesn't he come in?

As he drove off, she was left alone with her questions, questions that she had held inside over the years, not sure if she would ever find the answers.

Not today, either. Maybe never.

Lila sighed and went back to her work.

***

Fischer drove north through the city, processing through a checkpoint before arriving at the Berliner Ring, the *Autobahn* that circled the city. He got the car up to speed for a few kilometers and then joined another highway, the E28, which went straight north. It was a bit of a longer route, but the road was better. It was well maintained because it headed towards Wandlitz, the small enclave where most of the party bosses preferred to live, and to and from which their big cars commuted daily. It was an exclusive gated community, restricted to the communist elite. There they could live in luxury away from the prying eyes of the proletarian masses.

Fischer would have no trouble driving through the area with his documentation. His car alone was validation; its registration numbers were from a series reserved for government officials of the highest rank. His passing would be recorded, of course. But that was fine. He had nothing to hide.

Fischer was thinking about his long-ago adopted credo of hiding in the open. If an agent hides his life and activities from others, then eventually he will come under suspicion. Fischer did the opposite. His life was an open book. Everything he did had a real purpose at its core. It was only in the very fine print of his life that there were secrets and someone would have to be very good to even find them, let alone read them.

Großmann had been lucky, it must have been the Soviets who recognized the Americans' mistake and compromised Gypsy.

But that was the nature of the business; it's the small details that can kill you. Luckily, Großmann must have screwed up the arrest and probably no evidence was found. Despite that Fischer knew he must leave; the Americans could have mistakenly left other clues. He just hoped the people working to get him out were all trustworthy. Unfortunately, the one thing he had learned in the business of espionage was that trust was something you didn't give easily and sometimes those who received trust weren't worthy of it in the end.

Fischer silently apologized to his dead friend as he drove and thanked him for his sacrifice. He only hoped it would be worth it in the end. Now, he had to be careful not only of Großmann, but of Markus Wolf.

He committed himself to one thought. *If the plan works, I will soon be free. Failing that, I won't be taken at all.*

Passing through the small orderly village of Wandlitz, he turned to the northwest and made his way across country on the small roads that crisscrossed the countryside. He much preferred driving at a relaxed pace, away from the routes intended to be high-speed military highways for some future Warsaw Pact attack on NATO. That wouldn't happen anytime soon, he knew. For one, Wolf wouldn't have sent him away if any sort of conflict was looming in the near term.

Relax, he told himself. He was thinking too much and needed to focus his thoughts on the next few days. He drove on towards his refuge in the forest.

It wasn't long before he arrived. The detour had made the trip a bit longer, but he wasn't in a hurry. He drove through the village and continued up the road and into the forest. He turned onto his side road and stopped to open the gate. It was always a routine if you were alone: stop, get out, open the gate, drive through, get out, close the gate, continue on. Today, however, it was different for him. He knew he would not be coming back here again. He stopped before he got back into the car and stood looking wistfully at the road and the dark green forest beyond.

It is truly peaceful here.

He got back into the car and continued up the dirt road slowly. As he did, he reacquainted himself with the environment, the trees, and the animals. He was sure he would soon see the deer that lived in the deeper forest nearby. It was about as far removed from Berlin as possible. He was alone here except for several neighbors, all farmers. Even so, their properties were a kilometer or so away. This was his sanctuary.

I hope they can find me something like this in the United States, maybe in the mountains.

After nearly a kilometer, the *Dacha* appeared ahead. It was a single-story house built of heavy wood timbers, quite modest compared to the villas that some of the senior officials had been given. A small front porch with an entryway led to an inside hall. A small library at the front, a couple of bedrooms, a living area, and a large kitchen comprised the living space. There was a patio and a shed for the tools he rarely used. Beyond that, there was just the green of the forest that seemed to be creeping closer and closer to the house every time he visited.

My forest needs Lebensraum too.

There were paths that led off into the forest, but he would leave them until later.

He parked the Tatra on the side of the house and took the groceries inside, returning to grab a small suitcase he had packed with his country clothing and a few essentials. He had brought several new books acquired on one of his long walks in the city. He had meant to read them before but, perhaps unconsciously, left them closed on his table because he read too much at work. Now he might have a chance. It would be a good diversion from thinking too much about the future—or the past.

26

The big Mercedes-Benz sedan pulled up to the barrier on Glienicke Brücke. The bridge was named after a nearby palace but, to be different, the communists in East Germany had renamed it Unity Bridge because it linked the East German town of Potsdam with West Berlin. In reality, the bridge did little to promote unity and linked no one on either side of the Havel River.

Its most appropriate name was probably "Bridge of Spies" because it was occasionally used for Cold War exchanges of people who had been arrested by the United States or the Soviets, including the spy Rudolf Abel and the U-2 pilot Gary Powers. But those events were rare. Today the Mercedes was participating in a routine that took place more often: the passage of Allied Mission vehicles back and forth between the West and East.

The Mercedes was unremarkable except for its non-reflective, olive-green paint job and license plates with the number "23" and an American flag. Beneath the flag were Cyrillic words that translated to "US Military Liaison Mission to the Commander-in-Chief of the Group of Soviet Forces Germany." There were many other interesting and unique tweaks to the car, but they were hidden beneath its skin. Its 6.9-liter engine purred contentedly as it sat waiting to be released from its enforced stop while the driver and passenger sat and chatted. The guy in the trunk was quiet. A Russian border guard was trying to have a conversation with the passenger who, for the most part, just ignored him.

Sergeant Jason Marazano was trying to make a point.

"Listen, just because Michigan squashed Wisconsin like a bug last week doesn't mean a thing."

"Purdue doesn't stand a chance. They're totally inconsistent. I'll bet Michigan wins by ten points."

About that time the Russian private who had been standing outside the door chattering, leaned down and looked in the window.

"Are you going to give me your documents, Major?"

"Ah, yes," Bright said, handing him their identity cards.

"Okay, you're on. I'll put ten bucks on Purdue."

"Your loss," Bright said, "that will buy me two six-packs for the next game."

"Ha, fat chance," Marazano replied, "and what are you drinking anyway, PBR? That's not beer, it's dish water!"

"Nah. I only drink the golden nectar of the Rockies."

"Coors? Christ, why don't you drink one of our local brews? Granted, Berliner beers are garbage, but anything from Munich is great."

"Two reasons, I'm cheap and I'm nostalgic for American beer, especially when I'm watching football."

The Russian came back to the car and spouted the usual litany of warnings and threats while Bright and Marazano bickered about beer and football. They'd heard the same rehearsed speech many times before and would ignore or violate most of the warnings anyway. Eventually, the passes were returned and the gate boom was lifted. Marazano accelerated away and off the bridge towards Potsdam.

It was early afternoon and they were the last of three US Mission cars scheduled to cross the bridge that day. The Russians didn't know beforehand that three cars would cross and the intervals were close

186

enough that anyone who chose to follow the first two would not be able to re-orient on the third car. At least, that was the theory. They hoped that the bad guys didn't have enough assets ready to follow them at all.

So far the plan seemed to work. Marazano pointed the car on a southwest heading, first through a bit of the town paralleling the river, then along the Zeppelinstraße through a park and out of town. With no traffic on the road, Bright turned his head to the rear of the car.

"You still alive back there?"

A muffled reply came through the backseat cushion.

"Just fine. I was taking a nap, it's so comfortable in here."

"I'm glad you like it. I'll give you a shout when we're ready for you to come out of the cave."

"Okay, I'll be here if you need me."

After they broke out of Potsdam, Marazano continued west crossing the Berliner Ring towards Brandenburg.

As usual, Marazano was calling out landmarks while Bright recorded anything interesting in his logbook. There wasn't much of military interest to see. On a section of straight, open road, he yelled back to Becker.

"Drop the hatch and come on out."

Becker struggled with the latch, finally succeeding in popping it free. The rear cushion of the seat folded forward and he rolled out enough that it could be shut again. He lay on the seat awhile.

"The ventilation in there sucks."

"Not that it helps now, but I'll get someone to improve the airflow when we get back. We don't get many stowaways on these trips."

"I'm sure the next one would appreciate that."

He popped his head up to look out the front windscreen.

"Where are we?"

"Nearing Groß Kreutz, west of Werder. We'll head north soon and do our fishhook. We're gonna come close to a couple of installations, but not too close. We don't want to attract too much attention."

They drove on, kilometer after kilometer, through the countryside. Small villages were easily negotiated. The bigger ones they avoided as much as possible. There was no need to be slowed by traffic controls. Out in the country they were only hindered by farm machinery and empty hay wagons. It was amazing to see how East German farmers still used horse-drawn equipment alongside more modern "technik" like diesel tractors.

"The farmers are not all collectivized." Bright liked to throw out tidbits of his socio-economic observations when there was nothing military to talk about.

"I know. The government has realized what would happen to their economic production if they did. They've formed farmer cooperatives but, at the core, they still control everything."

Becker kept tabs on the system as well. It was all part of the unit's continual in-depth area studies program. Beyond studying the uniforms, equipment, and tactics of the East Germans and Russians, the unit's soldiers also looked at the cultural part of life in the East. It was one aspect of life in SDB that contrasted heavily from life in the regular army. It was also very different from nailing a tight 300-meter shot group with a sniper rifle or fifteen words per minute in Morse code, which were just two of the other esoteric skills everyone needed to master.

An interesting life…

Marazano had been quiet for a while and decided he needed to be heard.

"It was around here that one of our cars got clobbered last March."

"What happened?"

"One of the teams was parked on the edge of a forest and a Soviet convoy passed. They got some good info and photographs, but they decided to follow the trucks. By the time they caught up, the convoy had stopped, so they started to pass it doing the usual vehicle identification and count and getting photos of bumper identification. They reached the head of the convoy and an officer stepped out to stop them and then waved them on after they had slowed. It was just enough of a ruse to let a BTR-60 run out of a side road and T-bone them as they passed. The thing must have been doing about forty, because the Merc flipped twice and landed on its roof. Major Nelson got a broken collarbone in the crash. He was out for about four weeks."

"What happened then?"

"The Russians swarmed the car and stole everything inside, including the coffee thermos. The gave most of it back, but without any film or notes. Said it was our fault. 'The car was driving too fast,' they said. Total B.S."

"What did we do?"

"The usual protest letter. I think they detained a couple of Russian tours in West Germany for like twelve hours each. Hardly the same thing."

"It would be good if we can avoid that."

"I'll do my best."

Bright said, "We've been fairly lucky. One tour driver was almost shot a couple of years ago. Luckily the Russians are either bad marksmen or they're just trying to scare us. We're not sure 'cause the driver got a bullet through the door that hit him in his boot. We just keep driving on."

"Good thing. Your intel helps us all out."

"We aim to please."

"We're coming into range of Object 41," Marazano said.

"Object 41?" Becker asked.

"It's an East German munitions depot. They give them numbers instead of names. And, unlike the Soviet installations, you have to be careful. The civilians will report us when we're near their own facilities, but they don't care so much for the Soviets."

"There might be a good reason for that."

Becker saw a sign on the road that appeared to be military. It pointed off into the woods and as they passed the access road he looked down it. In the distance, he could the red and white marked barrier pole that closed the road to outsiders. It was the first perimeter of security.

"We'll skip them today, I think."

It was early evening and they continued on to the north, passing more villages and many more farms. There were a few National People's Army trucks on the road but no signature vehicles and no convoys, which was disappointing and comforting at the same time.

Finally, Marazano chimped out.

"Oo, oo! Look at that!"

He was pointing out into an open field about 2 kilometers distant. In the dwindling light, a semi-circle of military truck vans could be seen parked together with a big Zil 131 in the center. A large antenna loomed over it.

"Any guesses?"

Becker squinted around the curtain and out the window.

"It's air defense radar, but I can't tell what type. Maybe a 'Bar Lock'?"

"Close but no cigar. It's a P-19 'Flat Face.' It's a Russian unit," Marazano said, using the NATO codename for the air defense radar.

"We'll come back and find them again after we drop you off. They'll be worth a closer look."

"If they stay around," Becker said.

"They'll be here. It takes too much effort to set up after they leave their base and the Russians are pretty lazy. They must be monitoring an exercise or something."

"They're not watching the air corridor?"

"No, I doubt it. For one, they're oriented in the wrong direction. Two, they have fixed radar for that."

Becker felt a bit of unease thinking about the air support part of the mission. That was. scheduled to happen just about twenty-four hours from that moment. What the air force was about to do had been done many times before, but never in this area. He hoped it worked as well this time.

Trust the experts, Kim.

Bright made a couple of annotations in his notebook as they drove on. At the minimum, they had a sighting. If the radar did move before he and Marazano got back, they might be able to track its movements. But first, the priority was getting the "package" to the drop-off point securely and safely.

Before the village of Pritzwalk, they turned east and began the fishhook.

Soon they were heading south, crisscrossing the first section of territory. Once they were convinced no one was tracking their progress, they turned in the direction of the drop-off.

It was dark and they had 10 kilometers to go when Marazano asked Bright,

"Are we ready to go dark?"

"How long?"

"At this speed, six minutes."

"Wait a bit, the road is clear."

Marazano pulled his NVGs out of a pouch. He slowed for a moment and then hit a switch and the lights went out; it was pitch black inside and outside the car. He had his NVGs on in a second and accelerated again. Becker watched, blind in the back—all he could see was the green glow of the NVGs that illuminated Marazano's face. Bright hadn't put his on yet. He had a small red light on the odometer that he shielded so it wouldn't blind Marazano and was calling the kilometers as they clicked past.

"Seven clicks out, six, five, four, coming into range, three, slow down… now! Stop!"

The big Mercedes' speed was arrested by its powerful braking system. Marazano controlled the car well. The tires rolled to a stop without any chirping or squeals. Becker got out of the car quickly.

No brake lights showed to betray the stop and no interior lights illuminated Becker when he got out. Marazano had turned all the lighting systems off.

The trunk lid popped open with a command from a dashboard switch. Kim grabbed his rucksack and made sure it was securely closed before he swung it over his back. He quickly adjusted the straps as Major Bright silently closed the trunk lid. He grabbed Becker's hand and whispered to him.

"Good luck and God speed."

"Thanks. I'll see you back in Berlin soon."

Becker hoped he wasn't being overly optimistic as he plunged into the forest.

Bright turned and looked back. The road was empty. He hopped back in the car. The Mercedes disappeared into the night as silently as it had arrived.

27

Lila closed up her shop and turned towards the street to walk home. Up and down the avenue, it was dark. The street lights put out barely enough light to indicate that they were on, and even less made it to the ground. The apartment blocks also suffered from the same starvation, the inhabitants making do with small lamps and sometimes candles to light their worlds. It was only the major streets that were well lit, but the dark buildings above them showed that the electricity went only so far.

She looked across the street to make sure that Max wasn't there. Lila was still wondering about Max's recent appearance. It had been two days and there had been no news.

I hope he's alright.

She started on her way home along the familiar streets that she walked each day. The city's monotone sameness surrounded her but she took no note; there was no other life for her, the grayness of East Berlin was all she had ever experienced. She would often think about what life might be like in West Berlin. The lights and sounds of that part of the city, so long denied to most East Berliners, occasionally drifted across the Wall.

"The West is permeated with decadent capitalism," the State organs always said.

Lila had always wondered.

It had been a late day. Her shop was well visited and she was tired. But not too tired to realize there was a shadow behind her. At first, she just sensed the presence. The person made the same turns and walked in concert with her. She felt her heartbeat begin to race. Although Max had taught her the basics of counter-surveillance, she had never actually experienced being followed before.

Should I speed up or just keep cool and walk slow? Maybe it's a thief?

At a corner, she took the opportunity to look back in time to see a van stop behind her. A man got out and walked in the same direction she was walking. Now they were on both sides of the street. The van rolled past her and turned the corner—it was the same direction she intended to go. As she approached the corner she could see the dark green vehicle—parked. A third man was standing next to the van.

Now she remembered what Fischer had said: "Don't just worry about what is behind you, the danger could be in front."

She stopped. She had no idea which way to go.

"*Fräulein, stehen bleiben.*" Don't move. The voice came quietly from behind her.

She turned to see a woman who flashed her identification wallet and returned it to her coat.

"*Fräulein,* are you Eva Maria Pfeiffer?"

Lila hadn't heard her true name in over twenty-five years and she was too shocked to lie.

"*Ja?*"

"We are State Security. Please come with us."

The woman grabbed her roughly by the arm and pushed her into the van. The men followed them.

"*Los!*" Go! They took off down the street as the van's side door slammed shut.

28

Becker knew from his map reconnaissance and the odometer that he was within 100 meters of where he wanted to be. He knew he would be able to find OZ's *Dacha* without a problem. He just had to get there without being seen or heard.

The forest floor was damp. He could tell because he felt the water soak through his pants when he knelt on the ground. Not soaking wet, but it was damp enough to make moving through it quieter than it would be in summer when the dry leaves and pine needles crunched and the sticks snapped with each step if you weren't extremely careful. Becker walked a few paces deeper into the greenery and stopped. He listened to the sounds, trying to accustom himself to the normal noises before he crashed further into the woods. He wanted to know the forest and become part of it so he could tell when its mood changed, when something disturbed its normal rhythm. Above him, he could hear the wind rustling through the pine branches, a sound that would have been relaxing if he was anywhere but where he found himself. It had been several months since he had been in a forest at night—not since an exercise in the Swabian Black Forest the previous spring—but his senses were already becoming attuned to the environment.

***

195

It was times like these that he remembered why he came to be in Special Forces. Becker's father had been in Europe during World War II. He survived and came home after the war none the worse for his experiences. He liked the army and stayed in the reserves as much for the camaraderie as for the extra money it brought in. One year, it might have been 1964, Dad came home from summer training camp and dropped an Army Special Forces recruitment brochure on his son's bed, along with a P-38 can opener and a couple of boxes of C-Rations. It was the only reason Becker didn't mind his father's absences too much. He knew Dad would always come home with something interesting for him.

The brochure was especially cool. He studied its photos, as well as the descriptions of the "Green Beret" missions. The different jobs a man could fill on an "A" Team and their specialized equipment were described in a way that made Becker feel like he was reading Ian Fleming's *James Bond*. Then there were the gadgets, parachutes of course, but there was also the scuba gear, radios, explosives and many different foreign weapons. One image captivated him more than any other—it was of a soldier descending under parachute at night into a small forest clearing. On the edge of the moonlit clearing stood a wooden cabin, its windows glowing from the firelight inside, and a tendril of smoke curling up from the chimney into the dark sky. It was the epitome of everything he had imagined when he read books about the OSS working with the partisan fighters against Nazi Germany in World War II. It was there and then that he decided he would join the army; there was really never a question of him serving in the navy or the marines. Later events in life, some unfortunate, others fortuitous, conspired to ensure he followed through on that dream.

After five minutes of listening, he walked onwards, from time to time checking the luminous dial of his compass for his azimuth and picking out a landmark in front of him to stay on track. There was a waxing gibbous moon that gave him plenty of light despite the scattered clouds that were racing high across the sky. He wouldn't use his NVGs unless the moon disappeared and he lost all the ambient light. He didn't want to lose what night vision he had.

Becker had memorized the detailed map and carried only the map that showed the whole area up to the Baltic Sea. If he got caught he didn't want to be carrying anything that might give away his true objective. Still, he knew he was close to the target; if he was caught the East Germans might guess where he was headed, but there were always risks involved in these operations.

He went back to the business of walking. He had around 8 kilometers in front of him. Eight thousand meters, roughly 88 football fields to go. He wanted to be in place before daybreak and had all night to do it. He paused again for several minutes. Walk five minutes, listen for several, then walk again. It was the same routine for any patrol in "Indian country."

***

He first learned patrolling techniques during infantry training at Fort Polk's "Tigerland."

Polk was a shit-hole place. How much can they teach you when you're one of 200 newbies and the drill sergeants are training to the lowest common denominator?

And there was the hippy turned drill sergeant who kept saying, "Be one with the forest and the enemy can never see you."

Right, tell that to Charlie. I think that guy later got fragged in an outhouse in Da Nang.

When he got to the 82nd Airborne Division he was retrained by a squad leader who had served in the Marines during Vietnam. After he managed to escape from the 82nd a year later, he was retrained again in long-range patrol tactics at Camp Mackall. And then came Vietnam. He did two tours with 5th Group before he and a friend volunteered for a third with SOG.

SOG. Someone told him it was a good deal. The rule to never raise your hand for anything notwithstanding, he did just that. Special Forces training was rough, but getting prepared for the cross-border missions SOG ran in Laos was another story altogether. Even their train-up was live-fire from almost day one. They practiced with real bullets and a real enemy who didn't know they were being used as training aids.

I imagine they would have been pissed off to find that out. It was almost like the Union regulars getting their butts handed to them by Citadel cadets.

But he survived that year and here he was again in the badlands. The saving grace was this forest was nowhere near as hostile as a war zone. All he needed to do was avoid being seen. There weren't active enemy patrols seeking him out. He was not nearly as anxious as he had been in Laos; he just had no inclination to be shot as a spy. He stopped for a moment and listened. It was still quiet. As he stood in the dark, he smelled the forest and the tilled earth from the distant fields that surrounded it. For a moment he was lost in thought and his concentration wandered.

Never volunteer, indeed. Just what exactly am I trying to prove here? Nothing, I've done that already. What am I doing then? Freeing the oppressed? Hardly, I'm preparing to kill Russians and now I am saving a spy's butt. And why exactly is he worth even one soldier's life? Is this why I don't have any family other than my team? Are they who I am protecting? We need to think this through better when we get home.

He thought of Rohan and where he had left the conversation he might have had with her.

Tell me about her.

Who?

The woman you didn't mention. The one you're holding back on, the one that hurt you.

He paused before he answered. This woman should be an interrogator, she's good.

She didn't hurt me, I did. I killed off what should have been a good relationship.

How?

Have you ever heard of time and distance? And not in the mathematical sense. They always say that absence makes the heart grow fonder—it may for some, but time and distance actually tore us apart. If a couple doesn't communicate often, as we didn't, you lose something. Intimacy and trust disappear. That's what happened to us.

Did you love her?

I thought I did, until I discovered she didn't love me.

How did you know?

I just found out. Let's not go there.

Okay, but that usually means you were both at fault, not just you.

The loss of friends, the loss of a lover: it seems my life is defined by those kinds of things, Becker thought. He looked around again. He couldn't let his mind wander.

Concentrate!

Becker walked on through the night.

He had to cross several dirt roads in the forest. Like the West Germans, the *Ossis* also subdivided their forest lands into blocks for management. That meant tracks and pathways to clear the brush and overgrowth, danger areas he had to clear carefully before he crossed them. Being on his own required him to be extra careful, but it was nighttime and he didn't expect to encounter any one out here. At most, he might run into some civilians who decided to take a night-time walk, but he couldn't afford that kind of contact either.

It was like the one of the questions they often asked during the final selection board.

"Your team is moving in enemy territory, heading to blow a bridge. You come upon a shepherd watching his flock. He sees you and could report you to the authorities. What do you do?"

There is no perfect solution to the problem, but there definitely is one incorrect answer. And that answer would never cross Becker's mind even if he did come across any unlucky innocents.

Becker crossed a small ravine and saw a slice of silver moonlight across the ground about 50 meters in front of him. He approached it quietly and stopped short of the forest edge. If he had a full patrol he would have sent flankers out to check along the danger zone, before he sent another pair across to check out the other side while the rest of the patrol covered them. But he didn't, he had only himself and in some ways that was better; a single shadow flitting across the gap might be mistaken for an animal if was seen at all.

He crawled forward slowly until he could see down the road in both directions. Satisfied, he stood up, made his way quickly to the road and scampered across. He had to trust in the probability that no one would be out.

On the other side, he waited for a couple of minutes before he continued through the forest. It was mostly flat ground and he was not carrying much weight or equipment, at the most 30 pounds. For that, he was thankful. His usual combat load was more like 80 to 100 pounds and it was the reason he never became a communications sergeant. Their rucks were always the heaviest at well over 100 pounds. In winter the load was even heavier.

I am traveling light.

Pushing on, he moved slowly through the tall trees until he saw another cut in the forest. It was a big one, the biggest he had encountered and he knew he was very close to his objective.

The road cut was 50 meters wide. Again, he approached it carefully and observed.

At least I can see if any headlights are coming.

The grass was tall enough to hide him if a vehicle did come down the road. For the moment it was clear.

This time he bolted across the road, only slowing at the far edge to trot into the forest. Dropping into the grass, he listened and gained control of his breathing. It was dead quiet.

Now he had to find the access road. He walked along the road inside the forest, first north and then south until he saw it. He checked the gate to see that it matched the description OZ had given him and he knew he was there. Turning north again he walked a few meters and clambered over the fence before moving deeper inside the forest. Then he paralleled the access road until he could see it open into a large clearing. He moved towards the house.

Close enough.

The binoculars came out of his rucksack so he could peer at the house. There were no lights except for a solitary dim bulb over the entry door. He looked over the tool shed and the car.

The moon came out and lit up the scene. He looked again. A thin wisp of smoke curled up from the chimney into the night sky. He smiled and knew he was almost home.

Becker backed off and plunged deeper into the forest until he found a copse of small pine trees. It was as good a place as any, he thought. The trail he had chosen was not too far away and the location was secluded enough. He felt secure enough to pull out his poncho liner and wrap himself up inside it.

I shouldn't have to worry about anything other than the rabbits and deer, or maybe a herd of wild boar. That would be bad.

As he set up his camp, he ate some of his food and thought about next steps. He would sleep a bit and then get ready for his contact.

There were still a couple of hours until dawn.

29

It was late evening when the six-truck convoy entered Checkpoint Alpha at Helmstedt-Marienborn. Captain Welsh, the commander of the convoy, ostensibly an officer in the Army Transportation Corps, got out of the lead truck and walked into the Military Police post. He handed over the orders and identification cards for all the convoy drivers to the MP on duty behind the high counter.

"We need the drivers inside to compare them with their papers, sir," said the MP sergeant.

"That won't be necessary this time, Sergeant," said Major Wise.

The MP looked at his unit operations officer who had shown up about fifteen minutes before "just to see how things were going." Now he knew why the major was here.

"Yes, sir." He stamped each set of Flag Orders after making sure the ID card matched and then handed the sheaf back to the captain. He looked at the clock one last time.

"It's 2310 hours. You need to reach Checkpoint Bravo not earlier than 0110 and no later than 0310 hours, sir."

"Thank you, Sergeant. We'll be fine," Welsh said as he took the papers and turned to the major. Saluting, he said, "And thank you, sir."

He walked out the door and handed each driver his copy of the order and ID card before getting in the cab of the first truck. The first five vehicles were identical US Army Heavy Equipment Transporters—HETs—big olive-green tractors that pulled long, green, closed trailers. The last truck was a Chevrolet pick-up.

Staring out at the convoy as it departed the sergeant said, "What was that, sir?"

"A special equipment convoy, probably classified stuff."

"It's pretty late. No escort?"

"Obviously not. I guess they're not worried about being hijacked. Good night, men."

The major was bored. He had been told to show up to make sure the convoy got through without being hassled. It had. Now he was going back to his quarters, a beer, and a football game on Armed Forces Network.

Outside, the convoy rolled forward towards the Soviet checkpoint where they would undergo a similar ritual. Each driver's Flag Orders and ID would be checked and the Soviet guard would roam around the truck trying to figure out what was inside.

Each driver had been given packs of cigarettes, cash, and copies of *Playboy* magazine to tempt the guards into trading badges or whatever they had in an effort to occupy them. They didn't have to worry. The Russians didn't give a damn about the trucks; they had come loaded with stuff to trade. Out of sight of the officers on the dark side of the trucks, they pulled belts and buckles, hats, and cheap military badges from their pockets and out from under their coats. They were happy to get something from the West to take home, be it *West Marks*, cigarettes, or alcohol.

As each truck cleared the checkpoint, it rolled forward on the side of the four-lane *Autobahn* to wait for the rest. When the final truck cleared the inspection, the convoy rolled forward. It was 180 kilometers to Checkpoint Bravo and traffic was light.

East into the night the convoy rolled, the light from their headlamps bouncing as the trucks rolled over the regularly placed expansion cracks on the poorly maintained highway. The West German government paid the upkeep for the road. The East Germans spent the money on other things. It was all part of the game. The Russians didn't care because they rarely used it.

The commander stopped the convoy twice at lay-bys along the road. He walked the convoy line and spoke with each driver and waited a few minutes. Satisfied that no one was really paying attention to them, he got back in the cab and continued the trek.

About 50 kilometers short of Berlin, he saw the road was clear of traffic and gave a signal over the radios each driver was monitoring. The convoy slowed a bit, from 85 kilometers per hour down to 60. The last tractor trailer moved into the left-hand lane, pulled up next to the truck that had been ahead of it and stayed put, both of them slowing even more. Lights flashed.

As the number three truck moved to straddle the center of the lanes, its rear doors opened and a cargo ramp slowly tilted out of the truck until it hit the pavement. Even with the big truck traveling at low speed, there was a shower of sparks across the road.

Inside the truck was a green and white Wartburg 353. Nick Kaiser and Stefan Mann were sitting in front, its engine was running, and they were just waiting for the signal from the Agency officer who had released their tie-downs. When the ramp stabilized, he gave the thumbs up and Kaiser slipped the transmission into reverse so the car could roll backwards out of the trailer and down the ramp. He put it in neutral when it started down the ramp to prevent any damage to the transmission or engine.

A small puff of gray smoke and a squeal of the tires when they hit the pavement was the only sign of protest as they began rolling in the opposite direction. Once all the wheels were on the ground, he clicked the gear shift into third, let the clutch out, and accelerated to match the truck's speed. The rear ramp was pulled up, the doors closed, and the trucks got back into their single-file line. Four minutes had passed.

There was now a *Volkspolizei* patrol car in their midst. Nick pulled into the left lane and cruised up the line of trucks until he reached the front of the line. The trucks were back at their cruising speed of 85 kilometers per hour.

"That went well," said Kaiser.

"So far, yes," said Mann. He waved at the lead truck as they accelerated away from the convoy.

"No need to hang around here then. We'll get off the *Autobahn* and head for the house. We will get into the area by late morning and then we'll be able to lie low and observe things before we go in to pick them up."

The car had come out of a warehouse near an airfield somewhere in Europe. It was part of a collection of odd things that someone thought might come in handy one day. The warehouse had one of everything and sometimes two, including hang-gliders and hot air balloons, cars and trucks, and even a Gulfstream jet. There was also a selection of clothing, which explained where Mann and Kaiser got their uniforms.

The Wartburg, on its own merits, was a piece of garbage compared to western vehicles. The one Kaiser was driving had been acquired from some Third World country that had been forced to accept the cars as part of an East German police training package, probably paid for by the United Nations at greatly inflated prices.

Kaiser was told that "we gave them a fleet of Toyotas" because the locals hated the Wartburgs and Toyotas were better, of course, but also because some savvy quartermaster realized the Wartburgs might come in handy someday and shipped a couple of the best examples back to the States. He was right.

When the cars were sent to the motor pool, they were given to the wrench magi who were told they could have their way with the cars as long as they still looked like a Wartburg when they were finished. The mechanics stripped all the identifying serial numbers and rebuilt them using parts that actually worked and electrical systems that actually electrified, which is to say, not Lucas. The three-cylinder, two-stroke engine and transmissions were pulled and thrown away. With a small-block, German Ford four-cylinder and a four-speed transmission as replacements, the cars actually had power and reliability. Then they redid the suspensions so the cars would stay on the road at high speed. And they had real brakes; although they were drum brakes for appearances' sake, they stopped the car, which was a very important consideration in the balance against velocity. When the guts of the car were finished, the outside was redone. It was thought prudent to repaint several in colors that might be useful, in this case, the colors and markings of the GDR's *Volkspolizei*.

With a sub-eight-second 0–100 kilometers per hour time and a top speed of over 180 kilometers per hour, Kaiser told Mann that he better understood the phrase "bat out of hell" after his test drive.

Kaiser said, "I wonder if it's happy to be home?"

"It's probably confused, being part *Ossi* and part *Wessi*."

"Well, it now has a chance to serve the greater good," Kaiser said. He turned off at a highway interchange and took the road north.

By the time the pair got to the village of Neurippin it was mid-morning. They had taken a circuitous route to avoid population centers and known police stations. Their radio scanner kept them attuned to the situation. Only occasionally did they have to acknowledge another *Vopo* car but they kept driving after the obligatory wave of the hand.

It was only when Kaiser spotted an *Imbiss* fast food stand that he insisted on stopping.

"I need a *Currywurst* and fries."

"Okay, but stay in the car. I'll get us something. I don't trust your German."

"What, my '*Wie geht's?*' won't make it here?"

"It's not that bad, but you do still have a touch of Minnesota in your accent. Wait here."

At the stand, Mann was doing his best "chief goose guarding the flock" act, constantly scanning the neighborhood, turning his head from side to side and back to front watching the cook, the passersby, and their car to make sure Kaiser didn't do anything stupid. Kaiser, the only other SOG veteran on the team besides Becker, had a penchant for acting on the spur of the moment, despite his combat experience. And, although his heritage was German, his Minnesota accent came through when he was stressed or had drunk too much. This was not the place to test his fluency.

When he turned back to the stand to pay for the food, Mann saw reflected in the glass that a woman was approaching Kaiser's side of the car. Kaiser was totally absorbed in listening to the radio chatter. She rapped on the window.

"Shit," Mann muttered under his breath and quickly paid the proprietor in crisp, new *Ost Marks*. He made it back to car just as Kaiser rolled down his window to talk with the woman. He heard her say something about a husband drinking in a bar and asking for help to get him out.

Before Kaiser could respond with a full sentence, Mann interrupted him over the top of the car.

"I'm sorry, we're *Kripo* and we're on our way to investigate an incident. We can't help with a domestic issue right now," he said.

He tossed the paper-wrapped *Currywurst* trays onto the back seat and climbed in.

"Let's go."

The last thing they heard was a furious East German housewife yelling at them, "You Criminal Police— you don't have time for an abused woman but you've got time for a god-damned *Currywurst!*"

"That was your fault," Mann said.

They drove on.

30

It was still dark when Becker stirred. He listened for a while and heard only the whispers of the forest pines.

Time to get rolling.

He rolled out of his bivvy sack and repacked. In the cold morning air, his warm breath created a small steam cloud as he worked. He preferred that to oppressive heat and insects. There was something about a green forest that the jungle didn't offer.

The first thing he did was to pull his pistol from its waistband holster. He dropped the magazine and cycled the action. A cartridge flipped out into the air where he deftly caught it. He slid the round back into its place in the magazine, which he then snapped back in place. Pulling back the slide, he allowed it to slowly slide back into battery. He clicked the toggle to safe. Satisfied the weapon was ready, he returned it to its holster.

Ready condition.

He risked using his *Esbit* cooker to heat up some water for the freeze-dried chicken and rice patrol ration he was carrying, as well as some lukewarm coffee from of his thermos bottle. He had contemplated bringing C-Rations, as a can of "Chopped Ham & Eggs" with Tabasco might have been a tastier breakfast, but thought better of it. The problem was that anyone within half a kilometer could smell "C-Rats" cooking. Finishing his meal, he buried the unmarked packaging and carefully covered the hole so only a bloodhound or a wild pig would be able to find it.

Time to scout the trail.

Becker did a 360-degree scan of the area before he stood. It was technically the time known as BMNT or Begin Morning Nautical Twilight, that period when a person can just see things distinctly but when the sun hasn't broken the horizon. Some people simplify things and call it "dawn." In any event, it was the ideal time for an Indian attack or to look at an objective.

The eastern sky was brightening from the dark blue of night to apricot as he moved towards the trail. When he finally reached it, he remained in the forest and observed how it snaked through the trees. He was looking for a specific point and then found it. It was as Fischer described it, a slight bend in the path with a rather large flat rock next to the track. It was several hundred meters from the house and isolated, as was everything in this neck of the woods.

When he reached the rock, he gathered up a handful of stones— not too big, not too small—and reached over the big one to pile the smaller ones on the dirt trail in a symmetrical pyramid shape, three stones high. It was an obvious sign if you looked for it. It would have looked unnatural to anyone paying attention, but he hoped no one else would be walking the trail this morning.

He backed off, set his rucksack down in the brush, and found a space where he could sit leaning against a tree and disappear in the undergrowth to watch. He remained alert to avoid missing anyone or anything that might approach.

He remembered the first time he saw what happens if you sleep at the wrong time in the field. A student on the qualification course had fallen asleep only to have the TAC, the instructor, discover him asleep as the patrol got ready to move out. The TAC wordlessly motioned for everyone to move away and then dropped a grenade simulator at the sleeping man's feet. Eight seconds later there was a bright flash and an explosion, the equivalent of a quarter pound of TNT. It was a hell of a way to wake up, but better than having a bayonet thrust into your chest.

Point made.

It was two hours later when he heard someone approaching. The sound was too loud and too irregular to be an animal. He knew it was a person. The appearance of Fischer confirmed that. Fischer was walking slowly, looking from side to side, inspecting "his" forest. Becker sat silently in his place and watched him walk by. He didn't look back but continued up the trail.

Becker knew that Fischer had already walked down to the gate and checked out his other trails to make sure no one else was near his house before he came up this trail. Now he would continue on to check its further reaches as well. About thirty minutes later he reappeared and walked to the bend. This time he looked back in the direction from which he had come and then turned back towards his *Dacha*. Before he moved on, he swept the stones from the trail with his feet.

That was Fischer's sign. *The area is clear, you can visit me.*

Then he disappeared down the trail.

Becker looked at his watch, waited ten minutes and stood up, all the while continuously checking his 360 for unwanted guests. He put on his rucksack and walked along the trail's edge until he could see the open area and the *Dacha's* porch. The front door was open and a long-handled spade stood next it. It was still safe to come out of the cold.

He left the shelter of the forest and trotted towards the house.

Fischer was watching and stepped out the door. He reached out and grabbed Becker's hand and shook it while dragging him inside.

"Welcome, welcome," he said, shutting the door. "We meet again."

Becker looked about as he followed OZ into the parlor. He put his rucksack in a corner where he could quickly grab it and continued to study the interior. It was rustic. There were no paintings or photographs, but there were several trophies on the walls. He saw a big ten-point fallow deer rack and a smaller one near it.

"Is that a *Rothirsch*?" he asked pointing at the smaller rack of horns.

Becker was deliberately taking his time to avoid ratcheting up any apprehension Fischer might have. He felt the tension in his own body rising like someone was slowly increasing an electrical charge to his nervous system. He had to keep himself and his charge calm.

"Yes, I shot these when I was younger. I stopped hunting a while ago. I don't see the need. If I want some venison I just go down to a restaurant in the village. But I have a question for you. I don't know what to call you, what's your name?"

"Kim. My father liked Rudyard Kipling, hence Kim."

He wasn't under cover and was carrying an ID card in that name, so he thought it best to use it with Fischer.

"Another spy and an adventurer who ran before you. Your father must have been prescient. But, tell me how your night went. I was nervous all night long that something might happen to you."

"Uneventful," he reassured Fischer. "Some friends dropped me a long way off and I walked here without anyone seeing me. And then I waited out there in the bush for you."

"I felt someone watching me when I came to the rocks. I assumed that was you."

"Yes, I was probably staring at you too hard. People often feel it when someone stares at them intensely. It's your sixth sense."

"I hope you didn't have a weapon pointed at me."

"No, just my binoculars. I was just watching you, trying to see if you were under stress or any pressure."

"Was I?"

"Not that I could see."

"That's a relief. How much time do we have here?"

"Several hours. A team will show up here around mid-day, we will need to put a signal on your gate so they know it's safe for them to approach."

"What then?"

"We set up your disappearance. There will be a fire and the authorities will find a body—not yours, but someone that resembles you. It's been arranged."

"No one was killed on my account, I hope?"

"No. We found a candidate that had nowhere else to go. He's serving a higher purpose now. Then my men will move us to the extraction point."

"Extraction point? Where is that and how do we do it?"

"It's not far. It's south of here and closer to the main air corridor. We'll go out by air. We have some aircraft with special capabilities. One of them is coming tonight. I'll explain the procedure later. No worries."

"I have no worries at all, this is all just like a walk in the park," Max said facetiously.

Fischer kept himself busy for the next hours. He would read a bit, but the anxiety would overtake him and he would pace around the house before settling down again. Around noon, he walked down to the gate alone and put the safe signal in place; a bow of rope tied on top rail as Becker showed him.

Becker wandered through the house as well, but mostly he kept his eyes on all the approaches. He didn't want to be surprised.

***

It was mid-afternoon and he was in the parlor staring out the rear window when he heard the crunch of car tires on the gravel. Becker walked up the hall to a small study at the front of the house where Fischer was standing.

"This does not look so good," Fischer said as he watched the big black Zil sedan roll up the drive. Seconds later he confirmed his thought, "I thought so: it's Mielke's hitman, Großmann, driving in his Russian status symbol."

"The one that thinks you're the American spy."

"Yes. You know they always send someone you trust if they want to arrest you," Fischer said. He turned to Becker, "But, in this case, Großmann is not the man they would send. General Wolf knows I hate him. That probably means he came on his own. He must think I am about to run away. He's probably afraid he might lose his quarry."

He took Becker's arm and guided him back to the parlor.

"You are my neighbor, Jurgen Weiss. I hire you to keep the property in shape while I'm in Berlin. You live down the road. I'll handle the rest of his questions."

Becker accepted his new identity.

"No problem. Give me a sign if you think he'll be a problem and I will step in."

"I will resort to that only if I think this will end badly. I would prefer to get out of here without any additional evidence left behind."

"That's what we were hoping for too, but things may have changed."

Fischer nodded, "Yes, yes, but we'll see how this goes."

He walked back down the hallway to the front door. Before he got there, he heard the thump of a car door slamming. Someone was walking towards the house. Fischer reached the door about the same time as he saw a bulky shadow cross the opaque sidelight windows. He knew it could only be Großmann. Opening the portal, he saw a clearly incensed man in a long wool overcoat. He was wearing a Russian *Ushanka* fur hat, like a Cossack general. Fischer wanted to laugh. It wasn't even cold. Großmann loved to wear his general's uniform but he couldn't outside the confines of *Stasi* headquarters, so he compensated by trying to look like one in civilian clothing.

"Bruno! To what do I owe this honor?"

"General Wolf told me you were here."

"Please, come in."

Fischer said the words like he was actually surprised, but he had anticipated a visit might come. He turned and walked back into the parlor where Becker, having no other place to go, was standing.

He walked through the room and pivoted in front of a large lounge chair.

"Come in, come in."

Großmann came into the room and looked at Becker, then back at Fischer.

"Who is this?"

"My neighbor. He keeps things in order around here while I am in the city."

"Do you have a name?" Großmann threw the words at Becker like a superior who expected his questions answered before he asked them.

Becker stood rock still. He had put his field coat back on and was looking very much like the countryman he was supposed to be.

"I do. I am Jurgen Weiss." He didn't offer anything else.

"From where?" Großmann asked.

"From down the road," he turned and pointed generally towards the village.

"I meant from where do you come."

"Originally? From Suhl. In the south."

"I know where Suhl is. You don't sound like you're from there."

"I am. Are you from Mecklenburg?"

That startled Großmann.

"I was born up there. How did you know?"

"You sound like you're from there." Becker knew where Großmann came from not because he heard the vaguely *Plattdeutsch* lilt in his voice, but because he had read his Agency profile.

"Surely you didn't come all the way out here to discuss dialects," Fischer broke in.

"It's not so far when you have a job to do, Fischer," Großmann said. There was a threat implicit in his words.

"Job? What job? Is there some sort of an emergency?"

"You know exactly what I am talking about, Fischer."

"No, I don't have any idea. And is this a subject to be discussed in front of a man who does not have a security clearance?"

"I don't think it matters, really. He's probably in on it with you, anyway."

Fischer paused for a moment. He knew what was happening and what Großmann was about to say.

"He's in with me on what? Perhaps you should come to the point."

"Wait a minute!" Becker said. "I don't know what's happening here but I know it doesn't include me. So I will excuse myself now. If you need me, *Herr* Fischer, I'll be at my place."

Becker took a step towards the door, and closer to Großmann.

"Just stay where you are," Großmann said. He pulled a Makarov pistol out of his coat pocket and pointed it menacingly back and forth at both Becker and Fischer.

Becker noted that. *He doesn't know how to handle that thing in close quarters.*

"Are you crazy, Großmann?" Fischer enquired.

"No, not crazy, I am quite lucid, actually. I know what you are and I think this guy," he pointed at Becker with the pistol barrel, "will help me prove it."

"I am sorry, Jurgen. I think my colleague has lost his mind."

"He does look crazy, *Herr* Fischer," Becker said. He turned to Großmann, "I don't know who you think you are to come in here and pull a gun. I am going to get the police."

Becker took an oblique step towards the hallway as if to leave, one that was ever so slightly closer to Großmann. He touched the cold plastic grips of the pistol in his pocket and thought about pulling it out, but decided to wait.

"I told you to stay where you are!" Großmann was turning red.

Fischer saw what Becker was doing. He turned and began to walk towards the kitchen.

"Now where do you think you're going?" Großmann said, swinging his pistol back towards Fischer.

"To make some coffee. I think we need something to drink."

"I am not going to drink anything with a traitor!"

"Is that what this is about? You think I'm a traitor? On what basis did you decide this? I hope you told General Wolf before you decided to come up here."

"No, he would have just tried to protect you. He knows of my suspicions, and so does Mielke."

"Suspicions? You decided I was a traitor based on suspicions? I am sure that wouldn't stand up to scrutiny even in front of the State Security court. Or did you come out here just to shoot me?"

"You know we don't do that anymore. You are guaranteed your rights under the law."

"The constitution of the GDR assures civil rights? That may be true but we *Stasi* people don't care about such laws, now do we Bruno?" Fischer said.

"You people always think you're better than the rest of us."

"I take that to mean you don't think much of General Wolf's Directorate? He did always say that a good intelligence officer should have clean hands. So did Dzerzhinsky, as I remember."

"Dzerzhinsky shot his share of traitors," Großmann sneered.

"Perhaps, but then he was Polish. General Wolf never killed anyone nor has he ordered his officers to do so, while Mielke's hands are stained with the blood of innocents."

"In the defense of the nation, it is necessary to crush those who wish to destroy it. But, sometimes the wrong person gets shot."

Fischer decided that he was not going to play any more games with Großmann. He was already sailing far too close to the wind to care.

"Yes, yes, I know you are quite willing to overlook the mistakes of the system. I remember all those so-called theories about the dictatorship of the proletariat and the need to get rid of the 'counterrevolutionaries.' But if we had reacted differently to the uprising of fifty-three, I don't think we'd have half the problems we do now. Suppression of the opposition only breeds more opposition."

"I detect dangerous deviationist thinking in what you say."

"Ah, now I hear the true Großmann speak. 'Dangerous deviationist thinking.' What is that supposed to mean? I hear echoes of Stalin's propaganda in your voice, isn't that true? Anyone who is not for us is against us and must be dealt with. All opposition must be ruthlessly crushed. Are you still longing for August 1953? I have heard that you were involved in a lot of 'wet work' back then."

Großmann was shaken. He had never heard Fischer or anyone else in the Firm speak so openly against him or even Stalin for that matter. More than ever, Fischer was confirming his suspicions. Großmann was turning red again, his finger tightening on the trigger.

"You are against our cause. We were… we are protecting the Party and the nation from the Fascist West!"

"'Let the ruling classes tremble…' Remember that?" Fischer said.

"You were a supporter of the uprising?"

"No, you idiot! It's from Marx's *Manifesto*. The Party lost its way with the people. I am not anti-anything except the bourgeois class of party hacks, the cognac-drinking communist cadre we created and the controls they use to keep the people in their place. And from whom were we protecting the nation? A bunch of construction workers, farmers, and low-level bureaucrats who didn't want to work one hundred hours a week for less money than they used to earn from working fifty? Some threat they posed. We are not a perfect society as our leaders would like us to think. They have stolen the cause and just want to perpetuate their hold on power over the people."

"The traitors were being incited and led by Western agents, you know that."

"Do you still actually believe that tripe, Bruno? You know very well no help came from the West. That was an excuse Ulbricht made up to cover for the failure of his leadership. The people just wanted free elections and the things that went with democracy—you know what 'democracy' is, don't you? It is that thing we call our country—a democratic republic. Those words both belong with another word—liberty. In reality we have none of those things."

"Bourgeois freedoms," scoffed Großmann. "We need order, not freedoms."

"What do you know of bourgeois freedoms? I am wasting my time trying to lecture you. You're nothing more than Mielke's attack dog."

"Do you agree with his thinking?" Großmann asked Weiss/Becker.

"I don't think about such things. But I am surprised to hear you think *Herr* Fischer is a traitor. I've always known him to be a loyal citizen, but we don't talk politics. We talk about the local citizens—the animals and the forest mostly."

Weiss/Becker was telling the truth, he just wasn't saying to which country Fischer was loyal. Everything else was just being consistent with his cover. He was also trying to dial Großmann's anger back or at least redirect it. He wasn't sure if he could get his own pistol out in time and he didn't want to exfiltrate a dead agent if there was any gunplay.

Großmann stared at him, wondering if he was really dealing with a simple farmer or perhaps even a simpleton.

"Do you know what *Herr* Fischer, as you call him, does for a living?"

"No, other than he is some sort of official in Berlin. He must be important because he owns two homes, but we haven't talked about that. Do you work together? If you do, there must be a lot of conflict in the workplace."

"That's none of your business. I still can't place you, Weiss. Where did you say you came from again?"

His attempt was a very ham-handed challenge to trip Becker up.

"Suhl, as I told you. This is how I speak. My parents gave me their accent."

"Bruno, enough of the language analysis already. Why did you come here? Are you going to arrest me and drag me back to Berlin or do you have some other purpose for being here?"

"Well, for starters, I think it would be a good idea to take you and your 'Jurgen Weiss' down to the village to verify his identity. Then we'll see what happens next."

For the second time that day, there was a crunch of tires on the driveway. And then a car door slammed.

Becker couldn't help but think the timing, if unplanned, was perfect.

31

It was early afternoon, when the Wartburg growled its way north out of the village. Earlier, they had done an area recce before settling down in the forest to wait.

"We did this all the time when I was driving with the Mission. Hide and go seek," said Kaiser.

When it was time, he did another short circuit to make sure no one was following them and then followed a couple of tracks to get back on the country road that led to the *Dacha*.

Turning into the driveway, they saw Becker's safe sign on the gate, but it was partially open and unlatched, which puzzled Mann. He got out and closed it fully once the Kaiser drove their car through and then locked it with a chain and a big Chinese padlock. He had brought several for those times when it might be prudent to slow down anyone behind them.

"Take it easy. Keep your eyes open."

The last meters into a target were always the most nerve racking. It was always smart to come into a target slowly as you could never be sure of what might be waiting. As the *Dacha* slowly came into view, so did the big black Zil. A driver stood by the door watching them approach. The license plates on the car were nondescript in a way that still said, "don't mess with this vehicle, there is a VIP on board."

Kaiser gave out a low whistle.

"Houston, we have a problem," he said.

"Christ, just what we need. I'm going to go in. You stay here and make sure he doesn't go anywhere."

Mann got out the car and walked forward towards the house. Kaiser could see him speak with the man briefly and then continue on towards the house. The driver turned as if to follow Mann, so Kaiser did what he was supposed to do. He stepped out of the car.

"*Stehen bleiben!*" Freeze! Kaiser said.

The driver spun towards him. Kaiser was smiling as he approached him.

"You don't want to interfere with a police officer's official duties now do you?"

"No, of course not. But why are you here?"

"We are here to check on *Herr* Fischer. We heard reports that there might be something unusual going on, like a burglary. You aren't a burglar now, are you?"

"No, can't you tell by the vehicle? We're here on official business," said the driver.

"Maybe, but cars can be stolen and plates forged easily enough. *Herr* Fischer is an important man and we wouldn't want anything bad to happen to him."

"My boss is also an important man."

Mann stopped just short of the door to the *Dacha* and turned to watch the encounter. He sensed something was about to happen. He assumed it would not go well for one of the two.

Mann heard the driver say something but he wasn't sure what. Kaiser said something in return. He couldn't make out quite what that was either, but it sounded angry.

And that's when things did indeed go downhill.

The driver tried to reach under his coat to pull what Mann assumed was a pistol. Mann saw Kaiser's moves coming as the driver had mistakenly allowed him to get inside his circle of defense. Nick took a long step forward and smashed the driver's nose with an open palm strike that stunned him and slammed him up against the Zil. The second move was so swift, Mann barely saw it. Kaiser pinned the man to the car with his knee and disarmed him. Then he grabbed the driver's head, pulled it straight back and crushed the windpipe with a swift punch of his fist. He held the man and waited. When the body went limp, Kaiser dropped it to the ground. He stared at it for a second and then looked up at Mann and shrugged his shoulders. He took a couple of steps toward Mann and said quietly, "He didn't like my accent."

Mann spread his arms in supplication and looked at the sky. "Why me, Lord?"

He pivoted to the door and grabbed the door handle. Pulling his pistol from its holster he entered the house.

32

With the second car's arrival, the atmosphere inside the house became tenser still.

"Expecting visitors, Fischer?"

"No, it may be someone from the village, maybe the *Bürgermeister*. He checks in from time to time."

"Good. Then he can identify this Weiss person."

"Don't get too excited, Bruno." With the arrival of what he assumed were Becker's men Fischer wasn't as worried.

They didn't hear the front door open, but a disembodied voice came down the hallway.

"*Herr Fischer! Alles in Ordnung?*" Is everything okay?

Fischer remained quiet. It was Großmann who answered.

"Come in here."

All eyes were on the hallway as the tall *Volkspolizist* walked into the room. His Makarov was out and its barrel followed his eyes as he surveyed the room taking in the details. Only Großmann's pistol concerned him.

"Please put that on the table," he said.

"I–I am—" Großmann said, stammering.

"I don't care who you are. Do as I tell you until I can get this straightened out."

Großmann put his pistol down on the table.

"Now step back."

Großmann complied but he noticed something.

"*Polizeihauptkommisar*, what is your name? You have no name tag."

"Ah, that… Yes, I seem to have misplaced it somewhere. I am Franz Gruber, *Polizeihauptkommisar* Franz Gruber."

Gruber/Mann stepped forward to the table where the Makarov lay and picked it up. He holstered his own weapon then checked Großmann's. Deliberately, he dropped the magazine out, checked that it was full and snapped it back in place. Then he pulled the slide back a bit to see if there was a round in the chamber. The brass case glinted out at him and he let the slide slip forward. Making sure it was on safe, he pulled out his own pistol.

"*Feuerbereit*." Ready to fire, he said as he gave Großmann's gun to Fischer, butt end first.

Turning back to Großmann, he chuckled a bit.

"No," he said, "not really. I'm actually a lowly sergeant. Seems we've arrived in the nick of time, Boss."

Großmann looked completely baffled.

"Seems so," Becker said. "Sit."

Becker had pulled his Walther P38 out and gestured to Großmann.

Großmann sat.

"You are *BND*!"

"No, we're not *BND*. Try further west, much further."

It was finally starting to dawn on Großmann that he might be caught up in something he couldn't handle.

"I knew you were bad a long time ago, Fischer. I just didn't have the proof. Now I do."

"I don't think you had a clue until recently and right now I think you're a bit late with your proof."

Fischer turned to Becker.

"Well, Jurgen, what is the next step? Things have become a bit complicated."

"We continue as planned, although this man has, as you say, complicated things. We'll have to come up with a way to deal with that."

"If I may, Boss?" Gruber/Mann said.

"Go ahead," Becker said. He was always very open to new ideas. Großmann's arrival had thrown a wrench in the plan. He was that one variable they hadn't really contemplated.

"Nick, come in here!" Mann yelled.

There was a feral look in Nick's eye when he came into the room. He took in the scene and assessed there were no dangers to deal with, then holstered his pistol and spoke.

"Where do you want me to put the bodies?"

"Bodies?" said Großmann.

"Bodies?" Becker said. "I thought we only had one?"

Mann said, "The guy outside—I guess he was the bodyguard—didn't like Nick's German and started to pull a pistol on him, so Nick crushed his larynx."

"Yeah, he said I sounded like I came from the docks in Hamburg. He was a rude little shit," Kaiser said.

"He is insane!" Großmann cried, looking about wildly. He was truly frightened by Nick.

Nick took a menacing step towards him, but was stopped by Becker's hand.

"You have no idea what combat does to a man," Becker said, "but then we really don't care if you do."

"The driver's body will add to the story, Boss, believe me," Mann said.

Fischer took it all in and said, "I take it we are at the point of no return?"

"It does seem that way. Sometimes you have a plan and then sometimes you just have to make shit up."

Großmann was about to pee his pants.

"Well, *Herr* Großmann, it seems you have two options. Stay here or come with us and try out for a Green Card in America," Becker said.

"Are you all mad? How do you think you're going to get out of here? You will all be arrested and shot. I will make sure of that."

Fischer stepped closer to Großmann and around the side of his chair.

"I think I see your plan, *Herr* Gruber. It's rather interesting, I think. Your name… are you aware of another Franz Gruber?"

"Not really, no."

"It's appropriate, I think. The other Franz Gruber composed 'Silent Night.' But, I digress."

Fischer turned back to Großmann.

"Remember Heinrich Pfeiffer, Bruno?"

"No, who is he?"

"I didn't think you would; you murdered him. This is for him."

The pistol was under the man's fat chin before he could react. Fischer pulled the trigger and Großmann's head jerked back. His eyes and mouth remained open, seemingly in an expression of surprise. Doctors would tell you that it wasn't surprise but the instant relaxation of muscles at the moment of death. In either case, Großmann couldn't be surprised anymore, because he was dead.

"Good bye, Bruno," Fischer said.

Becker contemplated the corpse for a moment. When the smoke cleared and his ears stopped ringing, he asked, "Perhaps you would like to explain our new plan to me, *Herr* Fischer?"

"Happily," Fischer said, "your sergeant there gave me the idea. This is what happened: Großmann came here to kill me. His driver tried to intervene and Großmann shot him first. He fell over there," Fischer pointed to a chair across the room. "Then he shot 'me' in that chair. That's where you put my *Doppelganger*. Finally, Bruno was so despondent that he killed himself out of whatever delusional thinking brought him here."

"That's better than what I was thinking," Mann said, "the simplest explanation is best."

"Okay, we go with our new plan," Becker said. "Nick and 'Franz,' you guys bring in the bodies. We'll pose them, set the devices and then get the hell out of here."

"Should we take photos of this guy?" Nick asked as he looked over Großmann's body.

Becker shook his head. "God, no. We don't need to be carrying evidence of any kind of crime. Just being here is bad enough."

Turning back to Fischer, Becker said, "That was rather a quick decision on your part."

It was a question not a statement.

"Not at all, I have always wanted him dead. Unfortunately my professionalism kept me from realizing that goal until today. He was an evil man."

"Who was Heinrich Pfeiffer?"

"A journalist, he was the father of a friend."

"I think your people will thank you someday."

"Ah, they will never know. The Firm will hush this up and dispose of the evidence. It will be reported as a tragic accident."

"If we get out of here."

"Yes, if we get out of here."

Nick and "Franz" came into the parlor carrying the body of the driver and dropped him into the armchair with his pistol on the floor next to him. Kaiser wiped down the face to get rid of the blood and straightened the nose a bit. Satisfied with that piece of the puzzle, they went back outside and pulled a long, canvas bundle out of the car and walked it into the house.

They laid the body bag on the floor and unzipped it. The corpse inside was a little stiff, but it had lost much of its rigor mortis. It had come out of a cooler to be loaded into the Wartburg before they crossed Checkpoint Alpha.

Mann and Kaiser pulled the bag off the body and stuffed the dead man into the chair, flexing the limbs to look mostly correct. When they were finished, they stood back to admire their work.

"Not bad. He even looks like you, *Herr* Fischer. The doctor told us he would pass for you after the fire, so your disappearance will be most complete."

"Go on and get the car ready," Becker said.

Kaiser and Mann stripped off their gloves and tossed them into the body bag. The bag would go with them. Kaiser dropped a small satchel on the floor close to Becker as they left the room.

Fischer chose to remain distant from his stand-in. Standing next to the dead Großmann whom he hated seemed preferable to being close to the dead man he didn't know.

"Who was he?" he asked.

"An unknown, an unclaimed person, perhaps a homeless man, that's all we know. No one will miss him, I hope," Becker said.

Fischer bowed his head and said a prayer for the dead and asked for forgiveness once again. After a moment he lifted his head and sighed.

"Are we ready then?" he asked.

"Yes, go ahead, sir."

Fischer raised the pistol and carefully fired two rounds into corpse and then two into the driver. He handed the pistol to Becker. Becker pulled a cloth out of his pocket and wiped the Makarov off, before pressing it carefully into Großmann's hand. He walked over to the driver and looked at the lifeless body for a moment. It looked a little like a toy doll with its arms and legs askew, the head flopped over to one side. Becker leaned over and tipped the chair over onto the floor with the body splayed over it. The crime scene was complete.

"What about the fire?"

229

Becker reached down and rummaged around in the satchel Kaiser had dropped. He pulled out a metal tin, unscrewed its cap and dumped the contents over the chair and corpse and across the floor to where Großmann's lifeless body sat. He then walked into the kitchen with the satchel in hand and poured more fluid on the wood floor near the stove. That done, he placed a small device on the floor next to the stove. When it was properly situated, he took a tube out of the device, crushed it, and inserted it back into its hole. Then he turned on the burners and hurried out the kitchen. He placed a second device in the puddle of fluid on the floor near the chair with the corpse and activated the delay ignitor as he did with the first.

Standing up straight, he took off his gloves.

"It's a Russian *Spetznaz* sabotage device," he said. "A simple incendiary, mostly paraffin mixed with aluminum oxide. The ignitor is an acid delay that will give us about one hour to get far away. It's virtually undetectable after it burns."

"And the fluid?"

"An accelerant that will also disappear in the fire."

"A ghastly business. I hope no one else gets hurt helping me. I wish I could have escaped on my own without endangering you or your men. And your woman—she is okay, I hope?"

"Yes, she's not mine but she's fine. This is all unfortunately necessary, but it's what we do. We agreed that you needed to disappear completely. This will be our best chance and Großmann may have given us an advantage."

"I hope so. Where to now?"

"We head north then southwest to a pick-up point. You'll see. Are you ready to go?"

"Yes, I have one small valise with papers and a few mementos, that's it."

"Then we're out of here."

Becker grabbed his rucksack and the can and waited for Fischer to get his bag. Taking one last look around the parlor and hallway, they walked out. Fischer turned in front of the house and took a final look at his sanctuary.

"I hope what they say is true."

"What's that, sir?"

"You know—that dead men don't tell tales."

33

"Everything in the car?" Becker said.

"Yes, we are all loaded up, body bag included. The other car is clean, no evidence of a scuffle there. So I think we're ready to go," Mann said. "You climb in back and look like a couple of perps. We'll head for the LZ."

"What's a perp?" Fischer asked.

"A perpetrator, a criminal."

"That's easy, according to East German law we already are 'perps.'"

"We'll call it self-defense when we get to the West. Besides, you said he killed someone. Were you a witness?"

"Only at second hand. I read his reports and spoke to a Russian who was present. And it was more than one. There's no doubt he crossed the line many times, but those were very different times."

"Maybe, but there is no statute of limitations on murder. You don't regret what you did, do you?"

"No, not at all," Fischer said.

"Good, because we are all soldiers in this cause. Now, let's get out of here."

They climbed into the car and drove down the track towards the gate. The silent green forest seemed to suck up any idea of the violence that had just occurred. Each man was quietly absorbed in his thoughts. Behind them was a break with the past. In front was a path to an uncertain future.

"Stop short of the gate. I'll check out the route and wave you on," Mann said.

"Roger," Kaiser acknowledged. He halted the car about 75 meters from the gate. Mann got out and crunched down the pebble-strewn road. Inside the car, it was deathly quiet.

Fischer broke the silence. "Sergeant Nick, would you have actually killed Großmann?"

"Yes, I would have. I read your notes about him; he was a nasty man."

"You have no problem with killing?"

"I don't, not anymore, but generally only the bad ones. I got used to it a long time ago."

"What does your religion say about that?"

"It says that the sacrifice of a life is often necessary."

"What religion is that?"

"I am a Reformed Druid."

"Is that a recognized religion?"

"It is for me. My parents tried to make me a good Catholic but I failed both the written and practical exams. Then I joined the army and went to Southeast Asia and by the end of my third tour I decided to go my own way."

"Kim, you have some interesting people in your organization."

"Indeed we do."

In front of them, Mann opened the gate and walked out to the road. He turned and motioned for the car to approach. Kaiser let the car roll forward until the car cleared the gate. Mann pitched the lock and chain into the trunk, knowing that some supply officer would try to charge him for lost goods if he didn't, and hopped back into the car.

"*Vamos!*"

Kaiser accelerated onto the road and away from the scene. He turned off the main road as soon as a side track appeared and plunged into the countryside. After a few more turns, it was clear no one was behind them.

"You drive my country like you know it well," Fischer said.

"I have spent some time around this neighborhood."

"Then I would guess you were a driver for the USMLM."

"*Klar, Herr* Fischer."

"Kim, your organization is beginning to make more sense to me now. Mielke hates the Allies and their liaison missions. He thinks you are trying to subvert East German government."

Becker smiled to himself. Fischer obviously didn't understand the differences between SDB and the MLM or that the army was sometimes capable of working together as a team rather than a bunch of disconnected quarterbacks. But then, neither did most senior combat arms officers who thought Special Forces and Intelligence to be anathema to the American way of war.

"I'm sure you will be asked about all that when we get you to safety."

"You say 'when' and not 'if'?"

"There are no 'ifs' anymore. We'll do this."

Kaiser was taking the car north away from the *Dacha* and was moving at a sane pace for once.

"We have four hours and forty minutes until H-Hour."

"H-Hour?" Fischer said.

"Our exact time for the pick-up. To be melodramatic we could call it our 'rendezvous with destiny.'"

"Melodramatic is right, I am starting to get nervous the closer we get to the moment."

"Why?"

"I feel like I am one of my own agents on an operation. I am about to do something that I don't have any control over. I don't know what might happen next but I am committed. It is all risk versus gain. I hope to live to see the gain."

"What do you want?"

"The satisfaction of seeing the government fall and the people free."

"What do you worry about most?"

"Being arrested and interrogated. You should not let that happen to me. In your country, I would go to prison. Here I would suffer far worse than that."

"Do you regret what you have done?"

"No, never. Much of what I have done was unpleasant. Not anything like what Bruno did, but I have a cause, something worthwhile, to help win the Cold War."

"That's my goal too. Although sometimes I question our methods, especially when we support tyrants in the name of facing down communism. That said, there is no other country I would want to serve."

"I have found that no man or country is perfect. We can only do our little bit to try to make them better or change them completely. I have faith in your country and its people. At least they try to improve with age. The country I am about to give up is only concerned with winning by any means—most of their ways are bankrupt of any ethics or humanity," Fischer said.

"I don't know if I could find the courage to do what you have done."

"As long as you are an American, I doubt you could. There are only a few of you who have been persuaded to join forces with the communists. Yes, many have rebelled against society or things like Vietnam, but few would be a traitor to their country because your country can change, the pendulum can always swing in another direction. East Germany, and I suspect most countries of the Soviet Bloc, are filled with potential turncoats because the system is deeply flawed and can never change without a revolution. They are the people who will finally say 'We have had enough.'"

"You're one of those people."

"I imagine in some regard, although I am not without my own flaws."

Fischer was thinking of Gypsy and the others, especially Lila, who he had abandoned. He hoped there would be no repercussions for any of the living left behind in his wake.

There was a flash of light in the rearview mirror.

"We've got company," Kaiser said.

"What kind?"

"It looks to be undercover *Polizei* or *Stasi*. A black Lada with an antenna."

Fischer turned to look at the car.

"It could be either, I can't tell. But there appears to be only one man inside," he said.

"We could outrun him, but that might raise some questions."

"Boss, what do you think?" Mann said.

"Do you feel up to some more role playing?"

"Sure, I'm good with that."

"Then let's stop and you can figure out what he wants and get him off our backs."

"Right. Let's do it and, Nick, keep your damn mouth shut this time."

Nick brought the car to a halt on the edge of the road. Mann hopped out and walked toward the Lada, which had also stopped. Nick got out and stood by the door.

"*Verdammt*," Fischer said as he turned and saw the driver of the Lada get out and step into the headlights of his vehicle.

"What?"

"I know him and he knows me. He is Weber, the district security chief. He's been to my house several times."

There was nothing Becker and Fischer could do to affect the situation outside.

"Why are you following us?" Mann said.

"I haven't seen that car around here before, so I was wondering who you might be."

"And who exactly are you?"

"Major Weber, *Staatssicherheit*." He offered his identity wallet to Mann and left him holding it as he walked up to the Wartburg. "Who do you have here?"

"This is a criminal matter. It's not your concern."

"You should know better than to question my authority. Everything and everyone in this district is my concern," Weber said as he leaned over to peer in the window.

Mann positioned himself on the opposite side of the car from Kaiser and looked down to read Weber's identity card in the light. Weber stood back up and peered at Kaiser and then back at Mann before he looked into the car again.

Weber took an abrupt step back from the car.

"Why do you have General Fischer in your car?"

Inside the car, Fischer fumbled to try to open the door, but he couldn't find the latch. The panic was evident on his face. Weber was confused.

Why wasn't I informed if there was going to be an arrest? Are they trying to kidnap Fischer?

Weber reached under his coat for his pistol and pulled it out. It was almost aimed at Mann.

Shit, not again. "Stefan, drop!" Kaiser yelled.

Mann dropped. He turned to see Kaiser move in and grab Weber's wrist and twist the arm downward as he punched Weber in the head. They struggled for a moment and there was a loud report as the pistol went off.

Kaiser kept rotating the officer's arm and then threw him down to the ground face first. He completed his takedown with a knee drop to the back of the man's neck that was punctuated with a loud crack. The man was dead.

"Christ, I fucked that up," Kaiser said.

237

"How? If you hadn't put him down he would have shot me."

Kaiser looked up at his partner with the face of a man about to go into shock. Mann saw that he was holding his inner thigh.

"Yeah, but he shot me."

"Damn. Sit down."

"At least he didn't shoot the medic," Kaiser said, suddenly glad to have a school-trained Special Forces medic as his partner.

Mann pulled the medical kit he had insisted on carrying from the car and went to work. He cut away Kaiser's pants and inspected the entrance and exit wounds closely with a flashlight. The injury was bleeding slowly. Mann saw dark red and knew it was venous not arterial. The femoral had not been hit. He washed it with sterile water and watched it closely for a bit.

"You're good, brother. It's clean through and through and it didn't hit anything major," he said, as he began to staunch the flow with a gauze bandage.

"It stings a bit. Got anything for me?"

Kaiser laid his head back on the ground and closed his eyes.

"I'll give you something in a bit. Don't fall asleep on me, I think we need you awake right now."

"How is he?" Becker asked. He had climbed out of the car and was kneeling next to Kaiser.

"It's not too serious. The femoral is intact and there's some bleeding but I've stopped it with combat dressings for now. But, most importantly, he can't drive."

Becker's philosophy of "first, my men" jumped into action. Later he would say that he wasn't even aware that he made a decision.

"I've got some bad news for you, Nick. You won't be going back with Mann tonight," Becker said.

"What's that supposed to mean?" Kaiser said. He was wondering if he was going to be put down like a dog.

"You are going to take my place on the exfil tonight. You'll be in good hands in a couple of hours. I'll get out of here with Mann."

Becker stood up. Fischer looked at him questioningly.

"He'll be okay. But it means I won't be going out with you; we have the capability to get two men out quickly and only two. His safety is more important."

Mann continued to patch his comrade up, while Becker searched the ground with his flashlight. He caught a flash of brass and picked up the spent cartridge case. He switched the magazine from Nick's pistol with Weber's so the pistol appeared not to have been fired. Taking out a cloth, he wiped the pistol clean and put it back into the owner's holster.

They loaded Kaiser into the car. He was half in Fischer's lap when all was done, but his leg needed elevation. Then they took Weber's body and put it in the front seat of his Lada.

"Follow me," Becker said as he put on his gloves and climbed into the driver seat of Weber's car.

He took off down the road with Mann and the others following behind in the Wartburg. About 2 kilometers down the road they saw the Lada's brake lights flash. They came up behind the car as Becker stepped out and pulled the body over to the driver's side. The car was pointed off the road at an angle into the forest.

"Not elegant, but is there anyone out here who actually witnessed this unfortunate accident and can speak against the evidence?"

"That sounds like you've been reading too much Agatha Christie, Boss."

The engine was still running and Becker stuffed Weber's limp foot onto the gas pedal and stepped back.

"Help push it when I back out the door."

Mann and Fischer were behind the car as Becker reached in and shoved the gear shift forward into third gear. They gave it an extra push and the little car lurched down the embankment and slammed into a tree. The driver's door was still open and Weber slumped halfway out of the car.

"I'm convinced. He must have been a lousy driver," Mann said.

"He was also an *Arschloch*," Fischer noted.

They piled into the Wartburg.

"Kaiser, you are stacking the bodies up like cordwood," Mann said.

"I'll plead that it was all in self-defense. That Weber guy went off half-cocked and didn't even give us time to explain anything," Kaiser said. He was still in pain and fully awake.

"Not to worry, gentlemen. I think you just sped up the inevitable," Fischer told them.

34

Jamie Wheeler and Team 5's Paul Stavros and Fred Lindt had all arrived at Tempelhof Airport separately that day but were presently waiting together in the flight center for their hop down to Rhein-Main Airbase. An Air Force T-39 Sabreliner sat on the tarmac waiting for them while the crew filed whatever paperwork was required to get off the ground. The three men, the only passengers, clustered around an ancient Air Force coffee dispenser that had cooked the beverage into a dense brown sludge that refused to be either diluted by hot water or flavored by the industrial-grade powdered cream offered as a condiment.

"Look, my spoon stands up in this slime."

The pilot walked over and watched them. "You guys aren't actually trying to drink that crap are you?"

"It's the only thing around, isn't it?"

"Heavens no, we have real coffee on board, that's the beauty of flying VIP aircraft. They outfit them for the generals not us normal people."

Hours later they made the flight to Rhein-Main and waited. After all, waiting was what military personnel do best. They made their introductions and reviewed the pick-up plans. A day earlier, the 7th Special Operation Squadron crew had been given a classified pre-mission order which let them determine their flight plan into and out of the area and, most importantly, how exactly they would conduct the pick-up itself. Once everyone was satisfied with the plans, they retreated to their respective waiting points to make peace with their own gods and to prepare themselves for the night to come.

At 2130 hours, Aircraft 0561's crew had finished their pre-flight ritual and were still waiting. Now, two hours later, waiting for the final okay that would "green light" the mission and permit them to launch, they were sitting in the squadron briefing room adjacent to the hangar. They were drinking more coffee and trying not to get anxious.

US Air Force Colonel Frank Cantwell was the lead pilot and aircraft commander. His co-pilot, Major Steve Bannerman, and navigator, Major Ron Tuck, would fill the remainder of the seats in the cockpit. It was a high-ranking crew for a high-priority mission, Cantwell just happened to be the squadron commander.

In addition to the three guys driving the plane, there were six other Air Force personnel on the aircraft: an electronic warfare officer or EWO, a safety officer, a flight engineer, a radio operator, and two loadmasters. Then came the straphangers—the guys who had no specific role on the aircraft but were part of the operation nevertheless.

One of them was sitting with the A/C commander listening to the flight engineer explain a detail.

"Our transponder is spoofed to send the ID of another C-130," Senior Master Sergeant Lucas Hernandez said.

"So that our signal will show up on radar as a different aircraft? Why?" Jamie Wheeler asked.

"We don't want the Soviets to know what kind of 130 we really are, so we use the ID of a conventional airframe, one that often transits the Berlin corridor," Hernandez explained.

"Unless they see our plane in broad daylight, they won't be able to tell the difference," Cantwell added.

"Why do we have to ID ourselves at all?"

"Because the flight must be coordinated with the Berlin Air Safety Center before we enter East German airspace if we don't want to get shot down. We're pretending to be a regular Airlift Command mission; by the time they figure out something isn't kosher, we'll be back over the fence and in West Germany."

The squadron operations officer came into the room and looked around for a moment. He saw Cantwell just as the commander waved to him.

"Over here, Skip."

Captain "Skip" Gordon walked over to the table and handed his commander a message print-out. The group had been joined by Stavros and Lindt. Along with Wheeler, the three would be the straphangers on board to monitor the mission and validate any of the ground-to-air communications.

Cantwell looked at the message and announced, "We launch in one hour. Saddle up!"

"Let's go pilgrims, we're burning daylight," Lindt said.

"Who was that supposed to be?" Stavros asked.

"John Wayne, you know, the 'Duke.' I was building off the colonel's Western theme, couldn't you tell?"

"No, you really need to find another hobby. And, by the way, it is nighttime."

The crew and their passengers pushed the squeaking, GSA-approved folding chairs out of the way and made for the door. It was dark outside, but their aircraft was bathed in the light of ten high-intensity sodium lamps from the edge of the airfield apron.

In front of them was a Hercules MC-130E painted a sinister flat black and dark green. Even its insignia were in black which made it very difficult to read them close up, let alone at a distance. Only the number "0561" next to the forward entry door was visible. Its nose was bulbous, larger than on a standard Hercules; it housed all sorts of navigational gear that permitted it to fly "nap of the Earth" or NOE at 250 feet above the ground without plowing into a hillside or the ground unintentionally. There were also two 30-foot-long, steel boom arms folded back against the side of the fuselage. It was an apparition.

"It's a Combat Talon," Stavros said to Wheeler. "Ever flown on one before?"

"Never. I flew on Spooky but this one looks pretty cool too."

"Yeah, unfortunately it doesn't have guns like Spooky. This thing is all about getting in and out without being caught. You're going to love the 'NOE' part at the end. It's like Mister Toad's Wild Ride."

"I hope they have barf bags on board."

"Those be standard equipment on this scow, Mister Wheeler," Colonel Cantwell said.

Cantwell reached the aircraft, grabbed the handrail of the stair-well, swung himself effortlessly up the metal steps in a well-practiced move and disappeared into the airplane.

"Usually they tell me to go to the back entrance," Wheeler said with a mischievous glint in his eye and followed the colonel through the doorway.

Stavros was too busy trying to remember if he had taken his Dramamine or not and almost missed the stairs until Lindt grabbed him by the shoulder.

"Get your head out your bag. If the prop had been turning you'd be chopped liver."

"If the prop had been turning, I would have been paying attention, now wouldn't I?" Stavros said as some sort of explanation. He looked at the blades and tried to regain his momentarily lost pride before he followed everyone else into the belly of the big metal bird.

The crew continued its equipment checks. The navigator plotted coordinates into his computers that would get the plane to the correct address, while the EWO prepared his equipment that would be turned on to confuse and jam any hostile tracking radars if necessary. The EWO was using "Raven" as his intercom codename.

Colonel Cantwell climbed down out of the flight deck and moved aft to where the crew were assembled. He spoke with the loadmasters and safety officer to make sure they were happy and came forward to talk with his passengers.

"You all ready for this?"

"We're just straphangers, sir. The navigator knows where to go, so if he gets us there, we're happy."

"I guarantee that. Our navsystem will put us there to within plus or minus 10 meters. I think I can steer us those last meters in either direction," Cantwell said. He was supremely confident in his aircraft and proud of its crew, not to mention his own abilities. "We did a similar mission about three months ago that went perfect. We're going to do that again tonight."

Shortly after Cantwell returned to the cockpit, the loadmasters began to secure the aircraft. The doors slid into their locked position while one man stood at the rear control station. He manipulated a lever and the high-pitched squeal of the hydraulic system filled the cabin. The tailgate began to lift off the ground. As its support disappeared, the tail settled slightly and the tarmac lights slowly disappeared from view until the gate thumped shut. The loadmaster locked it in place and reported the aircraft ready.

Four Allison engines began their start routine one by one. A whining noise signaled each turboprop was starting up and then the propellers began to turn. Soon the cabin was filled with their roar. Each engine was producing 4,200 horsepower and it sounded like being inside a giant howling wind tunnel. The engines settled into a constant harmonious thrumming, as the pilots ran through their checklists. The fuselage seemed alive, pulsating, almost imperceptibly rocking from side to side as it sat on the tarmac.

"Ten thousand nuts and bolts flying in close formation," Lindt said.

"You're always the pessimist. Me, I love the air force," Stavros replied. He leaned back in the web seats, closed his eyes, and tried to get comfortable.

"That's what you always say at the beginning of a flight."

"It's worked for me so far."

With a slight lurch, the brakes released and the aircraft began to roll forward. The plane bumped along as it ran over the expansion cracks on the tarmac. Everyone was silent, listening to the exchanges between the pilot and the tower in their headphones. For the duration of this mission at least, aircraft 0561 became Number 1805, a standard vanilla C-130E with call-sign "Hurky 05."

Cantwell rolled Hurky 05 down the taxiway towards the active runway, which for this evening was 07C. He brought the plane to a stop at its hold position. He then released the brakes and allowed the plane to roll forward a short way before he set them again firmly. The plane shuddered as it jerked to a stop. The pilot ran up the engines to around three-quarter power while he and Major Bannerman did a final quick check of the instruments. Then the propellers' noise dropped in pitch as Bannerman powered down again. Cantwell asked the tower for release.

The tower answered, "Hurky 05, you're cleared for takeoff, runway Zero-Seven Charlie."

"Roger, Zero-Seven Charlie."

Cantwell repeated the clearance back to the tower and rolled into position. He tapped the brakes and the plane came to a protesting standstill. Then he and the co-pilot grasped the power levers and pushed them to the firewall and the plane rolled forward, quickly picking up speed. The engines' combined 17,000-shaft horsepower moved the lightly laden aircraft down the asphalt like a cheetah in full stride. Minimum speed for transition was 125 knots, but Cantwell held it on the ground for a while longer before he pulled back on the stick. The plane leapt into the air and did a high-pitch climb out—Cantwell was showing off and wanted his passengers to get acclimatized to his style of flying quickly.

In the back, Wheeler found the air sickness bags and made sure he had one at the ready.

The plane leveled out at 15,000 feet and turned to the northwest, heading to a point that would allow them to turn east into the central air corridor. There was a southern corridor through East Germany into Berlin but using it would put them too far away from the LZ to execute their planned maneuver in the sky over East Germany without being unduly noticed by the Soviets. It was to be "in and out"—no one wanted the company of a Soviet fighter plane on this mission.

35

Mann nosed the car through the gate in the perimeter fence and stopped a few meters inside. Becker and Fischer got out of the car and walked down the track a few meters to make sure the field was empty of animals and farmers, then returned. Mann was occupied with lifting a couple of canvas bags out of the trunk. He unzipped both, pulled two flight suits from the bag and laid them on the ground. Then he poked his head inside the car and looked Kaiser over. The wound had slowed its bleeding and his chest was moving rhythmically, his breathing even.

"How's he doing?" Becker said.

"I think he's snoozing. His leg is okay, the bleeding looks like it has almost stopped."

Becker spread his arms wide and turned to Fischer.

"This is our LZ," he said.

Fischer looked the open space over once again. Although it was dark, he could see enough by the moonlight to estimate its size at no more than 75 meters from side to side in any one direction. He knew at once that it was not suitable for an airplane.

"LZ means Landing Zone does it not?" Fischer said. "Is your aircraft a helicopter? No plane can land here."

Mann paused to listen. *This will be interesting.*

"No, it's not a helicopter. It's s a big transport called a Hercules and it will not land."

"I know what a Hercules is, I've seen them in Africa. To get on and off one, it had to land at an airport. So tell me, by what magic we will get on the aircraft?"

"We've been calling it a LZ, it should be 'PZ' for Pick-up Zone. Anyway, it's not magic. It is a very good bit of kit we've used many times before. It's called the Fulton Surface-to-Air Recovery System."

"I'm listening," said Fischer.

"It's also called Skyhook," Becker continued. "You are going to put on a special flight suit with a built-in harness. Then we will snap you and Nick onto a line that is attached to a helium balloon. The balloon will go up and the airplane will grab it and winch you up into the belly."

"You are not serious."

"I am very serious. You two will be in the air for all of about four minutes. It is our best and safest way out of the GDR."

"How many times has this been done?"

"Over 160 times. Probably the best mission I've heard of was called Operation *Coldfeet*. In 1961, the Agency airdropped two men onto an abandoned Russian ice station in the Arctic to collect intelligence. When they finished their work a couple of days later, they were picked up with the Skyhook system."

"Successfully?"

"They were all successful, except for one, but that was a long time ago."

"What happened?"

"It was in 1964. The lift cable broke. They use a stronger cable these days."

"That is comforting. Have you done it before?"

"No, but I have seen it done. You and Nick are both virgins on this one."

"This is not how I wanted to lose my virginity."

"Actually, I have done it," Kaiser said from behind them. He was awake and slid to the edge of the car seat. He was looking around the LZ trying to orient himself.

Fischer turned to regard him more closely.

"Really? How was it? What did it feel like?"

"Windy. It was a bit scary at first. First, you lift off straight into the air, then you just fly along behind the airplane and wait for them to grab you at the tailgate. I will tell you what to do in the air after they get you suited up."

"And you are really not coming with us?" Fischer said, directing his question to Becker.

"No, we have another way to get out of here."

"Can't I go with you?"

"No, our way out is too risky for you. You will be in the West in a couple of hours."

"Wonderful, but I would really rather take a train to Finland."

"Unfortunately, that is not an option tonight. You will go out as a pair. As a safety measure, there is an emergency parachute."

"What would that do?"

"If —and this will not happen—if the line should break, it would let you come back down to earth safely."

"But I would still be in the GDR."

"Yes, that's true."

"Then you can forget the parachute. I am leaving this place one way or the other."

They moved a bit further into the center of the field to set up for the pick-up. As Becker helped Fischer into his specially modified coveralls, Mann carefully assisted Kaiser. He rechecked his wound and wrapped some more elastic around the bandage, being careful not to turn it into a tourniquet.

"How long, Boss?" Kaiser said.

"Not long, about forty minutes. Just chill while we rig the system up."

Mann and Becker laid the remainder of the equipment out on the ground. Mann pulled the balloon from one bag while Becker fastened the main lift line from another bag to the two men's suit harnesses. Mann snapped the balloon's anchor into the lift line and then checked Becker's connections. Then Becker checked the entire system to ensure nothing was tangled. Kaiser lifted Fischer's arm up and snapped a clip from his suit harness into his partner's. They were linked together and ready to go.

All around them was a quiet open field. Becker thought this must have been what it was like to be a member of the French Resistance on a reception party during World War II. Either no one would notice them or the *Gestapo* would suddenly appear and shoot them. He hoped it would be the former.

"System complete," said Becker.

"Check, ready to inflate."

Fischer and Kaiser were sitting next to each other on the ground facing the direction the aircraft would approach from. Kaiser was doing his best to keep Fischer calm by keeping his mind occupied.

"When we are in the air, keep your legs and your arms spread out. That will keep you stable and your back into the wind. Don't fight it, just relax and enjoy the ride."

"Don't worry, Nick, I will mimic what you do. Now, tell me a story."

"What kind of story?"

"A war story."

"Ha, that's an easy one. First, you know that you should never believe a war story that starts either with 'There I was' or 'This is no shit.' You know that don't you?"

"I didn't, but I do now."

"Okay, once a long time ago, I was on patrol in enemy territory..."

"Where?"

"Let's call it Vietnam just in case the lawyers are listening. Okay, we're a small, six-man reconnaissance patrol trying to find enemy supply depots when—Wham!—we get hit by what must have been a company-size force. We've been fighting these guys for what seems like an hour when I get hit in the lower leg and go down. The bad thing is, I got hit on this little footbridge that spanned a stream between two rice paddies, so now I'm lying on the bridge with bullets cutting through the brush and chopping down branches and thunking on the bamboo railing. I can't seem to do anything. Then I realize my rifle took a round and doesn't work and I am pretty much helpless 'cause I can't move. The fighting is going this way and then that way when I see an NVA soldier running up the other side of the bridge. I grab one of my last grenades, pull the pin, hold it for a couple of seconds, and then pitch at the bastard. What does he do? The stupid shit catches it and is about to throw it back when it goes off. I lucked out there, but I am thinking I'm going to get captured and end up in some rat-infested cage somewhere north of the Demilitarized Zone, when two more guys come running towards me. I can't do anything and then two bursts of fire take them both down and my teammate Peter's head suddenly pops up next to me with a big grin on his face. He says to me, and this is no shit, he says, 'Don't worry, Nick, it could be worse, we could be in Stalingrad.'"

Fischer smiled. "I like that story, Mister Nick, but you said, 'This is no shit.' So do I believe you?"

"Yes, you can believe that one. That was Peter's way of making me feel better. I just remembered it just now for some strange reason."

Becker, who had been standing by keeping a watch on the surrounding approaches, walked up to them.

"You two ready?" he said.

"Yes, go for it, Boss."

Mann had connected the helium bottle and began to fill the balloon. Two printed arrows on the nose of the balloon were coming together and when they did, Mann would turn off the valve. As the arrow-shaped balloon began to rise, Becker played out the cable and lines, making sure nothing was tangled. Mann disconnected the balloon from the bottle and secured the nozzle.

"Ready to release."

"Let her fly," Becker said and watched the balloon sail up to the full cable length of 150 meters, carefully guiding the cable out of the bag through his gloved hands.

Kaiser nudged Fischer, "Don't worry, we'll be getting our wings soon."

"As long as they're not angel's wings, I'll be happy."

Becker looked at his Rolex Submariner, its tritium hands glowing bright in the darkness. He rolled the sleeve of his commando sweater down over its face.

"I make it five minutes to snatch. Let's turn on the beacon. Nick, turn on the lift line lights."

Mann pulled one of the AN/PRC-90-2 survival radios out of its pouch and turned it on. Kaiser reached into his leg pocket and flipped a switch on the control box. Above them, just visible in the night sky, two sets of red lights came on, marking the one-hundred foot section of cable the airplane would attempt to grab. Mann pointed the beacon antenna east; its signal would help guide the aircraft in on its final approach.

"It's a perfect night for a pick-up," Becker said.

They all were quiet, straining to hear the aircraft engines. Waiting, the only sound was the wind rustling through the tall grass.

***

Hurky 05 had changed its heading and turned east some time before. The plane crossed the frontier between West and East Germany and was making its way towards the approach for Tempelhof Airfield when Colonel Cantwell called their position in the corridor to the air controllers in Berlin as required.

"Everything according to standard operating procedure," he said to his co-pilot, "but not for much longer. Ron, I need the warnings as we planned, when's the first?"

Major Tuck responded, "Twenty-minute warning coming up in seven minutes."

"Raven, how are we looking?"

"All clean, civil radars are painting us now. Tempelhof, Tegel, Schönefeld, and Gatow radars are all active. Nothing hostile. The military airfields and air defense sites are all quiet."

"Good, hope it stays that way."

"Safety, let's deploy the booms as early as possible."

"Roger, I'll deploy them at the twenty-minute warning. That'll give us time to ensure they are out, fully locked, and ready. We have retested the winch system and it's ready. We'll drop the tailgate fifteen minutes out."

"Affirmative, Safety."

The Hercules droned on through the night. Stavros and Lindt were crowded into the radio operator's space listening for any ground transmissions but the frequency was quiet.

"Twenty minutes, sir," Tuck said.

"Roger, twenty minutes. We're deploying the booms."

The hydraulics could be heard as the booms pivoted out and into position. A red light on the overhead panel went to green.

"Booms deployed and locked."

Cantwell throttled back to 220 knots and scanned his instruments. All the gauges indicated the airplane was well within normal operating limits. Cantwell felt himself tense up as they flew on. This was the closest thing to a combat mission he had flown since Vietnam. Everything else had been exercises or humanitarian operations. It didn't matter, he thought, this was one mission that wouldn't be recorded in the unit history.

Unless we screw it up, then we really make the headlines.

He could see the *International Herald Tribune* now: "American Spy Plane Crashes in East Germany." At least he wouldn't have to worry about the consequences. He would be dead.

"Are you ready, Steve?"

"Roger, sir."

"Good. The controls are yours. You have the honors tonight."

Cantwell released his hold on the wheel as Bannerman took over. Things were about to get hectic.

"Ten minutes, sir," Tuck said.

"Roger, ten minutes."

Bannerman pulled back the throttles and the plane slowed to 180 knots.

Cantwell pressed the radio transmit button.

"Mayday, Mayday, Mayday. Berlin, this is Hurky 05. I am declaring an in-flight emergency. We've just lost engines three and four. Possible fuel system problem. What emergency landing options do we have?"

"This is Berlin Center. Understand your problem. Can you make it to Tegel?"

"Negative, I think we may lose all four shortly. Give me a landing strip."

"Wait one, Hurky 05."

The US Air Force officer on duty at Berlin Center turned to the Russian liaison officer.

"What airfield can we land on?"

The Russian who had been listening in looked at the radar plot and did some quick map work.

"Hurry, these guys may crash land if they can't make an airfield soon."

"Here," the Soviet Air Force officer said, "near Wittstock."

The Russian scribbled down the geographic coordinates and handed them to the American. Then he grabbed the phone to call Soviet headquarters.

"I'll need to alert the base," said the Russian.

The American officer read the coordinates off the paper to the airplane.

"How copy, Hurky 05?"

"Good copy, Control. We are turning on a northwest azimuth of two-niner-one to get to that location now. Stand by one."

Bannerman turned the aircraft to the northwest for a moment and then put it into a dive while fingering the intercom switch.

"Hang on folks, we are going down for NOE flight."

The plane descended quickly from 15,000 to 1,000 feet in a matter of minutes. Cantwell continued to talk with Berlin.

"Berlin, Hurky 05, we are losing altitude. Number two engine has also shut down. We're holding at 1,000 feet. Wittstock appears to be about 30 kilometers. We'll try to make it there."

In reality, outside the cockpit all four engines were roaring but at reduced speed. They were cruising at 130 knots. Tuck, the navigator, typed a new azimuth into the navigation system and the aircraft heeled to port as it headed for the pick-up point coordinates.

"We're locked in on the intercept point and are about eight minutes out."

"Safety, what's the winch status?"

"We're locked and loaded. Ready for the pick-up."

They were flying low but not quite "nap of the Earth" low. They were at 1,000 feet not NOE's usual 300 feet when the radio operator said, "I have our beacon on two-forty-three megahertz!"

"Got it. It just appeared in front of us on our pick-up azimuth. It's about twelve miles ahead," Tuck responded. "At this speed, five minutes thirty seconds to intercept."

"Those must be our boys. Raven, any changes to our status?"

"We're still clean."

"Tuck, time?"

"Four minutes to contact."

"Roger. Take us off auto, we're taking it manual into the pick-up. Give us corrections if needed until I have the balloon in sight."

"Roger, you have control."

Bannerman felt the control column and did a slight left-to-right movement.

"I have it."

Bannerman took the plane lower, down to just below 450 feet. Both pilots stared ahead into the dark.

"There. The marker lights."

"We have target in sight," Cantwell said over the intercom.

In the rear of the airplane, the crew edged closer to the open tailgate, pressing their helmet earpieces to hear the instructions over the noise of the engines and wind.

Bannerman vectored the plane straight between the two red lights that hung vertically on the line. He wouldn't see the actual cable until the last moment.

"Two minutes… One minute…"

***

On the ground, Kaiser heard the sound first.

"I think we have an inbound bird."

Everyone else heard the noise building to the east.

The Combat Talon roared out over the tops of the trees like a sinister bird of prey and was overhead and then gone in a flash. As it disappeared into the night, the cable straightened out for a moment before Fischer and Kaiser began to lift into the air.

Mann yelled, "*Bon voyage.*"

In all probability he wasn't heard in the din.

The pair kept rising straight into the air for about 100 feet before they took off in an arc behind the Hercules. Then they too were gone.

***

Above them in the cockpit, Cantwell and Bannerman saw the balloon flash overhead as the cable slotted itself into the yoke of the boom arms. It was instantly clamped and locked in the jaws as the upper section and balloon were cut away. The rest of the cable

257

snaked under the belly of the plane. Bannerman had to hold the plane steady on the same azimuth until the cable could be snatched with a J-hook at the tail and locked into the hydraulic winch to reel the men in. Cantwell wondered on which side of the border the balloon would land but he didn't think it would matter as the equipment was completely sterile—unmarked and untraceable. The East Germans might even think it was a weather balloon.

It seemed like minutes, but it was more like thirty seconds before the crew reported in.

"We have the cable captured and secure. Winching is underway."

Cantwell punched Bannerman in the shoulder and gave a thumbs up as he hit the transmit button on the control column.

"Berlin Center, this is Hurky 05. We've managed to restart engines three and four. We're still minus one. We're heading for the Zone and will land at the first available airbase."

"Roger, Hurky 05, you had us worried there. You went off the scope and we thought you'd gone down."

"Berlin Center, we're good. Scared us too. We're going to take it low and slow out of here. Thanks for the help."

"Hurky 05, roger. Safe journey."

The American and the Russian control officers looked at each other and shrugged.

"I guess they're alright now. *Spasibo.*"

Stavros asked the radio operator to send the launch signal to the convoy at Checkpoint Bravo and then climbed down into the cargo area to watch the hoist operations with Lindt. One loadmaster was closely observing the winch as it reeled in the cable while the second loadmaster and safety officer knelt behind the fence at the end of the ramp. They were safely attached to the airplane in their safety harnesses and were watching the cable, waiting for the first glimpse of their catch.

The cable angled up from the winch to a pulley that hung from the top of the tailgate opening and then it disappeared into the dark. It was being reeled in at around eighty feet per minute. Five minutes had passed when the safety officer saw the men on the line.

"Trophy in sight, fifty feet to go."

The two men were flying relatively flat and stable as they were winched towards the tail. The winch operator gauged their approach and slowed their speed as they neared the ramp. An indicator flag on the cable told him when to stop their forward momentum altogether. The two men hung from the pulley, swinging like a pair of newly landed marlin while the loadmaster and safety officer grabbed Kaiser and Fischer and drug them into the airplane securely behind the fence. They snapped safety lines to each man before the lift line was released. Fischer and Kaiser weren't going to leave the aircraft until it was back safely on the ground.

"Trophy onboard and secure," the loadmaster reported.

"Roger, we're running for home," came the response from the flight deck.

The tailgate closed and dim interior lights came back on. Wheeler, Lindt, and Stavros helped the two new and slightly disoriented passengers out of their harnesses and onto the web seats. It was quiet enough to talk at a low shout. Hurky 05 continued its run for the border at low level, flying at 225 knots and just over 500 feet. Anyone sleeping underneath its path would know it had passed but only for a brief moment.

Lindt helped pulled off Kaiser's helmet and was surprised to see his teammate's face.

"What happened to Becker?"

"I did. I got shot. He's coming out with Mann."

Only then did they notice the big dark spot and the bandages over what was left of Kaiser's uniform. Lindt grabbed his M5 medical bag and went to work to make sure the bleeding was still under control.

Wheeler pulled a flask out of his pocket along with two plastic cups and poured Kaiser and Fischer each a good measure of bourbon.

"Welcome aboard, gentlemen," Wheeler said. "You are home free."

Both of them knocked the drink back. Kaiser held out his cup again.

"Please sir, may I have some more?"

As Wheeler poured, Stavros noted, "I think he'll survive, but I can't wait to hear the story."

36

"Time for Police Call," Becker said.

Stuffing all the gear into two bags, he did a quick sweep of the grounds to make sure nothing was left behind. Satisfied, he and Mann grabbed a bag each and trotted back to the car.

"That was pretty incredible."

"It was. I think we'll make the history books but first, we have to survive the next phase. Let's get out of here."

The car nosed out onto the road and headed south for the Helmstedt-Marienborn *Autobahn*. Mann used Becker's NVGs for the first kilometers before he turned on the car's headlights.

"At least we don't have as far to drive on the return route. We'll be there fairly quickly."

It was indeed a short drive to their designated contact point. They would execute the pick-up in the reverse direction. The convoy would be heading west and they would meet it at a lay-by on the *Autobahn*.

When they arrived, the lay-by was as deserted as they had expected and hoped it would be. Mann parked the car at the far end and both men got out. Becker walked the 100 meters of the lane to make sure it was clear. It was partially obscured from the main road by trees and it wouldn't be long before the convoy arrived.

Unlike the launch, the reloading of the car required the truck to be stationary. The trucks would roll in, and they would drive on to the truck and be away in minutes. As long as no one happened into the area they would be good.

Becker was walking back when he heard some commotion up ahead. Mann was standing with a couple, his flashlight holding them in place like deer in the headlights. It was a young man and a young woman. Their hands were in the air.

"What's this?" he asked as he came abreast of his teammate.

"I found these two kids lurking in the bushes behind the bench."

Becker looked them over. They were shaking but they appeared too old to be kids making out in the woods.

"What are you doing out here?" Becker said.

"We were just having some fun together. Our parents won't let us be together at home."

"Show me your papers."

The pair surrendered their papers, pulling them from a small pouch that was stuffed with documents. Becker looked at the identity cards.

"You're twenty-five and twenty-three years old. Don't you have jobs? Can't you afford your own apartment? Let me see the pouch."

As he expected, it was full of official documents, birth certificates, and diplomas. A life in paper—just what any German trying to escape would want to take with them if they could. Mann went back to the bushes and was rooting around when he stopped and turned to Becker.

"Boss, check this out."

Becker pulled out his pistol and made a show of intimidating the two.

"Sit on the ground and don't move."

The two sat. Becker walked over to where Mann was standing. Mann leaned over and grabbed two brown canvas bags, hefting them so Becker could see. They walked back to where the couple were sitting and dropped them on the ground.

"Rucksacks? You two trying to catch a ride? The only reason you two would be out here at night with rucksacks would be to try and escape our wonderful country. Maybe you wanted to stow away on one of those damned NATO trucks that pass by?"

The couple did their contrite best to explain their loyalty to East Germany and plead their innocence.

"We will never do anything like this again."

Becker had no time for excuses.

"So, essentially, you are admitting to attempted *Republikflucht*? Deserting the republic is a very serious crime and you could both go to prison for a long, long time."

Neither of them spoke or moved, but sat there gazing at him with wide, fearful eyes.

"Get in the back of the car," he said. He threw the rucksacks into the trunk.

The couple climbed into the car. The young woman was crying and the man was holding her close. They slammed the doors shut and then Becker and Mann stepped away from the car.

"What are you thinking, Boss? You got a plan for them?"

"I'm thinking that we've only got a few minutes before the convoy arrives. We *could* run them into the village and dump them with a severe warning."

"You seem to be holding something back from me."

"When you did the final interview panel during selection, did they ask you any hypothetical questions?"

Becker saw the lights of the trucks approaching. They had only a few moments.

"Yes, they asked me when I would know it was time to shoot my insane team sergeant."

They both laughed.

"No, not that one. The one about the shepherd?"

"Not that I remember."

"It goes like this, 'You're in enemy territory on a mission and a shepherd discovers your team. You realize he can compromise your presence. What do you do?'"

"I don't think we have time for me to think about the answer."

"Okay, one answer is that you can shoot him, which is not the school solution. Or, you can tie him up and leave him. Or, you can take him with you," Becker said.

Mann looked at the car, then at the approaching truck headlights, and then he looked at Becker. He grinned.

"We take them with us."

"Good answer," said Becker. "Go read them the riot act. Then tell them they're going for a ride with us and for them to keep quiet or we'll toss them back to the sharks."

"Got it, Boss."

The trucks came in single file and blocked the entire lay-by. The transportation captain climbed down from the first truck and walked up to Becker.

"Ready to load?"

"Yes, as ready as we can ever be."

"Who are your passengers?"

"Captain, this is one time when you just might want to pretend you didn't see anything."

Five minutes later, when the car had been winched up the ramp and the rear doors secured, the convoy moved west on into the night.

Good progress was made until they reached the Soviet checkpoint at Marienborn *Grenzübergangsstelle,* the western exit from the GDR to West Germany. The transport officer climbed down to process the Flag Orders with the Russians, but was met with something he had never before experienced. A Russian major met him on the road instead of inside the small metal shed. Actually, a major never came out to meet the convoys; it was usually an officious lieutenant who tried to pretend he was much more than a lieutenant. A major had more power and could actually talk down to a captain.

"We have a problem, Captain Welsh," the major said. "We need to inspect the contents of your trucks."

Surprised that the major knew his name, the captain responded, "You know that isn't going to happen, Major. You have no right to access American military vehicles."

"Then we wait."

"Wait for what?"

"For orders from my headquarters."

"How long might that take?"

"I am not sure, Captain. Maybe an hour, maybe a day. I can wait."

"We can't, Major. You're violating the treaty. Our rights of passage are well established. You don't want a repeat of 1949 do you?"

"It's not my job to question orders. We wait."

"Major, this will not reflect well on you and your career when the United States protests and demands you be held responsible."

"I am not responsible, Captain. The Commander of Soviet Forces in Germany is responsible."

"We'll see, Major. I have a job to finish and I will finish it on time."

Captain Welsh climbed back into the cab of the truck. Welsh grabbed the radio handset and spoke a few terse phrases into the mike. A short response came back.

"We wait. Fifteen minutes, no more," he said to no one in particular.

The Soviet guards wandered around the trucks and pulled on locks and levers and beat the sides of the trucks with sticks while the Americans sat inside, secure in the knowledge that all was locked up tight. At least they hoped so. Only one truck mattered, and it was secure.

Fifteen minutes passed very slowly. One more radio conversation confirmed his plan and then Captain Welsh climbed out of the lead cab and walked up to the shed. At the same time he signaled to each driver to start his engines. The junior Russian soldiers stepped back. They looked at each other with the wide-eyed stare of soldiers who had no instructions. Welsh saw that they were unarmed as usual. This was, after all, a largely ceremonial checkpoint meant to demonstrate the occupation treaty and irritate the Allies.

The major stepped out of the shed, clearly agitated. "Captain, what are you doing? You don't have my clearance to move!"

"Major, according to the occupation treaty you don't have the authority to stop this convoy. I have reported the violation to my command and at this moment the Berlin Brigade and the 3rd Armored Cavalry have been alerted and are moving towards the checkpoints here and in Berlin. Unless you wish to escalate this to Moscow and Washington, I suggest you tell your folks to get out of the way."

The major was about to pull his pistol, but Welsh put up his left hand.

"You don't want to do that, Major. My men are armed and will defend themselves if fired upon. That is in the treaty."

Welsh held his Colt M-1911A service pistol at his side and the Russian's eyes got very big when he saw it. Welsh thumbed off the slide stop and the hard steel slammed forward chambering a round with a ringing noise that made the major jump; it was a sound you don't forget.

"Captain, you will never transit this road again!"

"Major, I go back to the States in two months. I hope you enjoy your return to the Motherland."

The major stood back and watched, contemplating which Siberian outpost he would soon be commanding.

Whatever the Soviets planned, they hadn't prepared their stop well. Had a T-64 arrived and parked on the road in front of them, the Americans would have been screwed, but there had not been enough time. Instead, there were six oil drums lined up across the road.

Welsh motioned to the drivers to roll and the convoy edged slowly forward. The first HET nudged two of the barrels and pushed them until they crumpled and were crushed under the wheels. They were empty as Welsh had gambled. The trucks continued to move out of the holding area one by one. The Soviets must have thought the threat alone was enough to hold the convoy, but they hadn't blocked the road and there was no physical barrier to hold them in place.

As the last truck rolled by, Captain Welsh gave the Russian a half-assed salute and climbed into the pickup that followed. Welsh had counted on the time factor. "Too little, too late, and no specific instructions from higher up on how to hold us," he said to the driver of the pickup who was holding the steering wheel with a white-knuckle grip fully expecting to be shot in the back.

The Russians stood by and watched. The major fumed.

37

The farmer threw open the doors of his barn. It was early morning and the sun had yet to break the eastern horizon. To the northwest, he could still see the city lights of Wolfsburg and reckoned it would be a couple of hours before there was enough light to work the fields. But he had other chores that needed to be done before dawn.

Something, a feeling, made him turn and look across the field. A huge black shadow shot over the trees and hurtled past. It was only when the apparition was directly overhead that he heard the roar of engines. And then it was gone.

All the farmer could think was that his chickens probably wouldn't be laying any eggs that morning.

Above, the crew was jubilant.

"We are back in friendly airspace," Tuck said. They had just crossed the inner German border, leaving behind the Iron Curtain and East Germany with two more passengers than they had started with.

"Sembach is programmed into the box now," he said.

Up front, Cantwell and Bannerman relaxed. The plane was flying itself to their landing destination. Cantwell would only take up the reins again for the final approach.

"Go check on our new arrivals," Cantwell said. He looked as proud as a new father.

Near the front bulkhead, Wheeler and Fischer were together talking in seclusion. In the far rear by the tailgate, Lindt and Stavros sat on the floor talking with Kaiser, who was flat on his back across the web seats, his leg elevated. Bannerman came back and knelt by Kaiser.

"You guys did good out there. We're proud to be part of your mission."

"So far, so good, for us at least. We have two more guys down there still in harm's way."

"I'm sure they will be fine. If anyone can pull it off…" his voice trailed off as he saw Kaiser's eyes drooping. "I think it's his nap time. He deserves it."

"How much longer do we have?"

"We've got a little bit less than an hour before we land. I'll let you know just before we go final."

"Thanks, sir," Stavros said.

Bannerman spoke briefly with the loadmasters and the safety officer before he turned back to the nose of the aircraft. He pondered interrupting Wheeler but saw that he and the other man were deep in discussion. He decided whatever he had to say could wait and returned to the cockpit.

Wheeler saw the co-pilot walk by and was happy he hadn't interrupted their conversation. At first Fischer was fascinated by the airplane, everything from the winch that hauled him to freedom to the small luminescent panel lights that glowed in the dark when the main cabin lights went off.

"You Americans have some amazing technology that I have never heard about."

"Some of it amazes me too, *Herr* Fischer. We will help you to get accustomed to the differences, but don't worry, most of our daily life is pretty simple. But I must warn you, while there is a lot of freedom in our country, there is much aggravation as well."

"I think I will just have get used to both. Overall, I think it will be better and I am not going back there, even if you try to throw me back."

"We can't send you back. Besides, we need your help to get your assets out. One of the first debriefing items will center on how we can safely contact them and extract them."

Fischer regarded Wheeler for a moment and then looked down at the floor. "Thank you. That has been one of my biggest concerns—the people I left behind."

"We will find a way to help them, don't worry."

After the initial celebration, quiet returned to the crew and passengers. Almost everyone was alert and waiting for their arrival at the airbase, save Fischer and Kaiser who had settled back and closed their eyes. They were closely watched by their guardians.

Forty minutes later, Captain Tuck hit the intercom button.

"We're ten minutes out, Colonel. Ready to take it back over?"

"Roger, let's have her back," Cantwell said and took hold of the controls.

The runways of Sembach Air Base loomed in the distance, brightly illuminated in the night. Cantwell called their approach: "Sembach Approach, this is Hurky 05. Request direct approach clearance."

"Hurky 05, Sembach Tower, you are cleared for emergency approach on Runway 24."

"Roger, Sembach. We have you visual now. We're coming in low, require medical assistance on landing."

"Hurky 05, Roger. Emergency services have been deployed."

The aircraft hurtled over the threshold at 110 knots, the wheels contacting the runway 50 meters further on. Brakes applied and props reversed brought the big bird to a near halt close to a taxiway ramp. Red lights twinkled up and down the taxiway marking the fire trucks and emergency vehicles underneath. The plane turned and rolled to a hangar at the extreme north end of the base. The vehicles followed. The hangar door was open as was the ramp on the Hercules.

By the time Hurky 05 got to the hangar, two of its four engines were shut down. The last two were barely turning over as the plane jerked to a halt inside. An ambulance rolled up to the rear and waited, while on the flight deck, Cantwell and Bannerman shut down the systems.

Four men approached the ramp and watched as they heard it whine down onto the hangar floor. When it touched the ground they clambered up into the cargo hold. Stavros met them at the top of the ramp.

"They pulled it off with only one hitch. Kaiser got wounded in the thigh. Lindt checked it out and says it's non-life threatening. We don't know the story of what happened yet, but Becker put him on the exfil and stayed with Mann on the ground."

"And our guest?" Murphy asked.

"He looks to be fine. He's up in the corner there with your man Wheeler."

Stavros pointed at the forward corner of the hold where the two were still huddled.

Jelinek grabbed Stavros' hand and shook it, "Well done. The rest of the team should be out soon."

Bergmann thumped Stavros on the back and followed the commander to check on Kaiser. Kaiser tried to sit up when he saw the colonel approach.

Lindt put his hand on Kaiser's shoulder and stopped him. "Don't. You'll pass out, we haven't replaced any of the fluids you've lost and the alcohol won't help you much," he warned.

Jelinek and Bergmann both kneeled by Kaiser. "How are you? What happened?"

"My man Lindt here tells me I will survive, so I'm good, I think. A *Stasi* guy tried to stop us. He didn't but I got winged in the process and he's out of the game for good. Becker handled the rest, I think. Maybe the German can fill you in on the details."

"I think this is why we send you guys to the aidman's course," said Bergmann to Lindt.

"Don't worry about telling us the story. We'll get it from your teammates soon enough." Jelinek said.

Jelinek stood up and motioned for Captain Kelly to approach. "Dieter, I want you to accompany him to the base hospital and to stay with him through the whole procedure. We don't need anyone talking with him when he's under anesthesia."

"Got it, sir. We'll get him patched up and transferred back to the city, ASAP."

Kelly was beginning to think the old man was getting soft calling him by his first name. He went to get the responders from the ambulance while the others deplaned from the front exit door. The safety officer sat next to Kaiser and waited.

"Tell me about the guy who gave up his 'D' ticket to get you on a ride out."

"He's my boss and, right now, I'm glad that he is."

***

Murphy walked forward to where Wheeler and Fischer were huddled in conversation.

"I don't know if you two have noticed but you've landed," he said.

"*Herr* Fischer, this is my chief, Tom Murphy."

Fischer stuck out his hand, which Murphy ignored and grabbed the German in a bear hug.

"Welcome to West Germany and thank you for your trust in us."

"It wasn't for you, what I did; it was for my people. I am actually sorry I wasn't able to finish what I started."

"We'll do what we can to see it through to the end. You helped us very much."

"Maybe. But I want to ask you for your help once again. I have three sub-agents that I want to get out. I gave you the information on 'Flower' already, but here are all their names and contact protocols. They have not been compromised as far as I can tell, but they will be scared as hell when they understand I am gone. They have done much to help me. Get them all out if you can."

Murphy took the piece of paper Fischer handed him. Fischer had stuffed a leather portfolio full of papers and small things into his overalls just before the pick-up. It was all he had in the world now.

"We will do everything we can, *Herr* Fischer," Murphy said. He handed the paper to Wheeler. "We need to get on this as soon as we can. Coordinate with Bonn and start things rolling."

Wheeler took the paper and glanced at it. Nodding his head at Murphy, he didn't say a word, but he knew there would be a lot of work to get the people out.

"One more thing, I should give you this before anything else." Fischer handed Murphy a sealed A4-sized envelope, thick with papers. "Don't open it now, but it contains microfilm and notes on most of the *HVA*'s overseas networks. Unfortunately, the West German network information is in General Wolf's safe. I couldn't get you that."

Murphy smiled, "I think this will give us a good start. Maybe we can persuade Wolf to come over someday. He still thinks we don't know what he looks like."

"Good luck with that," Fischer shook his head. "He has it too good over there and he is committed."

"Yes, well enough of that," Murphy said. "We need to get you back to the States as soon as possible. You'll be going first to Virginia and then we can figure out what is next for you."

Fischer's eyes lit up. "I'd like to talk about Colorado."

38

The convoy moved out of the American holding area at Helmstedt and back onto the *Autobahn* heading west. There were safe in West Germany. Inside the third trailer, Becker and Mann sat on the hood of their trusty Wartburg, while the two Agency technicians chatted to themselves. The East German couple sat inside the car not sure whether to be elated or fearful of their current circumstances. Mann had changed into his US Army uniform but Becker was still in his mixed bag of an outfit. The watch cap on his head made him look somewhat like a pirate, which, at that particular moment, was how he felt. He was just happy everyone had gotten out.

"How do we handle them?" Mann said.

"We don't," Becker said, "remember, an action passed is an action completed."

The truck came to a stop. They heard a scraping noise as someone manipulated the exterior lock and the door opened. One of the technicians dropped the ladder out the door and climbed out.

Becker turned to the other Agency man. "Just keep them locked up until someone comes for them."

Clanging down the ladder, Becker hopped off the final rung. He could see they had come into a military outpost not far from the border crossing. There were two civilians, Agency types by their look, and an air force officer waiting.

"Welcome back, we have a lift waiting to take you to Sembach," the Air Force captain said.

Becker could see the "Super Jolly Green Giant" HH-53 helicopter, its rotors turning slowly, beyond him on the middle of the parade field.

One of the Agency types came up to their group and broke into the conversation. "My guy says you brought two civilians out with you. You may have jeopardized the convoy with your actions. Who are they and by what authority do you think you can do that?"

"You're kind of rude. I was just talking with this nice air force officer and you butt in. Here," Becker said, handing the Agency guy the passengers' pouch, "I have no idea who they are, but you'll find all their papers in there. They wanted to come to the West and I decided I would rather accommodate them than shoot them. You should find a nice home for them somewhere. And, if you have any problems with that, take it up with my commander. Captain, if we may?"

Becker and Mann turned and followed the air force captain to the helo. It was just beginning to spool up its engines. When the helo lifted off, Sembach was an hour and forty minutes distant.

Long before they landed, the last two days began to tell on both. Mann and Becker were slumped in their seats asleep and didn't notice when the wheels of the Jolly Green touched down on the tarmac. One of the crewmen carefully shook the two awake and stood back, fully cognizant that both were armed and presumably dangerous.

"We're on the ground. We'll be at the hangar in a couple of minutes."

The tailgate opened as they taxied and Becker watched the glare of the airfield lights breaching the darkness of the cabin interior as they passed each pylon. Then it went dark inside and his view of the airfield did a pirouette as the helicopter pivot-turned and came to a stop with its tail facing the big steel structure.

Mann shook his head to clear it and stood up. Becker got up and grabbed each crewman's hand to shake it as he walked down the ramp. The rotors were making their last turns with a slow whoosh as they passed overhead. Mann stepped onto the tarmac, knelt on the ground, and touched it. Sergeant Major Bergmann walked up to them and grasped Mann's shoulder. "Good job, Stefan." It was one of the rare moments when Bergmann would have gotten emotional had he not been so elated. He grabbed Kim by both shoulders and shook him a bit.

"Kim, you did it. Everyone in and out safely. Kaiser is fine, we sent him off to the medics with Kelly. You're going to have some storytelling to do now."

"I did my job, Sergeant Major, nothing more, nothing less."

"It was much more than that. I think you can let go of that demon now."

"What demon?"

"The one Greener told me about: the only thing that matters is getting everyone home. You did that. You did all you could for your men and you succeeded."

Becker was silent and then he remembered something told him at a Sunday school session long ago. The teacher, an army veteran of World War II, said something he would always remember: "Greater love hath no man than this, that a man lay down his life for his friends."

The verse came back to him now. There was nothing more important than that.

"I'll do my best, Sergeant Major."

"Good, because I need team sergeants like you. Mann, you need to start on your after-action report right after we drink a toast to this operation. Let's go find the rest of the team."

The crew of the Jolly Green paused to watch the men walk towards the hangar, wondering just what kind of mission they had witnessed.

A couple of air force security police sergeants were standing by the partially open hangar door, their M-16s at the ready. Bergmann walked by them without his usual dig at "Flyboys" because of his elation and the fact that the squadron had fulfilled every request without a single objection or waver of commitment. They headed past the resting MC-130 and into the conference room.

Of the crew, only Cantwell remained. Becker saw Jelinek talking with Murphy and Fischer while Lindt, Stavros, and Wheeler were off to the side contemplating their coffee cups. When Jelinek saw their approach he broke off the conversation and started walking towards them. He didn't say a word, he just embraced first Mann and then Becker in a bear hug. Luckily it didn't last long because Becker couldn't breathe—he was being crushed by the colonel's most Slavic greeting and expression of congratulations.

"You did a great job! Your team did great," Jelinek said, handing each a big tumbler of Scotch. "I would give you a cigar but the air force says we can't smoke here!" He glared at Cantwell.

Murphy came up next and shook their hands.

"Good job, Kim. Don't worry about the kids you brought out. The guy you met in Helmstedt is a real dickhead. We'll take care of getting them resettled."

"Thanks. When this is all done, you should recommend Captain Welsh for a medal. He must have watermelon-sized *cojones*."

Then Fischer approached. The German stood back a bit and exchanged a silent look with Becker before he approached. He first shook Mann's hand silently and then wrapped his arms around Becker and hugged him.

"Thank you, Kim. I can never repay you."

"You just did, *Herr* Fischer."

"Call me Max. I am no longer your charge, I am your friend."

Murphy spoke up. "I wanted to get him out of here as fast as possible, but he insisted on waiting for you guys to arrive. We are going to fly him home in the morning once we finish the formalities here."

"Formalities? What else do we need to do now?"

"Just a couple of things more," Murphy said, reaching into his pocket. "I don't think you quite remember me, but you might remember this."

He placed a small tarnished bronze coin into Fischer's hand. Fischer glanced at it and then looked up at Murphy. "I thought there was something familiar about you."

"There is. I recruited you."

Fischer smiled. "Actually, *Mister Frank*, I think it was I who recruited you."

"Perhaps. But there's still just one more thing we need to take care of," Murphy said and then looked at Wheeler who standing by a door to the room. Wheeler opened the door and motioned to whoever was behind it.

Fischer was frozen in place. "My God," he said.

Lila walked towards him quickly and threw her arms around her friend.

"My God," he repeated, "how did you get her out? How did you know?"

"I remembered you talked about Lila when we were on Zanzibar. Then you gave us the contact information for Flower. I put the story together and that was all we needed to get her out. Her exit was much easier than yours. She wasn't being watched," Murphy said.

Lila turned to the woman behind her. "And this young lady helped."

Rohan stepped out from behind Lila. "We've met once before, *Herr* Fischer, in Berlin," Rohan said.

Stavros was as speechless as Fischer.

"We borrowed your friend after you went to the Zone," Murphy said. "She is pretty good at this kind of stuff."

"So I see." Stavros wrapped his arms tightly around Rohan and she squeezed him back in return.

"It's a family homecoming and I think I want to cry." Wheeler effected to blow his nose for the crowd.

***

Murphy saw that Lila and Max needed some time before he rushed them off, so he sat them down at a small table and walked away.

"So can I ask, was it all worth it?" Lila asked of Max.

"What? You and I, or my work?"

"Both, I guess."

"The work was, I think, most of the time. I did what was probably the right thing; I just hope it will make a difference to our people in the end. If I knew that, I would feel good. But the people I had to work with, that was hard..."

His voice trailed off. He felt as if a chasm had opened and he was staring into it.

Lila was leaning in closely, looking at him intensely, her dark eyes shining.

"And us?"

She shook her head lightly, swinging her long, dark hair back and forth. Her necklace, a long gold damascene chain with a heavy pearl orb attached, swung as well. It tangled in a long tendril of her hair. She was looking at him and hadn't noticed.

He leaned over and reached out to disentangle the chain. As she watched him, her eyes narrowed a bit and a slight smile came to her face. He felt the warmth he usually felt when she did that. He smiled inside and knew.

He tugged on her hair and unwrapped the chain a bit. Then he watched as the orb swung around, spiraling down the tendril until it fell free.

And, finally, so was he.

"I'm sorry for making you wait."

"No need for that now. We'll make it work, we've waited long enough."

Their eyes locked. Without even the slightest blink, her hand slowly reached for the orb, her fingertips softly brushing the smooth skin of her neck where the necklace lay.

She tilted her head to the side and looked down at the hand cupping the orb. A soft curl fell, framing her left temple. He reached out in an attempt to sweep the strands away, but instead he pulled her face closer. He closed his eyes and kissed her.

39

Kim Becker took off the watch cap he had been wearing, stuffed it in his field jacket, and ruffled his hair. He watched as Murphy disappeared with Fischer and Lila. His teammates and Rohan were heading off in another direction with the colonel and sergeant major. He realized he was alone in the room. He turned and walked back out into the main hangar where he found Wheeler looking up at the nose of the "Combat Talon."

"Nice piece of equipment. It did the job and then some," Wheeler said. "It might have come in handy a couple of years ago for some of my missions."

"It's always like that, 'necessity is the mother of invention.' We either have it in the inventory or we have to invent it."

"Without this thing we might not have been able to get OZ out."

"He mentioned something about taking a train to Finland, maybe you should look into that next time around."

"I don't think you can get there from here."

"No, I suppose not. But I mean there must be other ways to do this kind of extraction, just in case. You Agency guys are supposed to be good at this."

"The Agency is good but sometimes we need outside help. That's where you guys come in; you have abilities the Agency doesn't have.

It's not like they can rely on veterans like me to bring their skill set over and put it into action. It doesn't work that way."

"I thought you had some special action teams or something."

"You know, when I was in Special Forces a while ago, I thought there must be a super secret unit that was better, even tougher than we were. One that was so classified, no one knew anything about it."

"And?"

"There wasn't. We were the best. We were a bunch of regular guys trained to do special things. You and I are the ones. What we have is the desire and motivation to be the best. And even if we sometimes make mistakes or things don't go as we wish, we always come back. SF is still like that—you and your guys are the best. "

"How about the Agency? You like it?"

"I'm well beyond my rucksack years, so it's better than nothing for a guy who wants to keep his hand in the game. But we work more as individuals and the one thing I miss are the teams. I miss the 'all for one and one for all' sort of spirit."

Becker nodded his head silently as he ran his hand over the cool, aluminum skin of the fuselage towering over him. There was more to this job than the things the recruitment brochure showed and more than what he had experienced in the jungle. There were larger problems in the world that he could actually affect. Sergeant Major Bergmann's words came back to him and that, along with Fischer's heartfelt bear hug, pushed Becker's soul imperceptibly in the direction he was meant to go.

"What are you going to do now, Kim?"

"I am going back to Berlin. I've got a great team and a job to do. What more could I possibly want?"

"Good answer, *kuaʻana*, my brother."

I think I am supposed to be right here after all, Becker thought.

"Jamie my friend, I think it's time for us to go home."

40

"What the hell happened out there, Hoffmann?"

"Minister, the coroner identified three deceased men at the *Dacha*. We believe they were Major General Fischer, Major General Großmann, and Großmann's driver. Although we are fairly certain, it's difficult to determine exactly because the bodies were badly burned in the fire. According to the investigator's preliminary survey, it appears it was a murder-suicide. From what we know, Großmann learned that Fischer had gone to his *Dacha* for several days of leave. Großmann apparently believed Fischer was our traitor and decided to take the matter into his own hands. Ballistics show that Fischer and the driver were shot with Großmann's pistol. And then Großmann was shot with his own weapon, which was found in his hand. The *Dacha* was a total loss because of the fire. The investigator thinks it started sometime later—after the shooting. He believes it to have been caused by the gas stove. The stove was found to have been turned on, probably by Fischer before he was visited by Großmann. What remained of a coffee pot was found on top of the stove."

"Who gave Fischer permission to take leave?"

"I did, Minister. I thought he needed a break," Markus Wolf said.

The end state at the Dacha was clean and easy, maybe too easy. Wolf distrusted puzzles that were too easy to solve.

"And who told Großmann that Fischer had gone to the *Dacha*?"

"That was me again. I didn't imagine that he would run off after him."

"And Großmann spoke to no one before he left?"

"Not that we're aware of."

"Was Fischer the traitor?"

"I doubt it. We have since received another report from the Soviet penetration agent. It was attributed to the same source, but it couldn't have been Fischer. As far as I can determine, it was specific information out of Department XXII to which he didn't have access."

"So Großmann not only killed his driver, he killed the wrong man."

"It appears so."

"Then who is our traitor?"

"Only time will tell, Minister."

There was an uneasy pause.

"Hoffmann, please have Special Tasks clean this up. It was an unfortunate accident, regrettable, but nothing more."

"Yes, Minister," Hoffmann said.

The meeting was over and as Wolf walked towards *Haus 15*. He still had one lingering question.

We didn't find your Petschaft. Where did it go? Where indeed, Max?

Wolf had never lost at this game before and he wasn't about to start. He made a decision that he would never—could never—reveal.

Dahle will take the fall, he's witless and worthless. I'll throw him under the bus and we'll move on. Sometimes you have to sacrifice a pawn.

He looked up into the evening sky, his hands deep in the pockets of his wool trousers. It was chilly, but he stood there and gazed at the darkening red clouds above him. He spoke to the sky with all conviction.

"Well played, Max. That's checkmate—you're safe now, my friend."

But, for the rest of us, the game is still on.

And with that the Grandmaster continued on his way.

An extract from *The Snake Eater Chronicles 2:*
An Appointment in Tehran

1

It was cool, as November mornings in Tehran often were. To the north, the Alborz mountains were shrouded in a blanket of gray cloud and a light rain was falling. The day had started out quietly enough. The city had been tense for months as internecine squabbles, demonstrations, and street fights broke out across the country between the moderates, the communists, and Islamists vying for influence. The hard-liners of the Council of the Islamic Revolution had only tenuous control. That would soon change.

In his apartment several blocks from the university campus, Abdul Mezad knelt on a carpet facing the Holy Cities of Mecca and Medina and prayed. He was one of the few people in the city who knew what was about to happen. Although the Shah had been overthrown and the revolutionary republic proclaimed months earlier, there was still an infuriating presence in the city, the den of spies—the American Embassy—that housed the very same snakes who had installed the Shah onto the Peacock Throne. It had been a quarter-century, but many Iranians still felt the insult deeply—that the Americans could overthrow their elected government and install their puppet, Mohammad Reza Pahlavi. It was a brazen act by insolent foreigners who knew nothing about the true nature of Iran and its people and cared only for oil. But, he also knew that many other Iranians—apostates all of them—were supportive of the coup and the Shah. He considered them all to be traitors, not true believers of Islam, and they too would be dealt with soon enough.

After his prayers, Abdul walked in the light drizzling rain through the stirring city. The early morning commuters passing him would have assumed he was a student, dressed in faded jeans and a loose sweater topped off with an olive-drab fatigue jacket he had bought cheaply in a market long ago. But anyone who looked at him closely might have reconsidered, not that he cared. The intensity of a zealot on *Jihad* burned in Abdul's eyes, his vision reduced to tunnel vision, focused only on his destination and little else. He had a mission and if he was to be a martyr this day, so be it.

The shops were still shuttered. Despite the dampness in the air, the smell of *barbari* baking in the neighborhood ovens wafted through the neighborhood. He ignored his hunger; there would be time enough for food later. Walking with determination, he covered the few miles to his place of appointment rapidly. He turned into Taleqani Street. In front of him he saw his goal. Abdul strode on, over the glistening, damp concrete and stopped outside the embassy gates where crowds had started to gather. He glared at the Americans inside the fence who looked back at him with a stare that conveyed their sense that this day would be unlike any they had experienced before. The Marine Security Guards gathered in small groups near the gates, the front entrance, and even on the roof as the embassy staff hurried to their desks inside the Chancery. They were worried; they were too few to contain the threatening crowd that gathered beyond the fence.

As the city slowly awakened, the crowd outside grew to hundreds, then thousands of young people outside the 27-acre embassy compound. As the rain tapered off, the throngs grew, made up mostly of students who had not attended school since the uprisings began the previous January. Most believed they were there for just a peaceful protest, but the rain had dampened their spirits. Wistfully, some thought of going home, out of the rain, to enjoy tea and savory cakes. They wanted the Americans out of their new Islamic republic, but had not come with violence in mind. They were not aware of the real plan. But a small group, "the Brethren," had something else in mind. Today they would finally swing the balance of power over to Ruhollah Khomeini.

Abdul was aware. He was one of the "Brethren"—a true insider. They were the core element, even closer knit than the "Islamic Brothers." They were the vanguard of the revolution. While the placards and shouts outside the compound announced to the Americans that they should leave Iran, the Brethren had other ideas. They wanted to consolidate the Imam's power and eliminate rival militias. By seizing the embassy temporarily, they would not only break the links between the supporters of the provisional government, who wanted a "democratic Iran," and the Americans, they would also destroy the power of the leftists who remained a threat to the Islamic revolution.

While hundreds of young men and women kept the Marines on the perimeter of the facility busy, others climbed over the barrier fence and engaged in a tug of war over the halyards of the flag pole. These distractions occupied the Marine guards. Unseen in the crowd, a small group of men pulled bolt cutters from bags and severed the chains that secured the perimeter gates. With that psychological barrier opened, the masses outside were easily pushed to storm the compound.

After a few hours, Abdul found another of the Brethren, Ervin Rajavi, his friend and confidant, in the Ambassador's office suite looking out the window at the thousands of students roaming the property below him.

The Embassy Chancery had succumbed to the tidal wave of humanity that stormed inside the now meaningless perimeter fence. Bedlam followed. Not only did they occupy the grounds; the students penetrated every secure building on the compound. The ninety members of the staff inside the compound, sixty of whom were American, were herded into the basement for safekeeping.

Abdul Mezad was ecstatic, he hadn't expected the den of spies to give up so quickly and certainly not without a shot. They had been prepared to accept martyrs, but the Americans held their fire.

Were they scared of us? Or did they just want to avoid a massacre?

Abdul regarded his ostensible leader, he knew Rajavi was wavering in his commitment.

Rajavi turned to Abdul as he walked in but said nothing.

Abdul spoke: "What now?"

"We read our declaration and leave," Rajavi said.

"But we have an opportunity here. We have their people and all their secrets. We can hold them hostage to embarrass and punish the Great Satan."

"No, we read our declaration and leave. That was our plan."

"I'm sorry my brother. The plan has changed," Abdul said.

I gave you an opportunity and you failed.

"On whose authority?"

"Imam Khomeini himself."

2

Master Sergeant Kim Becker and Staff Sergeant Paul Stavros walked up to the 500-meter firing range. Both were in full assault uniform, a Walther P5 pistol in a belt holster and a Walther MPK submachine gun slung over their shoulders. In their dark olive-green coveralls with two SMG magazine pouches attached to their gear, they looked more like German *Fallschirmjäger*—paratroopers—than US Army soldiers. Except maybe for their long hair. They called it "relaxed grooming standards." As Team Sergeant, Becker was fine with that. It was better that he and his men be confused for the local *Polizei* than be identified as Americans. They held back and together silently watched the two men on the firing line in front of them, not wishing to disturb their intense concentration. They knew better than to distract a man with a gun, especially one that that could swat a gnat 100 meters away in the dead of night. One of the two was peering through a 20-power M49 spotter scope; the other lay unmoving on the ground, a long black rifle extending out in front of him.

The firing range was old; it predated World War II and there was an air of Prussian Army formality about the place. But with no *Bundeswehr* in Berlin these days, it was normally used by the Berlin Police for training. Today it was closed to outsiders, reserved for use by a small team of Americans. The rifle marksmanship stands were narrow but long, room enough for three shooters side by side. On this day, however, there was just the one shooter on Stand Four. A small rise in the ground allowed the man to lie on the ground and see the target stands down range. There were old brick walls about five meters high on either side of the lane that guaranteed privacy, but more importantly prevented stray bullets from escaping anywhere but up. In the early morning, steam rose as the dew on the grass evaporated into the warming air.

The man behind the Heckler & Koch PSG1 rifle controlled his breathing as he had been taught to do a number of years before. He peered through the Hensoldt ZF 6x42 scope at the target down range and tightened his index finger on the sensitive trigger. Just so much pressure at first, then slowly increasing the pull while regulating his breathing. His mind was focused not on his body functions or the reticle in the scope, but on the target down range. Just at the pause between his exhale and inhale, the trigger released the sear and the firing pin sprang forward to impact the primer of the Lake City 7.62mm M118 Match cartridge. Propelled by the burning gases, the 168 grain Sierra MatchKing bullet left the barrel at a supersonic 2,550 feet per second and cracked through the cardboard target seven-tenths of a second later. It was his fifth shot. He waited.

Down range, the target slipped down into the pit so the sniper's shots could be graded. A voice came over the radio speaker.

"I have four rounds in the center of the ten ring, the group is a little less than two and a half inches in diameter. You're missing one round. Still, not bad for a cold barrel."

"Check the oblique target behind," said Fred Lindt, the spotter.

"Stand by… Okay. All five are there. One round must have gone through the same hole. You're good."

"Of course he's good," said Lindt back into the mike.

Of course I am, Logan Finch smiled to himself.

Becker finally spoke up. "Okay, good shooting Logan, but let's wrap things up quickly. We've been recalled to the building. Training is cancelled."

As they packed up their gear, Finch and Lindt exchanged glances, not sure whether to be disgusted or worried. Recalls generally meant one of two things, either some bullshit training exercise or the real thing—just possibly an alert and a live mission.

***

Five of Support Detachment Berlin's six Special Forces "A" Teams had assembled on the second floor of their headquarters building. They were waiting expectantly as it was unusual to have more than one formation in a single day. The teams had been recalled to the building from their training at the range or off the streets by the Motorola pagers they carried. It had taken about an hour for the men to gather. The only team absent was Team 3, which was training with SEAL Team Two in Greece.

Becker stood in front of Team 5, engaged in banter with Bill Simpson, Team 6's senior sergeant. Stavros tried to listen in but all he caught was what he thought to be a Serbian expletive from Simpson and Becker's counter in French.

Whatever...

Otherwise it was quiet, quieter than the usual raucous morning formation. Everyone was expecting something important but not even the bravest dared to hazard a guess.

Finally, Colonel Jelinek and Sergeant Major Bergmann came up the stairs. Without a word of command, the unit came to attention. Bergmann slowly surveyed the assembly before him—one of the best trained and most unusual units in the US Army—and then with his usual gruffness addressed the men.

"Team sergeants, are all your people here?"

Receiving an affirmative from each of the five, he continued.

292

"Stand at ease, gentlemen."

Colonel Jelinek stepped in front of the sergeant major. Everyone knew something was up; he rarely addressed a formation. Jelinek was a big man. At six foot three and around 240 pounds he stood several inches taller than Bergmann. He was also very fit for a man nearing fifty. He had his sternest expression on, not than he often showed any other. He rarely laughed, but when he did, the sound carried through the building. And you didn't want to be on the end of one of his counseling sessions. Luckily, he left most of those to the sergeant major, at least for the enlisted men. For the officers, it was a different story.

A refugee from Czechoslovakia during World War II, he had fought with the French resistance against the Germans. His English was still colorfully tinted with the accent of his mother tongue.

"Gentlemen, as you already know the US Embassy in Tehran was overrun and occupied by radical Islamic students yesterday. Approximately sixty American staff have been taken hostage. A planning group has been set up and I will be departing for Washington tonight. As for you, Special Operations Task Force Europe has put us on alert as of 0900 Zulu. I want to see team leaders and sergeants in my office now."

Bergmann waited until the colonel disappeared down the stairs before he spoke.

"In case it needs to be said, all TDYs and leaves are cancelled. We're on a twelve-hour string. Get your gear together and prepare to upload the alert package. Go to it!"

Acknowledgements

I want to thank Casemate Publishers for the steadfast assistance I have received, especially from Ruth Sheppard, who supported my concept from the beginning and made it happen, Isobel Fulton, one of the people who keeps Casemate running but who changes her name periodically to keep me guessing, Daniel Yesilonis who promotes like crazy, and David Farnsworth, who backed this idea in spite of his better judgement. I also want to thank my editor Alison Griffiths who showed me which questions my writing exposed and suggested how best to answer them. Sometimes I listened.

I also want to thank my Beta readers, Jon, Jim, and Pierce who told me where I was off base and provided much-needed tips to improve the story. Thanks very much.

Thanks as well to the staff of the Publications Classification Review Board. You do important if unrecognized work.

Next come my friends and *Kampfgenossen* who through the years have mentored, amused, and frightened me. You inspired my writing. You were and are all great friends and role models—both devil and angel—for Special Forces and *die Sondereinsatzkommandos*. They include Jon, Stu, Russ, Jeff, Stan, Peter, MG, Poncho, Ron, Howie, Juan, Dave, Doctor X, *das Boot*, Rick, Rich, Big Jim W, Monty,

Dieter, Christian, and especially Nick and Stryker who helped me break contact in the firefight.

Then there are the mentors from the Potomac River Campus who trusted me to run alone and with scissors, who counseled patience when it was warranted, and gave me valuable advice when needed. Among the giants are Gordon H., John B., Mike D., Billy H., and Joe K.

Most importantly, I thank my wife Wanda and the rest of my clan for their love, support, and understanding.

J. S.